REVEREND WENT *Walking*

*To: Sas.
Dare to Soar!
Wm T*

WILLIAM TEETS

outskirtspress
DENVER, COLORADO

This is a work of fiction. The events and characters described herein are imaginary and are not intended to refer to specific places or living persons. The opinions expressed in this manuscript are solely the opinions of the author and do not represent the opinions or thoughts of the publisher. The author has represented and warranted full ownership and/or legal right to publish all the materials in this book.

Reverend Went Walking
All Rights Reserved.
Copyright © 2016 William Teets
v2.0

Cover Photo © 2016 thinkstockphotos.com. All rights reserved - used with permission.

This book may not be reproduced, transmitted, or stored in whole or in part by any means, including graphic, electronic, or mechanical without the express written consent of the publisher except in the case of brief quotations embodied in critical articles and reviews.

Outskirts Press, Inc.
http://www.outskirtspress.com

ISBN: 978-1-4787-7393-1

Outskirts Press and the "OP" logo are trademarks belonging to Outskirts Press, Inc.

PRINTED IN THE UNITED STATES OF AMERICA

For Superheroes Everywhere

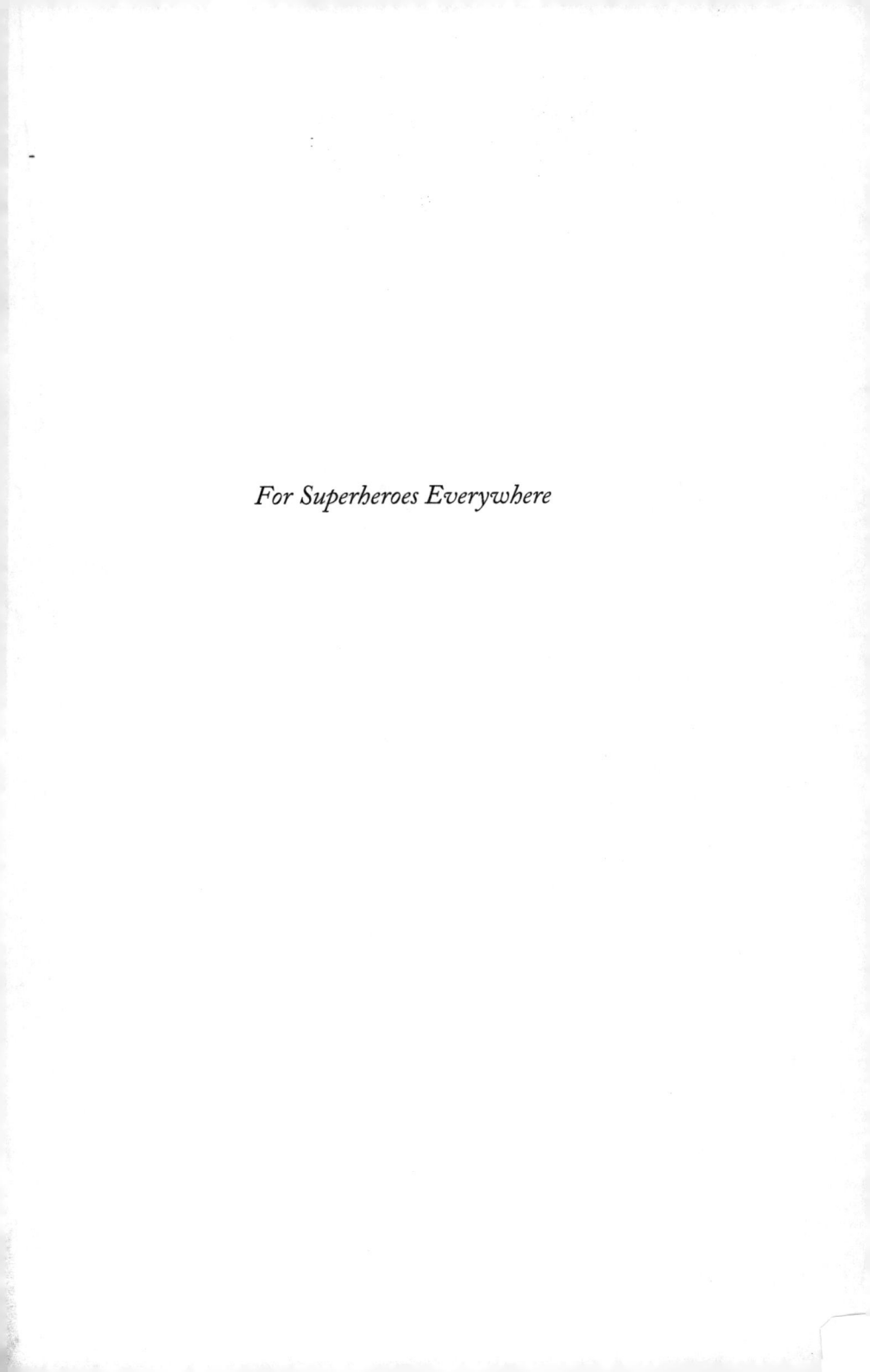

I, too, am America.

– Langston Hughes

Contents

Chapter 1	Dreams	1
Chapter 2	Kings Among Men	8
Chapter 3	Fresh Cut	17
Chapter 4	Secrets	25
Chapter 5	Built On Stone	36
Chapter 6	A Day In The Hood	49
Chapter 7	Cleaning Windows	57
Chapter 8	Who Really Knows?	66
Chapter 9	Can't Be Livin' In The Past	84
Chapter 10	Hopin' On Hope	94
Chapter 11	Heat Wave	103
Chapter 12	Runnin' Out Of Time	112
Chapter 13	Blood Rent	121
Chapter 14	The Train Kept Rollin'	135
Chapter 15	The Letter	144

Chapter 16	Balls Said The Queen, If I Had Them I'd Be King	155
Chapter 17	Is Miss Jones On The Bus?	162
Chapter 18	When You're Blessed The Sun Shines All The Time	169
Chapter 19	Just The Way It Is	179
Chapter 20	A Win For The Good Guys	188
Chapter 21	We All Pay In The End	197
Chapter 22	No Do Overs	208
Chapter 23	Pie In The Sky	218
Chapter 24	We Are Where We Are	228
Chapter 25	And A Child Shall Lead Them	240
Chapter 26	AWOL	252
Chapter 27	The Best Laid Schemes of . . .	263
Chapter 28	A Nickel In The Well	267
Chapter 29	On A Road	275
Chapter 30	Fickle	284
Chapter 31	Checkers	293
Chapter 32	Promises	303
Chapter 33	Row That Boat Ashore	314
Chapter 34	Whirlwind	324
Chapter 35	Salvation Teacher	342
Chapter 36	Reverend Went Walking	349
Acknowledgements		357

Chapter 1
Dreams

Reverend went walking on a cloudy fall day.

Lil' man walked straight and fast and hard, head held high. He had an almost bounce in his step like he was walkin' on a bumpy bed or some kind of funky moon shoes. Gravity's rules and physics that applied for most were absent for him.

Reverend walked so unlike his peers. Them, with their pimp-rolls-wanna-be-down-exaggerated-sidewindin'-gaits. Walkin' like they knew what time it was when they didn't have a clue about the next step in front of them.

Naw, brother, Rev walked different. Like Swiss cheese on a Frisbee type different.

He knew more.

Reverend walked like he didn't even belong on the block. Like he was above them streets. I mean shit; he had the

Timbs untied, colorful billboard-free advertisin' wears that others rocked, but that walk man, oh, that walk.

His walk shouted Reverend was special. That he was hearing some lost drummer in his head no one else could hear. That no one—from where he was from—had even ever heard of. Some Thoreau or Emerson type shit.

Too deep for the common brothers.

Reverend was headin' somewhere else, somewhere far away, a place no one else could see. A crazy unique-like place separate from all the grime and grit and dirt and shit that normally choked people's breath away. People who lived on top of landfills in fucked-up public housing, causin' asthma and other unwanted warrants and death knells for their children. But I'll speak about that insanity later.

Back to Rev, man, yeah, back to Rev's walk.

Now don't get it twisted, brothers and sisters, Reverend may have looked all cool and collected on the outside, but inside he didn't feel all that fly. Thoughts in his dome were all crazy and confused, as they should be for someone like him, but they was so much deeper and darker then any fourteen-year-old should be feelin', too.

See, people, when walkin', Reverend dreamed. Man, he loved to daydream. Rev's dreams took him to faraway places high above the noise and pollution, makin' him feel so special inside. But like crabs in a bucket or Icarus meeting the sun,

REVEREND WENT WALKING

Rev would start soarin' too far away, and the hood would snatch him back and the sun would melt his waxed wings. And man, he would fall hard—with a dud thud—onto the concrete corners of Hamilton, or Washington, or Lafayette, or some other street named after some other long-ago deceased, European, white man. White men who wouldn't be caught in the hood dead, if they were alive now. They would never walk and talk or live on these streets named after them.

No way, man, not in this part of town.

Just the way it is.

Just sayin' and all.

But Rev, naw people, he didn't know he, or his walk, was the bomb. He didn't recognize his glory or the sheen he shined. But his dreams made him feel that special way inside before he crashed like a daydream doper or some other fiend and *not* the kind on Halloween. Not that Casper cartoon shit, no, not that. Down here in the ghetto there ain't no friendly ghosts.

Crack-ass whores maybe. Runners and gunners and slingers maybe. But righteous self-esteem was extinct or at least heavily endangered. Just like Reverend's daydreams, just like the lost American Dream.

Endangered for real, bro.

But let me stop, I'm gettin' ahead of myself.

WILLIAM TEETS

Back to Reverend.

His daydreams of youth were fueled by the stories of his Uncle Luke. Not that Luke talked about them much, but the hood sure did. Luke being a hero and all. But them nasty ho bitches on the corner sellin' their wares and the drug dealin' barkers sellin' their work and always some wanna-be thug screamin' for the sake of just wantin' to be heard would break his dreams. Break them like a cheap bottle of wine, dropped by One Shoe, on the cracked *uneven* sidewalks. Shattering, like pool balls clattering, in back room bars, Rev was always reminded of where he was and who he was.

The good thing, though, was Reverend was still young enough to dream and not hardened or broken beyond repair by the streets.

Not yet, anyway.

Dig?

See, when he bounced his walk, Rev came up with some real intense type dreams; stick-up kids or drug crazies couldn't rob him. The Man couldn't bother him. PoPo couldn't stop and frisk. Life was paused on Rev's favorite hip-hop beat. A beat that played raucous rhythms in his head, promisin' him salvation or at least a chance at it. At least a respite before being swallowed by a Baku, who claims innocent souls and eats young brains for dinner.

Poison allowed.

Silent stiflin' deaths.

Fire and brimstone and the never-ending eternity of hell.

Not yet, not now.

Yeah, man, Reverend could still dream.

He dreamed of finding the Holy Grail with Arthur and green knights and dragons and damsels in distress. Love for all and all for love. He sailed Viking longboats and fought Attila the Hun. Sailed great ships for the Queen and collected gold for the King. He rode hard on a horse—even though he'd never seen a live one—across endless plains mapped on the broken globe in his bedroom/living room/dining room. He robbed from the rich and gave to the poor and always had a Friar or Squire or Wizard walkin' by his side.

A real fuckin' ghetto Harry Potter.

And oh, those marvelous elephants ridden by Hannibal and him. Smattering, battering, ragin', reckless beasts that trampled Khan underfoot and restored glory to the lands. Reverend traversed the Alps and explored the Rockies with Lewis and Clark. Cheering crowds and blowing trumpets welcoming home the victors of war.

Spoils for all!

Least that's how life happened in Reverend's mind.

WILLIAM TEETS

Well, I see we got a few more heads interested in Rev's story. Gather 'round, people, listen-up, y'all might learn a thing or two.

See, folks, Rev found sanctuary in the yellow-bricked Nathaniel Hawthorne Library, surroundin' himself with <u>fictions</u> and <u>memoirs</u> and <u>poetry</u> and <u>maps</u>. Even though the books were old and tattered, kinda like Ol' Hawthorne himself, Rev was at peace in the library. Hell, his only concern there was that the librarian might remember he owed eighty-five cents in past due fines.

That library, brothers and sisters, just like his walk and his dreams, made Reverend special.

But like I done said, Reverend was always brought back to where he was. Amazed how he could escape and be captured at the same time. Amazed how he could be so free one moment and then chained to his life and surroundin' streets the next. Shackled by life with Aunt Constantine on 163rd and Saint Stephen Boulevard, right on the Holy Corner of Saint Peter's Church.

Holy Saint Peter's by day, rock spot by night.

Fall, Icarus, fall. I told you not to fly so high.

Let me fill y'all in, folks. See, Reverend was baptized as Thomas. But after the crash, the crash he always heard of, but never heard with his ears, the one that killed his mother and father far away in someplace called Mount Pleasant—shit, how ironic is that?—Aunt Constantine, along with his Uncle Luke, took Thomas in. And, my dudes, Aunt Constantine changed his name from Thomas to Reverend.

All legal and shit.

Proclaimed to *all* he would be the greatest preacher the world ever heard.

Didn't tell Luke she was changin' names. Reverend was too young to know or have a say, but change names she did. How fucked-up is that? Like I said, not that Reverend knew, he was only two at the time, but he learned later his God given name was altered. Altered without him or anyone else knowin' or carin'.

Just happened, man, true story.

His name was now Reverend.

Oh, Luke raised holy hell and spewed some demon words towards Constantine when he found out. But check it out, folks, she committed that Abraham sin when Luke was overseas. See, with Luke bein' gone so much of the time, flip-floppin' names was easy to do. Constantine paid no mind to what anyone else said either. So, Thomas became Reverend, an uncle too busy savin' the world to save his nephew's name, and an aunt too crazy and lost and *holy* to care what others thought.

Just another fucked-up story from the hood, my peeps.

But oh, I've got lots more.

Chapter 2
Kings Among Men

Reverend was bouncin' on the block.

It was an October Saturday mornin', cool enough for long sleeves, but not for no jacket. Rev rocked his customary kicks and fitted hat—shiny gold seal and all—and looked fly in his understood uniform of the hood. He started to smile as he started to dream, but was interrupted by a voice lampin' on the corner.

"Hey, Rev, where's that uncle of yours? He been gone a minute now ain't he?" asked One Shoe.

One Shoe was a local wino, two-bit hustler from the block. Damn good baller in his day, but he got drunk one night on Mad Dog, fell asleep in a snow bank, and had to have half his foot cut off 'cause of frostbite. So now, he wore only . . . yeah, you get it . . . I know . . . and well anyways, he's been called One Shoe ever since. Sometimes, just Shoe for short. Kinda like calling a Robert, Bobby, or a William, Billy.

Nicknames being a motherfucker and all. They're big time used in the hood. Shit, everybody has one. Never use your government. That's understood 'round here.

"Don't know, Shoe, but I know he's coming back soon. Coming back for me," Reverend said.

"Damn, dawg. Seem like longer than usual. What's it been, 'bout two munts now?"

"Forty-four days, today."

"Right-on, Rev. See you countin' the days and all. Right-on, lil' bruh."

"See you later, Shoe, heading to the library."

"Sure thing, Rev, that's what's up. Peace out, lil' bruh, peace out. Get that knowledge."

Let me tell you cats the *real* story about Rev's Uncle Luke. See, Luke was in the army and all, had to travel a lot overseas. Folks in the hood talk about him bein' in Special Forces or some other kinda Rambo type shit, and everyone figured that's why he was gone so much of the time. That was true, but not totally true. Hood people always thinkin' they know everyone else's business and such. No one knew for sure what Luke really did or was up to. But follow me, my dudes, all you *really* need to know is Reverend loved Luke like a father. Hell, Luke raised him since he was two, and Rev missed him so bad whenever he was gone, no matter where he was gone to.

Reverend loved receivin' and readin' letters from Luke. They came from far away, exotic soundin' places like Somalia, Bosnia, Mogadishu, Arabia, well, you know the dilly. Anyways, Reverend loved gettin' those letters.

He would read them over and over before neatly sealin' them in a plastic bag and puttin' them in a Nike shoebox beneath his couch/bed in his bedroom/living room/dining room. After readin' the latest one at least twenty times before lying down to sleep, Reverend would smile, knowing some great dreams awaited him.

See, Rev didn't really know the deal. Didn't know Luke *was* in Special Forces and sometimes in harm's way. All he knew was that Luke was in the army—some kinda hero and all cause of mad shiny medals Luke brought home—and Rev knew that Luke traveled a lot. He figured Luke was probably into something kinda dangerous, but he didn't like admittin' that to hisself. Most important, though, Rev knew Luke would be comin' home soon. Back to the hood, back to Constantine, but most important, back to Reverend.

And get this, folks, whenever Luke came back home, except for school and sleepin', Reverend was always with him. Going to museums and zoos and even the library together.

REVEREND WENT WALKING

On some special weekends, Luke and Reverend would drive way upstate and camp in the woods. Man, listen, they would hike and fish and cook bacon over a real open fire—how dope is that?—and have a crazy cool weekend together. Reverend loved spendin' time with Luke.

Continue to follow me now, people. Luke made good money and always kept Reverend decked out in all the hottest styles and gear and kicks, as well as buyin' him the iciest gifts a fourteen-year-old boy could dream of. But more importantly, Luke kicked knowledge with Reverend about life and the hood and being a positive brother. He loved the shit outta that boy, too.

Somethin' special to see.

Yeah, Luke was Reverend's main man and Luke loved Reverend like a son. Strongest, most honest bond I'd ever seen between two people.

True Story.

I shit you not.

Well, well, even more folks wantin' to hear Rev's story. Make room, brother, step on up sisters, step on up and listen up, y'all.

See, my people, what Luke really wanted was to move him and Constantine and Reverend to a nice big house in the country—out of the hood—but Constantine, unfortunately, was havin' none of that.

"In the name of Jesus, no! This is where I was born, this is where I was raised, and this *will* be where I die," Reverend would hear Constantine boom at Luke whenever Luke brought up the subject of moving.

"But think about Reverend," Luke would say. "It's about getting him out of these streets, better schools and all."

"Nothin' wrong with Saint Peter's School. Lord knows, you know how much that cost a year, and besides, his grades are excellent. What, we too good for here now because we got some money?" Constantine would sermon, stare, and glare.

And Reverend would try to make his mind go away into *The Call of the Wild* or *To Kill a Mockingbird*, as Luke and his Aunt Constantine continued to argue over the merits, or the lack of, moving upstate and out of the hood.

Reverend loved the idea—mostly—because Luke did, and he thought about movin' often. Thought about wide open country spaces and clear blue skies where he could dream and soar and not worry about nothin' snatchin' him back or burning his wings.

Yeah, man, free for *real*.

He'd already made a pact with himself that after high school he was ghost. Far away at some college and spendin' semester breaks with Luke in some country home far from the hood.

Where the deer and the antelope *really* do play.

REVEREND WENT WALKING

Aunt Constantine couldn't say shit then.

Like I told y'all, Reverend was special, but don't be fooled. He understood darkness, too. Even at fourteen, he'd already seen so many friends laid to waste by booze and dope, poked-up, shot-up, jailed-up, or worse yet, dead-up.

He was smart enough to realize the streets held nothin' but <u>disease</u> and <u>death</u> and <u>decay</u> and he didn't want no part of that. He learned that stuff from Luke. Learned that stuff from books. Learned that stuff with his eyes. He didn't glamorize or get caught up in that false allegiance shit, like Constantine and others, that being from and survivin' the hood should be worn like a badge of courage. No, my people, Reverend knew bullets have no names, knew there's no future in frontin' and knew the streets lie—always—paved with gold or shit, the streets lie.

Naw, man, after high school, he was outtie.

But Constantine sermoned on.

"Besides, you know I can't leave my church. And that church and school only thing keepin' that boy straight and out of trouble. The Devil be anywhere you go, city streets or county fair. At least here, with Saint Peter's Church, the Devil don't stand a chance of claimin' our souls. Hallelujah, can I get a witness?"

And Reverend knew when Aunt Constantine started Holy Rollin' the argument was over. Luke couldn't win and he knew it too. With him being gone so much, Luke understood the final decision lay with Constantine. And he also understood—in a way—she was right. Reverend *was* doin' well in school and stayin' out of trouble, but those damn streets, man, those damn streets.

As Luke walked away from the argument and Reverend went back to readin', Constantine continued her holy homily in the kitchen.

"Move to some fancy house in some town called Pleasantville or Hopewell or Shady Brook, sinner, please. No strong church, no congregation. The Devil will collect his dues I tell you. Lord, no! We're safe and stayin' put. Satan be gone, you're not welcome here today. Praise, Jesus!"

"All right Constantine, you made your point," Luke would say over his shoulder.

"No I haven't, not even close. What about Thomasina, ohh, my loving sister, Thomasina, how'd that upstate livin' work out for her?"

"Constance, Rev is right in the other room, he can hear you. Stop talking that nonsense. Christ's sake, that's his mother you're talking about."

"*And* my sister. My beautiful sister. Moved upstate with those highfalutin' society people, lost God, lost her roots, and ended up killed by some drunk-drivin' hillbilly. The truth shall set *us* free! Nothing wrong with that boy hearin' the truth.

REVEREND WENT WALKING

Praise the Lord! And you, you taking the Lord's name in vain in our own home. Does *anyone* have *mercy*?"

And Luke would fast-walk into the living room/bedroom/dining room where Rev was readin', scared about answerin' Constantine honestly because he was not sure how much *mercy* he had left. Afraid he might show her what true *mercy* really is. Instead, he rolled his eyes, tilted his head, and gave Reverend that *oh, well* look.

"You OK, Rev? You know she gets crazy with that religion stuff. After your Momma died, she ain't been the same. Good woman and all, though, when I married her . . . still is . . . I guess. She good to you when I'm gone, she good to you? *You good*?"

"Yeah, Uncle Luke, I'm good. Always good when you're around."

And they both would laugh a little laugh, pretend everything was solid, and smile. Smile the way Reverend smiled into sleep after readin' Luke's letters.

In his dreams, Reverend always saw Luke as some great Moor warrior riding those magnificent elephant beasts into battle. A shiny knight in armor wielding a powerful sacred sword. Luke would slay barbarians at the gate and free bonded people. Sir Thomas—his God given name—not Reverend, would be saddled beside him.

Both would shout victory cries on the battlefield.

WILLIAM TEETS

Water for the horses, whiskey for the men!

Luke and Sir Thomas would venture into dragon lairs, behead Medusa, and shoot poisoned arrows from speeding chariots at Ares. They would repel the Gauls and Vandals and Visigoths who dared try to seize their castle and they would sink enemy schooners at sea. Winning over fair maidens and drinkin' the finest wines, Luke and Thomas would bathe in bodacious perfumes and garner the most coveted spices. All gifts granted by silk traders and Marco Polo, who journeyed from the Far East.

Luke and Thomas the Moor.

Kings among men!

Allies and protectors of the common man.

Leaders of Christ's Crusades!

How cool life would be, how dope their lives would end up.

Luke and Thomas, no doubt.

Luke and Thomas the More.

Sinfuckingsational!

Well people, I know different.

Chapter 3
Fresh Cut

"You want a fresh cut or are you going to sleep all day?"

"Luke!" Reverend shouted, as he bounced from his bed/couch. "You're home, you're back, I knew you would!" he exclaimed, hugging Luke so tight, fearful that if he stopped a Baku would swallow this too.

"Come on, man. Get yourself ready and let's go get that cut."

Rev loved goin' to the barbershop with Luke. They had to walk downtown—below 154th Street where the shop was—where all the ramblers and gamblers, slingers and lost saints, wanna-be OG's and *real* OG's hung out and prayed to their own altered gods.

In a weird kinda adolescent way Reverend romanticized, admired, and even envied a little, the street corner hustlers and all the action takin' place. He loved the cee-lo games, the pool halls and smoke shops, even that sickly sweet smell of weed wafting in the air. Most of all he loved the barbershop.

The shop was owned by Solomon, who everyone called Solly, naturally—remember what I said earlier about nicknames and all?—and Solly was Luke's best friend. Reverend loved sittin' in the shop and listenin' to all the men share stories and arguments about most anything you could imagine and some things you never could. He so enjoyed the camaraderie and the liveliness and all the salty language and diversified dialects banterin' about the room.

And the food, dawg, forget about it. Beef patties, jerk chicken stew, ox tails and rice, man, makes your mouth water just thinking 'bout all that food. Rev was mad hype. It was Sunday—no school—Luke was home and Rev had him all to himself.

"Un-Un, sinner, not today. Today's the Lord's day. The Sabbath. You and that boy ain't missin' service to go get some haircut down at that den of iniquity smack in the middle of sinner's land. Present day Sodom and Gomorrah . . . you'll both be turned to salt. Lord, no! Not today. Today is the Lord's day," Constantine bellowed as she pranced into the room.

"But Aunt Constantine, please," Reverend begged. "I'll make it up. I promise."

"Ain't no deal making with God, boy. Only the Devil makes deals. Like I said, not today, not on the Sabbath."

REVEREND WENT WALKING

"With all due respect, Constance, me and my son are going to get a fresh cut . . . to-day. Trust me, the Lord will understand and hopefully in a few years, you might too," Luke said.

And oh my, did that send Constantine into a tizzy. She grabbed her shawl, grabbed her purse, and stompin' her heeled hoofs like an angry water buffalo, stormed out the door wailing for the Lord to save us.

All of us?

That whole scene made Reverend smile, but what made him smile even more—inside—was that Luke had called him his son. See, Reverend didn't miss *his* mother—he couldn't remember her—but what he did miss was never havin' no mother. No father. And Luke's loving words just changed that, even if just a little.

On the low.

So many nights Rev would lie awake in the nighttime black darkness that made space infinite and think about his mother who he never knew. Who she was, what was she was like, what may have been, and then he would create her in his mind. That perfect natural woman you see in catalogs and pin-ups who sang in angel voices like sirens on lost shores. That perfect natural woman who had loving eyes deeper then the Universe. That perfect natural woman that the entire world yearns for, who can't be found, never was, taken away somewhere too soon, too suddenly, leaving us all orphans to our own fabricated fates. That was Reverend's mother in his mind.

Deep shit, folks, I know, but I'm gettin' ahead of myself again.

Don't mix it up, though. Rev loved Constantine, but as his aunt, not his mother. That special mother love was never fostered with her. Luke though, always felt like Rev's father. Reverend always loved Luke like his pops, and now Luke had even called Rev his son.

Yes, sir, this was going to be a day to remember.

As Luke and Reverend walked downtown, Rev's walk bounced so graceful and high he almost floated above the skyline. That electricity of true unconditional love between two people—without no words being said—currented between Luke and Reverend.

They chuckled and laughed low as they told silly jokes and broke on the people around them. Bumped into each other's shoulders on purpose and played the dozens. A perfect day for both of them and then, just before arrivin' to the shop, they heard a barking growl, rattlesnake hiss behind them.

"Well, well, if it ain't Cool Hand Luke. Welcome home, soldier boy."

Luke and Reverend turned around to see No Neck standing with his laughing hyena posse, as if what he had just said was the funniest thing them clowns had ever heard.

"Morning, Thaddeus," Luke replied.

And the corner went quiet.

A few snickers, a few guffaws, and a few *oh shit, no he didn't* sounds emanated from the crowd, but one look by No Neck, in the offenders' general direction, silenced all.

For real.

"Only my Moms called me that, Luke. And even though you a bitch, you ain't her," No Neck said, proud of his wit and now approving of the snickers and guffaws and *oh shit, no he didn't* clatters from the hood corner jesters.

"Whatever, man, whatever. Let's go, Rev," Luke said, placing his arm around Reverend's shoulders.

"Yeah, that's right, my man. Ain't no sand niggas here for you to beat up on. Just real niggas like me. What's wrong Cool Hand . . . need an army to fight your battles?"

Luke paused in his step, but when he felt Reverend's muscles tense, he continued to walk.

"Hey church boy . . . Reverend . . . ain't it? When you gonna come down this side of town where niggas is real? Not them church goin' faggots you fucks with. When you gonna come check me and find out how real niggas be?"

Oh man, no he didn't, tell me he didn't.

Yes, he did.

Luke stopped again and straight-armed Reverend behind him. He exhaled heavily and took two steps towards No Neck. No Neck—or Thaddeus if you prefer—more of that hood nickname bullshit I told y'all about—squared up and clenched his fists.

"Yeah, nigga, come on. This is what I'm talkin' 'bout. This beens a long time comin'," No Neck hissed.

"What's goin' on? Luke, you good?" asked Solly, walkin' fast from his shop, towards the growin' circle of people surroundin' both men.

"This don't concern you barber man. Fuck off and minds yours if you knows what's good for you," No Neck shouted to Solly without looking at him.

Solly went to step, but was hemmed up by two of No Neck's crew.

"Just you and me soldier boy. Just you and me. You gonna find out I ain't the next man. I ain't the next nigga."

And what happened next, my people, can't no one really say.

REVEREND WENT WALKING

Shit happened so quick, the confrontation between Luke and No Neck was done over before it got started. No Neck took a swing and then was on the ground heavin' for breath and groanin' all loud and nasty like. The corner got mad silent when Luke, all calm and peaceful Pacific, not fazed or winded in the least, leaned over No Neck and said, "As God is my witness, if you ever fuck with that boy, I will end you. Understand?"

No Neck grunted some words that sounded like, 'Fuck you, soldier boy, suck . . . ' but before he could finish, Luke touched his shoulder—I'm tellin' you, people, just touched it—and No Neck started screamin' like someone had beaten his momma.

"Say yes, if you understand, Thaddeus."

"Yes, nigga. I understands," No Neck gurgled through clenched teeth.

"Good then. Have a nice day, Thaddeus. Let's go get that cut, Rev. Get your hands off him! Solly you good?"

"Yeah, Luke, I'm good."

And just like that, a hood version of the O.K. Corral erupted and was settled and was dismissed. No Neck and his crew vowed revenge from across the street sellin' woof-woof tickets. No Neck tellin' his peeps, "Naw, dawgs, I wasn't hurt. He tricked me with that Kung-Fu shit. I'm a gonna bust his ass next time. Word."

WILLIAM TEETS

And people went back to doin' whatever it is they got to do in the hood and Luke and a wide-eyed Reverend walked with Solly into his shop to get a fresh cut, but not before Luke said to Reverend, "Not a word of this to Aunt Constantine. She'll fuck me up."

Rev smiled.

Chapter 4
Secrets

"What the hell was that all about?" Solly asked Luke.

"Man, you know, that beef between me and No Neck been goin' on since high school. We used to be best friends, you remember that, but some junk I can't even recall, and he's been ridin' my dick ever since."

"Yeah, man, but the balls on him . . . in daylight. We know he's a punk, but he's crazy and all too. Be careful he ain't packin' or setting your ass up. Don't sleep on him, Bro."

"Forget him. He might be crazy, but he ain't stupid. He's a two-bit hustler loser with no self-respect."

Luke looked over towards Reverend. "Never lose your self-respect Rev, never. Got it?"

"Got it, Luke."

And Reverend saw and needed to see that side of Luke.

Needed to see that a man can take care of hisself and not be a bully or an asshole or arrogant about doin' so. Another lesson learned by Reverend from Luke, from the hood, from his eyes. Reverend loved that man even more that day, if that shit was even possible.

Word.

As Rev peeped Luke's reflection in the mirror, he thought more about him. Thought about things he didn't know about him, about who the other Luke was, what Luke *really* did when he was away. And Reverend thought, w*hat's a sand nigga, how did Luke hurt No Neck so easily, why did Luke threaten to end No Neck's life*, and a harrumph grill formed on Reverend's face and he pondered hard before his thoughts were broken by Solly sayin', "You're up Rev, you're next."

Yeah, man, Reverend was next.

Walkin' home from the shop in early dusk—a fall breeze blowing—Luke and Reverend didn't talk much. Rev was all quiet, silent like, and Rev's mood wasn't lost on Luke. But Luke thought lettin' lil' man be, about what happened earlier in the day, was for the best. If Rev had questions that needed answers he would ask, and Luke would tell.

Simple.

REVEREND WENT WALKING

Right, folks?

The truth shall set you free and oh what a tangled web we weave and all that other type shit, right?

Always been.

Always preached.

Unfortunately, not always practiced.

In Rev's head, he replayed the questions the day asked and tried to understand the upside down feelings bouncin' 'bout his brain. Split-shit perceptions he had of Luke. Hell, he knew Luke—he knew that—but he ain't never seen Luke act, or be forced to act, like he done did earlier. Didn't bother Rev, though, Luke actually grew in his eyes, and Rev thought—*Fuck No Neck*—but the ease that Luke brought that big man to his knees with still swam in Rev's brain. Was Luke a superhero? What did he *really* do for a living? He must be a superhero.

Rev ain't learned yet that a superhero ain't but a step away from kryptonite.

That superheroes fail and don't *really* exist.

Even if you'd seen one.

Or think you did.

But that shit Luke did . . . nigga, please.

Now don't get me wrong, my people. Reverend's no pussy and he has street smarts and his props and all and can definitely hold his own. Hell, in the hood you have to, or you are sure to be a victim. Preyed on by anyone you allow to be above you in the jungle-hood food chain of survival.

Anyone.

Beat down, or get beat down.

But Rev was still only fourteen. Lots of stuff he didn't know or wasn't able to grasp or learn yet. He was perplexed by Luke chumpin' down No Neck so easily, not even breakin' a sweat, and then not even talkin' 'bout what happened. Like that scenario on the block didn't even really happen. Like it was some kinda covenant or secret.

See, Reverend didn't know or understand that everyone, and I mean everyone, brothers and sisters, has that one dark and hid secret they ain't never shared with no one. Not their best friend, not their wifey, hell, sometimes not even with themselves. And that dark secret lay hidden always and anyone who says they don't have one, well, son, they're a liar. Kinda like masturbating. Ninety-nine percent of people do it and the other one percent lie. Anyone who tells you anything different is straight up frontin'.

And that's what Rev was riffing with in his head. Thinkin' 'bout Luke, what kind of secrets Luke might have and had never shared. Why did No Neck challenge Luke in the first place? What does Solly know?

Reverend was havin' problems clearin' his cloudy thoughts into crystal ideas and recognizin' those confused feelings that come into our heads and then run away before we can grab them. Feelings that you have sometimes when you wake up in the mornin' and sense somethin' is wrong, but don't have a clue about what it might be. Some instinctual, gut feelin', premonition type shit, that's real as right, but unrecognizable at the same time.

Feelings and thoughts that can drive you insane. That lead you to self-destruction. Make you become a wino or start hittin' on that pipe. Tear your marriage asunder and make you sell your children. Needin' pills to sleep and pills to wake back up again. Followin' a faith that has left nothin' but burnin' brown bags of dog shit on your stoop that you step on to put out after you answer a knocking so loud on your door. Cymbalta, Xanax, ganja, a couple of forties, just to make you feel, or not feel. Fuck, to make you lie to yourself that you love your family, love yourself, and everything is groovy.

I know, I know, I'm gettin' deep and to the marrow, people.

I've got a tendency to do that.

But, hang on.

Let me take you back.

WILLIAM TEETS

Back to our story.

As the fall breeze scattered newspapers and empty coffee cups instead of leaves—see no trees really grow in the ghetto—that's just another story and all, kinda like Chicken Little or the Easter Bunny, Luke noticed Rev's face all scrunched up in deep thought. When Reverend looked up at Luke with his eyes sayin' *yeah, but* . . . Luke broke the silence and said, "What's up in that noggin of yours? Let's take a seat and talk. I've been trying to be quiet, not get inside your head and all, but it seems like we need to kick it."

And when they sat on the stone bench in front of Nathaniel Hawthorne, Reverend tried to express his thoughts into words, but his mouth couldn't keep up with his brain.

"Are you in danger when you leave . . . how did you do that to No Neck . . . are we really going to leave the hood someday . . . are you leaving again . . . soon?"

"Whoa, easy, Rev. One at a time," Luke said.

And Reverend looked at his kicks, feelin' stupid and childish that he blurted out his thoughts all at once, confused and jumbled and girly-like, and he frowned. Luke picked up on lil' man's feelings and put his arm around Reverend's shoulders.

"I'm not going to front, Rev. I did a lot of dangerous stuff in the army, but the past few years have been a breeze. I'm more of a consultant and advisor now and work out of big offices and buildings far from any danger."

"And?" Reverend asked, looking hard into Luke's returning eyes.

"And, I'm gonna tell you something I haven't told anyone else yet, not Solly, not your Aunt Constantine, and well, not even you, until now. I do have to leave one more time to go overseas. Just to wrap some stuff up and take care of business. But, that's it."

Reverend's eyes widened and a small smile began to turn up on his face, "And then?"

"Well, and then, I've been offered a position at West Point—remember where we saw those football games—I've been offered a post to teach cadets. We're going to be living there. That is, if you want."

"Hell, yeah, I want!" Reverend exclaimed.

"With or without Aunt Constantine. I'm hoping she agrees and there's no problem, but you know how she is. But believe me, we're gonna make this work. It's what I've been working towards for the last twelve years, ever since we took you in. And now, my man, looks like we made it."

And man, did Reverend ever hug Luke so hard and long. Not your regular sight in the hood—two men huggin' a lot longer than the normal, few, bromance seconds—but hug they did, right there under Ol' Nathaniel, who might've smiled if his concrete face allowed him to do so. Almost like Luke and Rev were one. Yeah, my peeps, a true proper bond of love.

And as another breeze from the fall blew over them, they started headin' home, but not before Luke said, "Listen Rev, not a word of this to no one. Not Constance, not Solly, not Old Man, not anyone. It's our secret for now. Got it?"

"Got it, Luke."

And Rev thought then that everything in the world was righteous and correct. Couldn't nothin' mess with him now. His dreams were comin' true, even on them streets that lie— always—his dreams were comin' true.

Better than that, y'all, he had a secret with Luke that no one else knew. A great special oath between only Luke and him. A secret only they shared. Luke's special secret that he chose to tell Rev.

Tell Thomas.

Luke and Thomas the Moor.

But before you all get happy and weepy, people, didn't I just tell ya that Reverend hadn't learned yet about everyone havin' that one hidden secret they don't share with no one?

I mean no one.

REVEREND WENT WALKING

Reverend poured some Aunt Jemima on his second helpin' of johnnycakes. Man, he loved Aunt Constantine's johnnycakes, and Rev smiled inside and out. Not just because of the johnnycakes, but because of the wink and knowin' smile Luke gave to him before Luke left to go back overseas. Overseas for the last time, with no one knowing it was the last time, 'cept for Reverend and Luke.

Their secret.

Yeah, man, their secret.

"What's wrong wit' you boy? Sittin' there smilin' like the cat who ate the canary. Usually you all down in the dumps when your uncle leaves. I knows my cookin' is good, but nots that good."

"Nothing up, Aunt Constantine, just chillin' and all, you know."

"Hmmm, chillin'. Looks like you hidin' sumptin'. You hidin' sumptin', boy? You know you can't hide nothing from God. He knows and sees everything. Ain't no secrets from God, you hear me boy, ain't no secrets from God. For nothing is secret that shall not be made manifest! He will bring to light what is hidden in the darkness and will expose the motives of the heart. Lord, have mercy! Whatever you have said in the dark will be heard in the light. Hallelujah, can I get a witness?" Constantine shouted, working herself into a hoof-stomping sweat.

And Rev just smiled.

The word secret danced in Reverend's head like MJ moon dancing. Back and forth, up and down, sideways.

Unh, Unh, Unh.

Yeah, man, the word secret danced. Danced like a wild stallion snortin' and pouncing and unable to be tamed. Come to life right off the pages of a Louis L'Amour novel.

Secret, from the Latin secretus, separate, set apart. Least that's what Reverend read in the big dog-eared dictionary down at the library. Secret, secretus, separate, set apart—but that didn't define the word for Rev, anything but. His and Luke's secret may have separated them geographically, may have set them apart for the time bein', but naw, man, their secret was goin' to bring them together—forever—once they could share their great secret with the world.

Unfortunately, my dudes, Reverend *still* didn't know some secrets can't or never will or never should be shared.

True that.

Good secrets, bad secrets, healin' secrets, or hurtin' secrets. Don't matter. A secret is a secret is a secret, and most just ain't shared proper. Ain't meant to be or can't be. Any secret has the power to destroy. Evil or righteous. But our boy Rev smiled anyways. No one could tell him that his and Luke's secret wasn't the motherfucker of all secrets. No, sir, their secret wasn't separate and settin' them apart, no, dawgs, their secret was special and joining them together.

What God has joined together.

Their special secret.

Let no man tear asunder.

Their special secret.

This is the word of the Lord.

Their special secret.

Praise be to God.

Their special secret.

How special, Reverend had no idea.

Chapter 5
Built On Stone

"Wake up, boy, your sinner uncle gone. They'll be no missin' service today. Haircuts, zoos, upstate campin' in Satan's wilderness, sleepin' amongst the beasts of the wild, no, boy, he's gone away now. The Lord will have his time. This Sunday you'll be spendin' with the Lord, yes indeed, rise up, rise up, I say, and greet the Word. Hallelujah!"

And Reverend groaned.

See, folks, goin' to service with Constantine wasn't your normal forty-five minute meet-and- greet the Lord. Oh, no, service at Saint Pete's was a marathon of madness that could last hours, causin' the most devoted and pious of us to roll our eyes, sigh to high heaven, and search for the nearest exit.

What with the wailin' and cryin' and talkin' in tongues, bonkin' one another on the forehead, people shakin' limbs and fallin' out, crazy wafting holy smoke, splashes of holy water, naw people, I tell ya, it's a madhouse for real.

REVEREND WENT WALKING

True story.

Believe me, y'all, I'm not frontin'.

And then, of course, there's our boy, Rev.

Lord, how that boy dreaded bein' dragged off to service on Sunday with his Aunt Constantine. She'd strut down the block like Attila the Nun, chastisin' Rev to pick up the pace and stop all his lolly-gaggin' and suckin' of teeth.

Sittin' on his couch/bed, tryin' to rid himself of wakin' up sleep, Rev could hear Aunt Constantine in his head. *Stop dawdling, boy, and lose that hang-dog face. Rejoice, I say, for today is the Savior's day. And you best not be rollin' your eyes at me. Mm-Mm, not havin' none of that sassin'. My sister may have brought you into this world, but Lord knows, I can takes you out. And don't even think of tryin' to sneak off. The Lord sees and I sees all. And pull your pants up, they'll be no saggy pants in the house of the Lord. Now move, boy, before I haves to put my foot where the sun don't shine. Hallelujah! Can I get a witness?*

And Reverend groaned a second time.

See, folks, he already knew the next few hours of his existence on this old spinnin' globe of ours was gonna be spent witnessin' all the madness I already told you all about. The wailin', the chantin', the talkin' in tongues and the bonkin' of foreheads, but also the dark shadows. Rev hated the darkness of the church. See, Saint Pete's Church is closed off from the sun outside, the once majestic missive is just so damn gloomy.

Wasn't always that way, but through the years, what with so many tall buildings and those damn 'jects being built, Saint Pete's was cast into a shadow land. The hood's own manifest destiny and fake-ass gentrification now dwarfed the church and blocked out the light of the sun. Damn shame too, people, cause that church got the most beautiful stained glass windows you ever saw.

I'd seen them—back when I was a youngster—and man, let me tell ya, the dazzling rays of the sun made all of Roy G. Biv's colors dance like flowin' rivers of M&M's or chalk colored orange and purple sunsets. Right there, right in old Saint Pete's.

Can you dig that?

Do you know what I'm tryin' to say?

The beauty of something, one time *real*.

People, I tell ya, that church and them windows was a sight to be seen. But like most everything else, down here in the hood, it ain't there no more or don't work no more. 'Specially those saintly stained glass windows that's s'pose to share the sacraments and praise the Lord. Just can't be, not with the sun blocked out.

Kinda defeats the whole purpose of havin' the glass in the first place, don't you think?

Kinda like lookin' through stained glass on stormy days.

REVEREND WENT WALKING

Just don't work.

Know what I'm sayin'?

Broke like.

Like most everything else these days.

Naw, shit just don't work no more.

Two tears in a bucket, fuck it.

Don't want to sound all negative and down, just keepin' it a buck for you all, just keepin' it a hundred.

Anyways, Reverend and Constantine headed off to Saint Pete's, to the great displeasure of Rev, but to the magnificent glory of Constantine. Gatherin' in front of the church, before service, Constantine would stand in a tight circle with other members of her holy herd. She would hold healthy to Reverend's hand, and lament on the sorry condition and disrepair of the corner of 163rd and Saint Stephen's Boulevard.

"The sin is encroachin' sisters. Did you see the broken vials, the drug remains, the Devil's handiwork right outside our door? We need to have Pastor Goodman-Brown organize another town hall. The wicked are multiplyin' and tryin' to lay seize to our sanctuary," Constantine sermonically said.

"Yes indeed, sister, yes, indeed. My Ollie went out for milk last night and said those corner boys were sellin' Satan's rock right here on the block. As brazen as King Herod hisself," a second member of the herd snorted in.

"Not right, sisters, not right. Miss Jones, herself, lost to the sin. Flaunting and making herself available to men in broad daylight. Saw her sneakin' off down an alley with that old, sinning, wino, One Shoe," a third harrumphed.

"Heard she's on that pipe. Satan's telephone, microphone, oh, sisters, don't make me say it. You know what they say, she's smoking Satan's . . . oh, I can't say it, sisters. "

And the word *dick* came into Rev's head. *She's smoking Satan's dick and who knows who else's dick to get more of the rock to smoke from Satan's dick. Just say it, you know you want to.*

And Rev smiled, for the first time that day. In a perverse guilty way, thinkin' them bad words made him feel a little better.

"Oh, I can't say it. I can't."

"It's all right, sister, we understands, we know what you're tryin' to say, but we must denounce the Devil and Miss Jones. She must be banished," a young calf mooed.

And the herd snorted a cacophony chortle, "Agreed. Praise, Jesus."

And Rev groaned a third time that day.

Thought I might've even heard a cock crow at that point. Naw, folks, just playin' with y'all, just messin' with your heads, but y'all know what I'm sayin', right?

But man, let me tell you, all those holy rollers worked themselves into a mini frenzy and began babblin' as if they shot an arrow to the high heavens, like Nimrod himself. Gotta give 'em credit though, they still gave a shit—about what, I'm not so sure—but they still cared about somethin'. When it seems no one else does and has already surrendered to what is they still gave a shit. Even in their blindness, they still tryin' to see.

For all of us?

"The end of days is upon us, sisters. Our holy refuge is goin' to fall into a sinkhole of sin, but with God's grace, we will be cleansed anew with holy water flooded from the harbor. Cleansin' the saved and drownin' the wicked. Michael will row his boat ashore, hallelujah, and we will be saved sisters, can I get a witness?" Constantine huffed.

And amens and hallelujahs resounded through the hood.

"Time to enter, ladies and gentlemen, time to pay homage," young Pastor Goodman-Brown said.

And all began to funnel through the majestic mahogany doors, but not before Constantine straightened Reverend up by grabbin' his shoulders. Wiping away any left over, wake up sleepin' sand from his eyes—nearly blindin' him in the process with her short stubby thumbs—she looked into his ears, patted his head hard twice, and said, "Boy, if you don't pull those pants up, I'm gonna . . ."

The echoes of the muffled hymns from inside the church quietly whispered onto the streets. Lost, lilting, faint words, which were heard only by a few. Almost like them words were rumored secrets or foreboded warnings or lost validations, swallowed up by howling alley winds before their message could be completely told.

Have you ever heard an alley cat screech or a hungry baby scream, people? Kinda like that, but so much less noticeable—just as much distress—but so much more covered up. Gagged. I guess like an oxymoron—isn't that an awesome word, folks, oxymoron?—or some other unknown entity or sound that not everybody can hear, or chooses to hear.

I know, folks, weird, I know.

Just sayin' and all.

Gets me to thinkin'.

What and who does God really hear or speak to?

Just sayin'.

REVEREND WENT WALKING

Just askin'.

Yeah, I know, my people, I be buggin' sometimes.

Anyways, back to our main man, Rev. Had to feel sorry for the lil' brother, surrounded by different beasts of the wild now. Man, he'd watch that insane church-service-show like it was some Bellini painting come to life right off the pages of an art book he'd seen in Nathaniel Hawthorne.

Shit, even Ol' Hawthorne hisself would have been aghast at this panorama. And let's not forget, people, his ancestors were Puritans who burned witches. Yeah, man, this scene would've definitely bugged out Old Nate.

So, see, how do you think Rev felt?

Well, let me tell you, people, let me tell you all what usually happened.

Rev would sit there, eyes dartin' back and forth, one on Constantine, one on the undercover ushers, both on the clergy covered and uniformed deacon constables, and he would plot his getaway.

No doubt.

Faithful faith.

Fire and Brimstone.

WILLIAM TEETS

Let my people go!

And just as Rev thought he'd found an escape route, just when he was gettin' ready to book, Constantine would horse collar him—like the hand of God Himself reaching down from the heavens—and she would proclaim to all, "Release this boy, Satan, he does not belong to you! Reverend, release your sin and denounce the false light of Lucifer! Allow the Lord to save you! Oh, me, oh, my, oh, Virgin Mary, Mother of God, spare this child. We've got a sinner in our house, sisters. There is a lost lamb amongst us."

And Rev would be instantly surrounded by four or five woman water buffaloes who would shake their mighty wooly heads and stomp their massive angry hooves and raise their cleft-hands in homage to the Baby Jesus. Chantin', screamin'—and lest not forget more wild wailin'—they would commence salvation amid their howls and grunts and proclamations and solemnly state, "Save the lost baby lamb, save the sinner child, Hosanna in the highest. Praise be to God! Spare the babe; for he knows not what he does."

Ain't no God about all that, if you askin' me.

Just sayin' and all.

For Rev's sake and all.

But anyways, the whole crazy inquisition, exorcism, fanatical farce, made Reverend's head swim so terrible he thought his ears would go soundless, his mouth would be sealed and

REVEREND WENT WALKING

his eyes would explode. He would be left forever deaf, dumb and blind.

Man, with all the hollerin', the darkness, with what I already told you about the burnin' smoke and splashin' water, there were *real* times Reverend thought he might die. Right there, right in Saint Peter's Church, right in front of the altar and tortured saints.

But just when Rev finally had enough, when he felt closest to death, when the dank musty smell and sweat beads from the herd dropped upon him, he too would wail and shake his limbs and cackle some unintelligible syllables, speaking in a foreign voice, like a rabid angel. Reverend would profess his love of a false Lord—a Lord so different from his Lord, the Lord he had learned from Luke—and he would shake and rattle and roll, people.

Just like Big Joe Turner!

He knew actin' all crazy-religious and such was his only chance at *present* salvation. To be bonded with truth and Luke again at a later time.

For now, the masses needed to be satisfied.

The beast had to be fed.

The truth had to lie.

He knew he had to plead for this false salvation. Reverend

knew it was his only hope at escape. His only *real* hope for survival. His only chance at bein' cleansed anew.

And brothers and sisters he sold his act.

Sold his transformation like some used-car salesman sells you a hoopty.

That smooth.

And oh, how the herd rejoiced.

They would praise Jesus, praise Yahweh, and then stampede to the next lonely lost lamb that had strayed from the flock or been led away by a wolf of deceit. Another lost soul in need of desperate salvation and grace. Or not. They would impose their glory on this next innocent lamb, savin' or bastardizin', raisin' up or puttin' down, bein' helpful or bein' hurtful, it's hard to tell the difference, but they pounced.

Fuck, I don't know.

Gave up judging a long time ago.

Don't want to be judged no more, myself.

Just ain't right for me.

Now, it's between me and *my* God.

No one else, people.

REVEREND WENT WALKING

Can't afford the price of admission.

Can't judge what was right or wrong for Rev either, even if I think I know.

You decide.

Like I said, I done gave up judgin' others.

But anyways, back to Reverend.

He knew why he did what he did. See, poor Rev, forgotten and alone now, would collapse in a pew, covered in his and the herd's musky sweat, and wish Luke was there to *really* save him. Save him and take him away. Take him somewhere he ain't never been before. Where all this bullshit couldn't clutch him back into the crab bucket, where all this fake ceremonial mumbo-jumbo couldn't strangle him, where a Baku couldn't eat his dreams so willingly, where he could soar so high, in a new beautiful blue sky, the sun could never melt the wax binding his wings.

To *really* be free.

To dance.

To sing.

He *really* believed Luke could do *all* that.

He still believed in a God he knew could do all that.

WILLIAM TEETS

Problem was, people, Rev was gonna get his wish—to find all this out—sooner than later.

See, folks, Luke was gonna do a lot more to that boy then Rev could ever imagine.

Fall, Icarus, fall. I told you not to fly so high.

Chapter 6
A Day In The Hood

Reverend hip-hopped down the block.

Damn, people, we got even more heads wantin' to hear about Rev's story. Pull up, take a seat, brothers and sisters, or stand quiet like and listen. There's lots more 'bout to go down. Grab that milk crate, shortie. My man, lean up over here. Youngblood, don't be shy, this here story might just change your life. Sit over there, brother, hear me now.

It was late December, but warm as hell. Some kinda Gulf Stream, low-high front, El Nino—or somethin' like that type-shit—was basking the hood in seventy degree weather. Our boy, Rev, was diggin' the smooth sunshine on his face. He replaced his standard-wearin' winter Timbs with a favorite pair of his Nike Uptowns, and yeah, people, he hip-hopped down the block. Wearing a fresh, blue-and-orange, Knicks' hoody he got for Christmas, days like this even made Rev think the hood wasn't so bad and could be saved after all.

Unexpected gifts can do that to a brother.

A little joy, a little holiday cheer, some unaccustomed winter heat wave and suddenly everyone starts thinkin' everything is groovy. Starts believin' that all is right in the world, everyone is blessed, everyone the same.

Damn, man, why can't those special happy feelings and times last forever?

Why can't we put them in an old cigar box or slip them between pages of an old book and have them ready for us, always? Have them there when we need them most? Kinda like emergency jumper cables for the soul. Why can't we hold tight to our wondrous special times forever?

Maybe Rev thought he still could.

He was only fourteen—after all—still three months from his fifteenth birthday, but don't forget people, I told you before, people, Rev was a deep brother and an old soul at fourteen, but on this blessed warm day, even Rev allowed himself to get caught up in false glory.

All need to be careful in the hood.

Someone slips, someone gets caught sleepin', and man, let me tell you, that there is a sure fire recipe for disaster and heartache.

Rev knew that—or he should've known that—hell yeah, he

knew that. But today he was sleepin' and slippin'. And in the hood that will get you got.

"Well, well. If it ain't motherfuckin' church boy," No Neck bellowed, waking Rev up from his early mornin' siesta. "What you doin' down here, church boy? Lost or sumptin'? Maybe you come to take me up on my offer, wanta earn a little cheddar, wanta roll with the big dogs? Is that it, church boy, is that why you on my block?" No Neck barked.

Rev tried to half circle, wide berth, No Neck, but Cool Breeze, one of No Neck's corner boys—another one of them anti-govment, nicknames—bounced Rev back straight with a laugh and a sneer and then a laugh again.

"Leave dat boy be. He ain't messin' wit' you," One Shoe shouted, as he stood up from the empty Crown Royal case he'd been sittin' on in front of Abdula's liquor store.

"Fuck you, Shoe, minds yours, you fuckin' wino, 'less you want some of this, too!" No Neck shouted back.

And as Reverend braced himself, not sure what to expect next, he heard a car horn honk and looked to see Solly pulled over to the curb.

"Still ain't learned your lesson, No Neck? Reverend, get in. No Neck, when you gonna join the human race—for real?"

And Rev jetted into the front seat of Solly's car before any of No Neck's goonies could snatch him. He closed the door behind him, but not before hearing No Neck shout, "Fuck you too, barber man. Your times is comin', same as that pussy-ass soldier boyfriend of yours times is comin'. Mark it, nigga, that's my word. All yours times is comin'."

"Get your ass back to the circus—clown," Solly dissed and pulled away.

"Yeah, clown, go join a circus," One Shoe cracked from across the street.

No Neck was heated.

"You good, Rev? You OK?"

"Yeah, Solly, I'm fine. I'm good."

But Reverend lied, people.

He wasn't fine.

He wasn't good.

He was hurtin' inside again, in his head, in his heart, fed up with how the hood always stole away any good feelings he had like a stick-up corner boy steals your rope or celly. No, my peeps, Rev was not good. He was beaten up in his brain, so damn tired of this shit.

Sittin' in Solly's car, Rev wished so bad Luke was home. Home to fuck up No Neck again, home to bounce down the

REVEREND WENT WALKING

block again, home to go to the zoo again, but really folks, Rev thought of Luke being home for good, their special secret shared. Home for good so they could move upstate and leave this cesspool city behind.

The fulfillment of a sacred creed.

A secret finally shared correct.

A faith unable to be tested.

Damn, people, that stuff sounds good, but down here in the hood...

Anyways, as Rev sat in Solly's car, he saw No Neck's reflection in the side view mirror. Saw No Neck holdin' court with his cronies like he was above everybody else. Like he was the grand poobah, the king-shit, the czar of the corner and that made Reverend angry. But as Solly pulled off, Reverend exhaled as the big man's reflection shrunk in the mirror.

What Rev didn't get though, folks, is that images in the side view mirror are closer than they appear.

———•((•))•———

"Start with the floor, Rev. I want to open by ten. After that hit the front door window."

WILLIAM TEETS

"Got it, Solly. Getting on it."

Reverend had begun working for Solly on some weekends and over school breaks to earn a little scratch since Luke was gone so long this time. Constantine didn't like the idea, Rev having to walk downtown, below 154th street, but she approved of Reverend learnin' a proper work ethic and earnin' his own money and ambivalently gave her approval. Besides, folks, weren't many opportunities for young brothers to work and get paid in the hood, 'lessen you want to count the game as a viable employment opportunity. And ain't no one, 'cept No Neck, wanted that for Rev.

Constantine understood this, as did Solly, and as did Rev himself. He was gettin' close to, or hell, already at that age, where so many youngbloods start making bad decisions and begin a never ending journey through the Man's system. A system so hard to get out of, folks, once you're in. A system that leaves people and families and children broken and defeated, and that ain't no good for no one.

I'll say it loud.

Jail ain't no good for no one!

Word.

Now granted, I'll admit some cats need to be locked away forever, but for most, jail ain't no good.

Just check the statistics.

Justice ain't blind.

I learned a long time ago—in the hood—the bitch can see.

'Specially if your skin is black or brown.

'Specially if you got a legal aide as your Cochran.

Just sayin', my dudes, check it out for *real*.

Justice ain't blind.

I know, I know, I'm preachin' again, people, but these are words that need to be heard. But right, right, y'all, I'll get back to Rev and Solly and the story.

"Rev, No Neck messin' with you on a regular? His crew, his boys, they pressin' you too hard?"

"Naw, Solly, nothing I can't handle. Most of them are straight up cowards. Only strong when they're all together. Get them alone, one-on-one, and they're straight up ass. I'm good, Sol."

But, ahh, people, Reverend wasn't being completely honest again. Remembers I told y'all earlier, how sometimes Reverend was excited and drawn to the corner action? Remember? Well a part of him still was. A part of him still sees some romanticism on the corner. All that action, all that stimulus, shit, folks, it's hard for a young brother to ignore that on a regular.

WILLIAM TEETS

Luke needed to get home.

He been gone too long.

That boy needed Luke.

Right then, right now.

Chapter 7
Cleaning Windows

"Rev, where you at, brother? You hear me?"

"Huh, Solly, what'd you say?"

"Damn, boy, you're gonna wipe a hole clean through that glass. What's got your attention out there?"

And Solly looked and saw what Reverend saw.

Mighty Missy Brown.

Missy Brown was a seventeen year old hood rat who ran the streets and fucked shit up. That was her job, folks. Tearin' shit up, makin' paper, and fightin'. I'm talkin' both girls and dudes. Oh, she could be sweet when she wanted something, but hell, most times she just done took whatever she wanted. Therefore, folks, you figure out how sweet she really is.

I know better.

WILLIAM TEETS

True story.

See, Missy's moms—no pillar of the community herself—sent Mighty Missy to Philly to live with her pops to see if he could straighten her out, but after Missy gave both the school principal and her pops eye-jammies, her pops had enough and sent Missy back to her moms. Had to be about three years ago that she was sent to Philly, I'd say. Shit, I'm surprised she lasted that long. But now, Mighty Missy Brown was back in town.

And not to sound like a dirty old man, people, but she was fine to look at. Yes, sir, easy on the eyes, as they say. A real tomato, a dime, bangin', smokin'. A young woman built like she was; well me and my boys—back in the day—would call a girl like Missy, a brick house.

Still would.

Still do, I guess.

And this wasn't lost on Reverend, either.

Know what I'm sayin'?

"Hell no, boy! Don't even be thinkin' 'bout that. Don't be messin' with Missy Brown. Nothing but trouble, Rev. Plenty of other shorties out there. Mighty Missy is bad news. You hear me Rev? Bad news. You don't know, son, believe me, I know, I know that fam," Solly said.

But Reverend didn't hear.

How could he?

Youngbloods his age always thought with their wrong head and were young, dumb, and full of cum. Hell, you know how that goes, people, and all Solomon could do was sigh. See, folks, he knew too. He was a young buck once and realized what time it was. He realized there wasn't much he could say that would stick between Rev's ears. Solly filed the thought away in his mind and understood this talk was best left for Luke to have with Reverend, whenever Luke got back home.

And like I already said before, Luke needed to get home.

Now.

"Think I'll sweep out front, Solly. Such a nice day and all," Reverend said.

"Sure you right, bro, sure you right," Solly sighed a second time.

As Reverend swept the entrance outside Solly's shop—hell, if you could call what he was doin' sweepin', damn broom hardly touched the walk—Rev kept his gaze on Mighty Missy. See, folks, Rev's been with a few girls from his school before, stealin' kisses and cheap feels, even swiped third base a few times with Naughty Midnight Noreen, but Mighty Missy Brown stirred a stronger feelin' in his body he ain't never felt before.

WILLIAM TEETS

And he liked that feelin'.

With that freaky warm December sunshine and heat on his face, staring at Mighty Missy and all her curves, diggin' the feeling inside of him, Reverend felt *real* happy a second time that day. Feelings he usually didn't feel down here in the hood. Good feelings he knew never lasted, but, for the second time that day, Reverend started takin' another siesta slippin' sleep. Not thinkin' about Bakus or those damn crabs in a bucket.

And just like earlier in the day, before Reverend could *really* enjoy his *present* moment and be truly happy with himself, the never endin' joke that the hood always played, of lettin' Rev see a glimpse of happiness before snatchin' happiness away again, laughed out loud. The hood howled and mocked Reverend and made his ears burn like fire as he watched Mighty Missy Brown walk over to No Neck's corner and give dap and high-fives to No Neck and his clown crew.

They hooted and hugged and Rev swore they were laughin' at him. Laughin' at the church boy from uptown. Sweepin' the barber man's stoop. Too square, too much of a pussy, too uncool to ever be able to hang with them. The final insult and pain to his pride came when No Neck and Rev's eyes caught each other's from across the street, and No Neck laughed louder. December sun glinted off his gold fronts and No Neck widened his eyes and cocked his head to one side, as if sayin', *This could all be yours too, homeboy, just come and see me.*

REVEREND WENT WALKING

———((•))———

"Damn, Rev, why you slammin' the door like that?"

But Reverend failed to hear Solomon a second time that day.

Failed to answer.

As Reverend headed home after his shift at Solly's, his usual bounce hip-hopped step was gone. He wasn't walking straight and fast and hard anymore, but with slumped shoulders and shuffling feet. He looked like so many of the other vacant-eyed ghost ghouls wanderin' the streets and avenues of the ghetto.

Damn near killed me to see it, people.

I shouted out to him, "What's good, Rev?"

He didn't hear, again.

I've seen too many youngsters in my time lookin' like Reverend looked, gettin' finally beaten down by the hood. Saw too many of their beautiful innocent souls become black holes of muck and mud and nothingness. The hopeful songs in their hearts quieted and quelled. Nothing more than faint sounds of faraway ringin' bells, which at one time promised so much love and joy. Almost like the muffled hymns echoed from Saint Peter's that I already told y'all about. Nothing more than vain whispers on the street gettin' blown into nihility by the wild winds of despair.

Just like young brother's souls and hopes and dreams.

So fucking sad.

So fucking useless.

So fucking true.

I'm not gonna front, people. Seeing Rev walking like that brought a tear to my eye.

As Reverend slogged along, his ears were no longer fire, but powerful, mixed-up, angry feelings raged inside him. You know the feelings I'm talkin' 'bout, people, feelings that can turn a good person bad and erase any semblance of common sense and intelligence. Madman feelings that make you swear if someone even says something simple like *good morning* to you, you'll stick a fork in their eye or an ice pick in their ear. Yeah, man, that's how Rev was feelin'. He tried to fight his emotions, to overcome them, tellin' himself when Luke got home and they moved upstate everything would be copasetic and groovy, but with Luke not home and Reverend still in the hood, *all* his thoughts were overpowered by more *real* raw ones, and Reverend had an achin' longin' to want to belong to something, to someone, to anything, to anyone.

And, folks, Missy's curves stayed in his head.

Believe dat.

REVEREND WENT WALKING

Luke or no Luke.

Hood or no hood.

Upstate or downstate.

Right or wrong.

Reverend wanted to belong.

Know what I'm sayin', my peeps?

Adolescent angst that ain't for adolescents only.

"There you are. Hurry here, boy, help me with these bags. The sisters will be here shortly. I needs you to wash up and get dressed in your Sunday best—hmmm—what's that smell on you? Cheap cologne spray and talcum powder from the Devil's den at sinner Solly's. Hmmm, boy, wash up good. You smell of downtown, you smell of Satan."

And Reverend's shoulders sagged even more in his defeat as he grabbed the grocery bags from Constantine. "What's wrong with you? All dog-faced again. And don't be snatchin' these bags, you'll break the eggs and they'll be no angel cake. Can't make no angel cake without no eggs. Be mindful of them eggs. Don't break the eggs. Not much time, we're runnin' out of time, I'm tellin' ya, runnin' out of time. The sisters will be here shortly, hallelujah, Bible study tonight, yes, Lord, Bible study tonight. The Devil is a lie. Put those bags down and go gets yourself prepared. And don't think about hidin' and readin' your heathen books tonight. No, lost sinner, not tonight. The only book you'll be readin' tonight is the Good Book! Amen, can I get a witness?"

And Reverend staggered away—beaten—his heart and mind still in fierce combat, his spirit and self-worth shot to shit. Makes you feel for the brother, doesn't it, people? And as Rev collapsed in a corner wooden chair he couldn't decide if he was going to scream, cry, or stick a rolled-up sock in Aunt Constantine's mouth and then duct tape it closed forever as she continued to sermon on in the kitchen about the virtues of being saved and the sisters arriving for Bible study.

"Are you gettin' ready, Reverend? You runnin' out of time, we're runnin' out of time," Constantine seered.

And Reverend didn't hear a third time that day.

Remember the cock, people, oh . . . Ok . . . I'll stick to the story. No jokes. No metaphors.

Just sayin'.

OK, y'all, the story.

As Reverend sat all bamboozled in a wooden chair—I love that word, people, bamboozled, don't you all?—a loud rapping

REVEREND WENT WALKING

knock on the door startled both him and Constantine.

"Who's that knockin' like they the police? The police here for you, boy? Let me find out, sinner. Let me knows you broke the law. The sisters can't be here this early. We still have a little time, hallelujah, a little time, I think," Constantine said, as she quickly hoofed herself to the door.

From his hard backed wooden chair, Reverend saw what looked like someone in a military uniform standing at the door with someone else in civvies, but when he caught sight of a pair of ultra-shiny, black, army boots, he thought it must be Luke—finally home—but he also thought, W*hy would Luke be knocking? Luke has a key.*

And then Reverend heard Constantine let go of a howling windswept wail that started deep in her bosom and resounded through the hood. A wail that awakened sinners and saints, stray sleeping dogs and feral alley cats, dealers and junkies, lightness and dark, angels and demons. The big lady's knees buckled and she slid to the floor, her girth supported only by the door jamb and the soldier standing at the entrance to the tiny apartment.

Luke was dead.

Chapter 8
Who Really Knows?

Stay with me now, people.

Keep diggin' the story.

I know, I know, quite a shock about Luke.

Settle down now, folks.

Cool out, sister, chill, youngblood.

I know, I know, you're all wonderin' what happened.

Well, everyone get grounded again.

Let me tell on.

What Luke told Reverend, you remember the secret—'bout him goin' overseas to tie up some loose ends and then comin' home for good? 'Bout Luke not bein' in danger anymore, about comin' home and working at West Point?

It was true.

All of it.

Just like Luke said.

Movin' upstate, gettin' a slice of that American Dream pie. A piece of that false Dream that's denied to so many. That they were going to finally be welcomed to the table of the privileged. Yeah, folks, Luke's words were all true.

All of them.

Luke would've never lied to Reverend.

Just like I done told, y'all.

But as the twisted cosmic jokes of the Universe do, playing havoc with our lives and dreams, Luke's flight home crashed into the Atlantic.

No survivors.

No recovery.

Least that's what was reported.

But what got me wild was that the government offered no sound story.

All the government told Constantine was that Luke was aboard a commissioned military flight home, back to the states, when the plane *unfortunately* crashed into the ocean.

No further details available.

Ongoing investigation.

Further information pending.

Must complete forms: Victor Tango Charlie-2764, Whiskey Delta-7963, Romeo Foxtrot- 8.

Unfortunately crashed?

Must complete forms?

Really, motherfuckers?

Unfortunate?

What did I tell you all about trustin' the government, folks?

Hell, you tellin' me they couldn't recover bodies or wreckage from that flight? Not even that black box contraption that's supposed to say what happened? The army unable to find a big-ass army plane? Don't know about you, my peeps, but I'm not buying it. Something else happened to Luke. Something covered up. Not hard to believe. We done believed and ate so much bullshit and lies for so long, I guess it's become status quo. Makes me angry, though, people, you feel me, folks? For once, can the *real* truth be told? For once, can we be in the mix?

REVEREND WENT WALKING

And what kind of coded, top secret, fucked-up forms are those, anyways? All army official and shit. Delta, Tango, Whiskey, nigga, please. I *need* a whiskey after hearin' that shit.

What about the families, the loved ones left at home? What coded form covers that type of catastrophe, that type of horror?

Shit, I don't know.

The Man, the PoPo, hell, once again, the United States Government is bending us over.

Who can we trust?

When do we get an even break?

Stop being exposed?

Stop being denounced?

Get a fair deal; stop being dealt the shittiest hand in the deck?

Aw, fuck, folks.

I never saw that shit comin'.

Did you?

Damn shame too, when a solid brother like Luke is taken

WILLIAM TEETS

away too soon and too suddenly. Like so many of our other black heroes. Ain't too many positive male role models like Luke left in the hood no more. I'm gonna keep it a hundred with y'all, I cried when I heard the news. Finest decent brother that I knew in this fucked-up and failed government experiment of segregation. You remember when I started early on in our story, 'bout people living on waste landfills, chemical dumps breeding asthma and God knows what else? CIA sellin' dope, that damn her'on, to people in the hood? Did I talk to y'all about that? White flight? Everyone selling out for the cheddar and that goddamned false American Dream, how the government . . . OK, OK, right, back to the story, but I'm just sayin', again.

There be mad lies out there.

Mad untruths bein' told.

Well, anyways, word of Luke's death moved through the hood faster than if you heard a hooker was givin' head for free, standin' on hers, while she shit out keys to a free Lexus.

My, people, word of Luke's death spread so fast.

Man, it was sorrowful.

Hell, me and One Shoe got so drunk, we drank like tomorrow was a rumor.

Yeah, man, the hood was hurtin' more than ever, but not as bad as Constantine and our son-son, Rev. I couldn't tell you

REVEREND WENT WALKING

which one of them was more devastated. I mean a straight up pick-em, folks.

Constantine and her herd were all dressed in black, spotted white veils and crazy church hats and they brought a new definition to that word, wailing. But at least she had her Holy Herd and was able to process Luke's death and put some kind of closure to it in a mature and adult way. All Reverend had was Solomon, but as hard as Solly tried to comfort that boy, Solly too was feelin' seriously hurt. Solly tried like hell, though, to bring some understandin' to what happened, but Rev was beyond pain and being consoled.

How could shit go so wrong, so fast?

Everything was a mess.

A hot volcano mess, folks.

In the days that followed the news of Luke's passing—never liked that word passing, what's that supposed to mean, passing?—Reverend existed with no feeling and no emotion. You could have placed that boy next to Nathaniel Hawthorne and people would have thought the library put up a new statue to keep company with Ol' Nate.

Yes, siree, a real messed up mess.

Reverend was so empty and so unable to explain his loss to anyone else, but worse yet to himself. You know what I'm sayin', folks, that empty, hollow, straw feeling of hopelessness and yearning. Knowing you ain't gonna never see someone you love more than yourself ever again. Wishin' you could trade places. Wishin' you were dead instead. That's how our boy felt, my peeps. Ugly thoughts that ran like an out of control locomotive belching and hissing white steam and smoke-like lightning and thunder through his mind, heading for a derailment.

So wrong.

So sad.

So not fair for our boy, Rev.

People tried to help, but it was usually done in some stupid, silly, ignorant kinda way. Tellin' Rev everything they thought they knew happens when someone dies. The religious zealots who told Reverend, Luke was in a better place and Rev would see him again soon, or the self-proclaimed realists who told him, Luke was worm food cause that's all that happens when we take a dirt nap, to the cynical folks who told Rev, why care what happens when we die, at least we're out of this goddamned hood and off this shit-stained Earth.

Like I said, folks, everything was a mess.

And I know, I know, you're all thinkin' what did Constantine do to help Reverend? Well, unfortunately, people, not much of nothin'. I mean in her defense, how could she? Whenever her or the herd spoke about the matter, it was always the same old rhetoric of salvation and grace. God's will. A bigger plan that no one is privy to. Naw, man, Constantine and the herd, like so many others, served the man-made machine of organized religion, leavin' the soul, the spirit, out of healing and love. You follow me, people?

Where's the love?

Glory to God in the highest!

Peace to his people on Earth!

Lord, God, Heavenly King . . .

That whole false original sin shit, with absolution included, for ninety-nine cents.

Two for the price of one.

'Cept that shit wasn't working for Reverend.

No way, my peeps, Reverend wasn't buying.

Are you?

I'm not.

Makes me wonder if future anthropologists are going to dismiss our beliefs like we dismissed Zeus and Isis and Apollo. If they'll laugh about arks and walkin' on water and talkin' burnin' bushes like we do about the Minotaur and Cyclops and sirens singin' so beautifully to Odysseus.

Know what I'm sayin'?

Can you dig it, folks?

Maybe in the year 2525, who knows?

We won't be around.

But really, people, who does know? How do you really console someone dealin' with the earthly finality of death? Especially a fourteen-year-old young man, three weeks away from his fifteenth birthday, who loses the only positive, constant, love force in his young life.

Answer me that, people. Give me some insight into that cold reality. And don't dare lay that greater God's plan, Jehovah jive shit on me, or I swear I'll cut you.

That's my word.

I'll tell you why, my brothers and sisters, I'll tell you why.

Shit, fam, I've seen preacher men gnash their teeth on their death beds and denounce a God they served their whole life. No sir, they were not willing to go quietly into that good night. I've also seen so-called sinner brothers bleedin' out from gunshot wounds, lyin' on cold concrete sidewalks, smile and say, *The Lord has come, peace out and spill a forty for me*, upon their untimely demise. I've seen loved ones slip away into an emptiness, never heard from again, and I've seen innocents sacrificed to a death due to no ill doing of their own.

So I ask you again, brothers and sisters, who really knows?

Who knows what darkness is out there and *really* all about?

I saw a friend of mine, Usman Buhari, baddest motherfuckin' brother you ever met, tell me on his death bed that the Devil has no horns or red face or trident but comes disguised as everything you ever wanted in life. But just as he said that, he told me everything turned into blackness deeper than rattlesnake eyes. Then something sucked the breath from his lungs, his eyes opened wide along with his mouth and he gasped for air and was gone. He became rigid and cold and dead and grotesque in a few inconsequential seconds that we take for granted. Did I tell y'all, his death bed was a cold city sidewalk?

True story.

Scared the shit out of me and I swear my hair turned grey on that day.

I'd done seen death's rattlesnake eyes.

I don't never want to see no shit like that again.

Like I said, folks, who knows?

I know I don't want to face death like that ever again.

WILLIAM TEETS

Too cold.

Too honest.

Too true.

So I ask you, if you know, who's *really* sellin' and buyin' and gettin' salvation?

For *real*.

And for how much?

And where?

Don't it, ain't it, supposed to come from our own souls?

But enough of that, let's get back to Reverend. I know I done ran off the rails again, my peeps, and took you all with me—screamin'—away from the story, but I'm back on track now, I'm good money.

I'm seeing even more new listeners joining the story. Gather round, gather round, people, you missed the beginnin', but the end is a doozy. Listen up, now. Here, brother, give some room to homegirl. Here, sister, get up in here and listen up. Man, we gettin' deep, people.

As the day of Luke's funeral arrived, winter back in full effect—it was brick outside—Reverend had dealt with, heard enough about, and thought enough about Luke's demise.

REVEREND WENT WALKING

Our little man was saturated with death. Rev didn't even want to look at or read the letters from Luke, in his hidden shoebox, anymore. They were lost lies as far as Rev was concerned.

They didn't help no more.

And whether some unconscious defense mechanism to keep him sane kicked-in, or that old fight-or-flight theory was silenced, Reverend exhaled sittin' in the first pew of Saint Peter's Church, and he told himself what is done is done and that he was done with everything. I don't really know if Rev, deep down inside, believed himself, but at that particular moment he convinced himself he was done with *all*.

He even mumbled beneath his breath, "Hallelujah to that, motherfuckers."

I guess those words helped, too.

Luke's funeral had all the glory pomp and circumstance that a true American hero deserves. American flags, gold and blue flags, black and white flags, hell, I couldn't see all the flags from my last row pew seat there were so many. Solly and a couple of Luke's army buddies gave eulogies, Pastor Goodman-Brown preached, and the herd huffed puffed and wailed.

Rev sat like stone.

Brought another tear to my eye. I could feel his broke heart.

WILLIAM TEETS

Wished I'd had some magic to make his heart whole again.

I had none.

Nothing.

Shit on a shingle.

I sipped rye from my flask instead and ignored the hisses of the so-called holy in the pews around me. Fuck 'em. At least I know my love and heart is real. Know what I'm sayin', folks? I know I'm real.

I sipped again.

I sipped for Luke and Reverend and Constantine and Solly. I sipped for Usman and One Shoe and my boys and the hood. I sipped one for me and one for the Lord, Jesus Christ. People, if I could've turned water into whiskey on that wretched day, I might still be sittin' in that pew and still be sippin' for all the world.

Know what I'm sayin'?

Feel me?

Sippin' for the world.

Like I said, folks, I know my heart is real.

Anyways, after the service, our boy Reverend was gettin'

surrounded by the holy herd. Their bellowing, mooing, and cooing was too harsh and abrasive for most mortal's ears. But Rev sat there stoic and stone-like—the herd's sweat once more drippin' upon him, mammoth mammaries suffocatin' his ability to breathe and waftin' smoke incense and candles blazin' his brain.

"Oh, poor child, don't be sad. Rejoice in the light. Rejoice I say, for your loving uncle, my loving husband, is home at last. Rejoice, poor child, rejoice."

"You are not alone, Sister Constantine, nor you, lovely lamb. We are all together in God's glory and grandeur. Let us rejoice, rejoice, glory to God in the highest. I have a beautiful angel cake to bring over later, sister. Amen."

And before Reverend could skulk or slink away, he was engulfed by the manic sect of holy rollin' water buffaloes and carried in the most crazy surreal clutch of human hands, bodies and fat- rolls one has ever seen—right out of the church—like Aladdin on some grotesque, Satan-inspired, magic carpet ride, as the herd sang out of tune, *Swing Low, Sweet Chariot*.

More pomp and glory with no substance or circumstance. Like I said before, no soul. Them church folks do what they been taught and be swearin' it's righteous. Just don't work in my book, folks. Too organized and aimed, too cold and calculated. The Good Word's supposed to be soft and filled with light, not that old time, sanctimonious, unforgivin' shit, that religion sells too well.

Hear me knockin', people?

I ask again, where's the love?

Absolutely insane, people, absolute craziness.

Religion, not love and compassion, was in full effect.

Luckily, Solly was nearby and seein' the distress Reverend was in, grabbed him by the arm and pulled him out of the circled herd and to much needed *real* salvation.

"I'll drive Reverend to the cemetery, Constance, no bother at all, I'll help you out," Solly said over his shoulder while half-draggin' Rev by his forearm down the granite stairs of Saint Pete's.

And before Constantine could denounce Solly's offer—and you best believe she would've if she could've—both Reverend and Solly were two-steppin' into Solly's car.

"Thanks, Solly. Couldn't take much more of that fuckin' shit before I bugged out."

"Yo, my man, no need to curse. I saw. I saw. You good now, Rev?"

"As good as fucking ever."

And Solly stared, with his head turned sideways, at our boy. Rev turned up the car radio and said, "Yo, son, this is my jam."

See, my people, don't sound like Reverend to you and sure as hell not to Solly. Not to me neither. Somethin' bad was goin' on inside that boy's head.

"Hey, Rev, no bullshit, I'm gonna keep it real, this is some crazy shit, bro, but we'll get through it. That's my word, homie, we'll get through it."

"No doubt, Solly, no doubt," Reverend replied, with empty black eyes that made Solly think of rattlesnakes.

At the cemetery, there were legal twenty-one gun salutes—not often shots are busted off in the hood and five-o don't respond. Everyone jerked at each crack-firing shot, tensing themselves and hearing the next sound before the shot was even fired. That lost second of silence which hangs in the air, never seeming to arrive, before it does, and you hear the sound a micro-second before your ears do. CRACK! And all exhale wails or sobs or cries just as the guns are fired again. Bosoms heave, heads jerk, shoulders rise and fall and misery cannot be drowned in echoes of spent rounds heard loudly before or loudly again.

Reverend stood like stone.

A bagpiper in a kilt, with hairy legs and a scraggly red beard, horned *Amazing Grace*. A young pale-faced soldier, not much older than Rev, bugled out *Taps*. Pretty flowers, dirt, and ashes-to-ashes and dust-to-dust was cast onto Luke's *empty* casket. I still ain't buyin' the army couldn't find no bodies or no big-ass plane. What about you cats, you buyin'?

Anyways, when all was done, a cold, brazen, winter-crazy, gust blew across the cemetery and sent proverbial chills through everybody's spine. The hair-like branches and limbs on dead and barren trees creaked and moaned and a few cracked like earlier gun salutes, before falling hard to the ground.

The sky was grey.

I felt so much for Reverend because I knew how much I was hurtin' and what he must be feelin' with Luke gone. See, folks, I'll keep it a hundred, I loved Luke too. Mentored him and Solly for years in the hood. Like they were my own. Maybe I didn't love Luke as much as Rev loved Luke, but I didn't even want to imagine the little man's pain. Hell, when a soldier presented a folded- up flag to Reverend—me watching from a moss-covered cracked stone behind a dying oak—Reverend stood tall and strong with one tear fallin' down his cheek. I wanted to run over and hug him and hold him so tight I'd never let him go.

That's my word, people.

That's my word.

But, hell, we can't always get what we want.

And you best believe, regardless of what you may have heard, sometimes we don't even get what we need.

True Story.

Word.

Chapter 9
Can't Be Livin' In The Past

Believe me, folks, for so many of us in the hood, Luke's death was a real kick in the head. Shit, I bet for y'all, too. And I ain't gonna front, people, but that picture in my head of Rev holdin' that folded-up flag, tear serpentinin' down his cheek, well, let's just say it haunted me. Stuck me like a knife in my gut—twisitin' and turnin'—and I ain't talkin' no Chubby Checker.

I ask again, how does God let horrors like that happen so bad?

What good was God thinkin' could come from Luke dyin'?

What was the greater purpose?

Damned if I know, but I guess that's why I'm not God.

Y'all feel me?

I did know, though, that I had to get myself together and get

REVEREND WENT WALKING

back to livin'. Can't none of us live in the past. Y'all best believe that. Ain't none of us strong enough to live in the past. Livin' there will kill you. Word. Need to keep on truckin' and keep hope alive. Ain't that what *they* say, folks? Keep hope alive? Well, hell, it was gettin' harder and harder to do on a regular in the ghetto and Luke's untimely death didn't make stayin' strong any more easier.

I mean I knew I'd bounce back from this ghastly shit. I'd done saw plenty of death in my time—remember my friend Usman Buhari?—remember that story, folks? Sure you do. But see, I was concerned about Rev. I was prayin' this tragedy wouldn't crush his spirit and soul and leave him so shattered he could never recover. Leave him broken and empty and hollow. I'd done seen that plenty of times too, my peeps, but like I said, can't none of us live in the past. Doin' that is a straight up death sentence.

I prayed harder that the Universe wasn't goin' to impart that verdict on Rev.

But who really knows, folks, who really knows?

As Luke's death slowly left the hood like a mornin' fog burnin' off in the sun, I was chillin' with One Shoe in front of Abdula's, knockin' back a fifth. "Can't keep doin' this, Shoe. Need to get my shit together. Hell, I've been drinkin' with your drunk-ass for three days in a row now."

"You need a break, my brother, a break from all this kookiness.

Need to get away somewhere—where I don't know—but you need to clear your head and go away."

"Joshua Moriel," I said.

"Who?" asked Shoe.

"You're a genius, Shoe. A straight up ghetto Rasputin."

"Who?"

"I'll catch you later, brother, be good to yourself. Here, hold this twenty and make sure you get something to eat."

Alright, my peeps, gather around now and listen up. I was gonna tell y'all 'bout Joshua Moriel later on in the story, but there ain't no time like the present. OK, dig this now. Joshua Moriel was an old friend of mine from upstate. I'd visit him on some holidays and such and those visits always eased me and seem to quiet whatever darkness was creepin' 'bout me. Without even knowin' what he was sayin', One Shoe put into my head what I needed to do to shake the blues that've been houndin' me.

I called Joshua Moriel.

"Old Man. What's news, my brother?"

"Too much to get into over the phone, Josh, but some bad juju been happenin' to some of my peeps down here in the hood. I need a break from life and I don't want to impose on you or be a burden, but I was thinkin' I'd hop the train and come visit with ya for a bit. That is if you're up to it and all."

"Hell, yeah. I'd love to see you, Old Man. It's been a minute since we've gotten together. Perfect timing, too. I have Monday and Tuesday off from the job. The kids are going on a home visit. When do you plan on coming?"

"Friday works for me, and it's great you got a couple extra days. Damn, the Hall still sendin' them delinquents on home visits, huh?"

"Yeah, man, crazy as it is. But I'll take the time."

"How's the job goin', Josh? How are things with you?"

"Like you said, Old Man, too much to get into over the phone."

"Word. I can dig that. I'll call you about what train I'll be on."

"I'll be at the station when you arrive with bells on."

"Right on, my brother, right on."

WILLIAM TEETS

Kick back and put on your listenin' ears, people. Let me bring y'all up to speed about Joshua Moriel and how me and him became fam and who he is.

In my younger days, after years of runnin' and gunnin' and ramblin' and gamblin' I did a bid for a B&E. After I got out from under the jail an uncle of mines pulled some strings and got me a gig with the city sanitation department. Gettin' that job saved my life. Believe that. That's what's wrong nowadays, folks, ain't no jobs out there for youngbloods. What else they supposed to do with their lives? How they supposed to support themselves and theirs? They got to hustle, they got to eat, but see the government likes it like that. Y'all know prison is big business now, right? Y'all know the Man keeps ghetto folk down by not givin' them jobs, right? Y'all remember that American Dream lie I been . . . oh, right, I'm startin' to rant again . . . OK, my people, OK, settle down now, I'll get back to the story, I'll educate y'all, later on.

I did my twenty-and-out at sanitation and continued to live my life pretty straight since then. I still drink too much, book some side bets and move a little ganja with Solly, but I steer clear of the PoPo and all the trauma drama in the hood.

Anyways, a friend of mines was working a night security gig at a juvy center upstate called Rutherford B. Hayes Haven Hall and told me 'bout a part-time maintenance job in the school there. Merely paid nine-fifty an hour, but with only my pension from the city to live on, along with the little bit of ka-chang I made with Solly on the side, I took the job.

I was still a few years short of collectin' social security at the time and the few extra bucks I made helped to hold me down.

That's where I met Joshua Moriel.

Josh is an English teacher at the Hall's school—that's what we call Rutherford B. Hayes Haven Hall for short, people, the Hall. We became friendly when I worked there—hell, he used to give me rides on a regular to the train station to get my ass back home—and we would stop at a few joints along the way and knock back a few. Like me, Josh likes to get into the cups.

Still does.

Maybe a little more then he should.

Definitely more then he should.

Just sayin'.

But don't get it twisted, people, Josh was the best damn teacher I ever seened. Had those baby convicts eatin' out the palm of his hand. Had those teenage thugs readin' Othello, Vonnegut, learnin' 'bout Socrates—hell, he's the one got me into readin' all kinds of books. Yes sir, my peeps, Joshua Moriel was one of those true teachers that only come around once in a blue.

A born teacher.

WILLIAM TEETS

The realest kind there is if you ask me.

And it was a pleasure to witness, folks. While kids in other classrooms were tearing shit up, throwin' books out windows, fightin' and cussin' everyone out, Josh's students were speakin' Shakespeare.

True Story.

Yeah, people, like I said, Joshua Moriel was a born teacher.

His name rang bells.

Hear me now, though, folks, when I tell y'all Josh has his share of issues, too. His drinkin' is well known at the Hall and doesn't go unnoticed by the higher-ups in administration. The only reason they tend to turn an eye and ignore his drinkin' is because of what I'd already told you. He gets results. He's good for the kids. One less classroom gettin' tore up. Hell, Josh hungover and runnin' on four cylinders is better than most the other staff firing on eight, if you know what I mean.

But I still worry, folks, if one day his drinkin' won't spiral out of control and be his Waterloo. What's Waterloo, you ask, brother? Waterloo. That's from Napoleon. Learned that from one of the books Josh gave me. Look it up if you don't know. I may have learned a little late in life, but readin' is knowledge. The key to success. Hope some of you folks learn that, if nothin' else from my story. Yeah, my brother, write that down. Waterloo.

And as far as folks abusin' the drink too much, people, let me enlighten y'all. Some people, like Josh, are dreamers and romantics. Develop some kinda adolescent awe from readin' too much Hemingway, or F. Scott, or James Baldwin, or some other fly alcoholic writer. They think that shit is groovy until they find out that shit is *real*, and by then, it's usually too late.

Other folks dive head first into a bottle because that's all they know. They grow up lookin' up to some drinkin'-drunkard, fake-ass-role-model in their life and become another monkey see, monkey do. They see, they learn, they do and then think that's the way life's supposed to be. Hear that, people.

Some other persons drink themselves to death, never knowin' why.

Not a clue.

Know what I'm sayin'?

Ask One Shoe why he's a wino and he'll tell you it's some curse some long ago Haitian voodoo witch-doctor cast on his ancestors. Mighty Missy will tell you all that her mom's says *real* bitches knock back Henny. No Neck, well, he don't think much about nothin' much. Sorry, bad example there, folks. Me, I hit them hard 'cause none of your goddamn business, that's why.

What I'm sayin' folks is drunkards are a strange breed.

WILLIAM TEETS

Strange indeed.

And Josh falls under wearin' that hat.

Hell, if you ask me, society should be more concerned about booze than someone puffin' on an L. What's worse, folks, the businessman who has a six martini lunch and drives his SUV down Main Street or some kid laid up doin' a bong hit? A group of cats sharin' a blunt on the corner or some soccer mom pickin' her kids up after practice, after she done picked up two bottles of wine? I know I'm goin' all over the map again, folks, but sometimes I just have to get this truth off my chest. And you know the truth, or lie, all goes back to big business and the almighty dollar, right? Just think about that, that's all I ask, just think 'bout a lot of the shit I be layin' down.

Anyways, all I was tryin' to do was give y'all a little intro to Joshua Moriel. Give you a little insight into who he is. There's more to come though, lots more. And like all of us, Josh has his plusses and minuses, but I think he has a lot more positive tips to offer then most cats I know.

Even if he is a dreamer.

A drinker.

A sentimental romantic.

He's special.

Special to his students and special to me.

I was lookin' forward to our visit.

Lookin' forward to a break from all this hood noise.

Lookin' to leave the past where the past belongs.

Lookin' forward to Joshua Moriel.

Chapter 10
Hopin' On Hope

Just as fate would have it, people—how's that sayin' go, *if it wasn't for bad luck I wouldn't have no luck at all*—my damn gall bladder started actin' out and I had to put the ixnay on visiting Josh. The doctor at the clinic said I would live and to get some rest, but travelin' on the train and knockin' some back with Josh would have to wait. I sent One Shoe to Yakabu's for some smokes and a couple of forties—for medicinal purposes only—and I chilled at home.

I thought about Josh.

I smiled.

I could picture the big man downin' some Busch beer chased by Crown Royal while he dreamed the day away. And like I done told y'all before, Josh was a dreamer. Man, listen, in his mind, he'd be off and runnin' with the snortin' bulls of Pamplona, then sippin' wine with Hemingway and Gertrude Stein afterwards. He'd be ridin' camels with Bedouins across the Sahara and then be chasin' fair-haired maidens with Falstaff through the moors. Maybe he'd picture himself swillin' wine and smokin' a blunt with Lord Byron, while everyone listened to Mary's story of *Frankenstein*. Yeah, my dudes, Josh was a beautiful dreamer.

For better or for worse.

For good or for bad.

Joshua Moriel was a dreamer.

And lots of times, folks, his dreamin' and innocence made me happy for him, but I felt for the brother, too. Josh was deep. Maybe too deep. Anyone who was tight with him—like me—could see he was fightin' some fierce demons in his soul. Don't know what they really were, or where they came from, but trust me, brothers and sisters, they were howlin' and gnashin' their teeth right next to Josh's spirit.

I think—naw, people, I know—that was one of the reasons Josh hit 'em so hard. The drinkin' helped to hide his dark shadows. Quelled the shrieking for a bit. His job helped, too, y'all. Yeah, folks, his job would help take his mind off dark thoughts. That's why he put so much effort into his work and into those kids at juvy. That's why he'd go in on weekends and do all kinds of extra shit with them kids.

It helped.

Helped the kids, but helped Josh, too.

WILLIAM TEETS

Helped him fight those damn demons.

Helped him not to hate himself.

Helped him to stay sober.

Made me think.

Don't we, ain't we, supposed to love ourselves?

Ain't there light in *all* of us?

Aren't we *all* worthy of salvation?

Makes you think about crazy Constantine and her water buffalo herd always hoofing and snortin' 'bout salvation and soulful peace bein' only an acceptance of grace away—doesn't it, my people? But, shit, I know better. See, the reality of our living is that life gets in the way. Dulls our thinkin' and clouds our sight. Muffles what we hear and gags our spirit's voice.

Y'all feel me?

Life can break our dreams in half and before we know what happened, the Wicked Witch of the West is rulin' the Emerald City. Hustler, rat-race runner, doctor, lawyer, Indian chief, garbage man, mailman, the fuckin' man behind the curtain, the corner boy, stick-up boy, or booster—too many of us succumb to society's accepted survival of low expectations and false successes.

REVEREND WENT WALKING

All our dreams, our songs, our souls, wither away and all we can focus on is payin' next month's bills and workin' for the Man. Havin' two-and-a-half kids, a dog named Skippy, a roof over our heads, and a great big fuckin' lie jammed down our throats that becomes our American Dream. We're tricked into bein' satisfied and happy while capitalist non-compassionate pigs right out of Orwell's *Animal Farm*, snort more lies and feed us leftover scraps as we live paycheck to paycheck.

Fuck that.

I ain't no peasant.

Let *them* eat cake.

I want to have a rib-eye and drink some Pinch.

Know what I'm sayin'?

In the ghetto.

Not in some fancy restaurant.

Right here, in my hood.

Ya feel me?

Ah, shit.

Sorry, ladies and gents, I went all fruit again, didn't I?

WILLIAM TEETS

Admit it though, people, I got y'all thinkin', right?

I mean honestly, my brothers and sisters, there should be more to that deceitful American Dream then slavin' your life away so you can visit the Grand Canyon at seventy, only to find out you're too old and sick to ride a donkey. Too banged up to ride some virtual roller coaster with the grandkids at Disney World. Who's gonna hold your shit-bag? Who's gonna jump start your pacemaker when it goes on the fritz? Who can even afford all that crazy stuff anyways? Or even afford to retire, for that matter? To save any money, to stop working? Hell, maybe if your name is Rockefeller.

Just askin' and all.

Just sayin'.

But let me get back on track.

Back to Josh.

Let me take a swig before I do, though, and settle my old ass down.

Gimme a light, pardner.

Good lookin'.

Whether he knew it or not—hell, knowing Josh, he knew—Josh was in a rut. Yeah, the drinkin' and job may have placated him—'nother great word, people, placate, right?—but he, like all of us, wanted more.

I mean damn near every mornin', Josh would slide his big-ass body into his nine-year-old convertible—he was always a rag top man—and start his drive to work. Windows down, AC cranked, singing to some seventies CD, Josh would drive to his job on autopilot.

Did ya ever drive like that people?

On autopilot?

I bet most of you do.

I bet most of you don't even recognize you do.

I used to before these damn cataracts fucked my eyes up. I don't drive much no more, but yeah, man, I used to cruise along to Marvin Gaye or War or Harold Melvin and the Blue Notes.

Straight up on autopilot.

Both drivin' and livin'.

Hell, is there another way to roll?

Damn autopilot just might crash us, though, folks.

If it hasn't already.

WILLIAM TEETS

Missin' the world and life whizzin' by.

Whizzin' by, 'cause we on autopilot.

Again, my peeps, just food for thought.

Anyways, while Josh's teachin' brought him some peace of mind, his job also strangled a part of him. I remember how Josh would arrive in the morning and low step into the teacher's lounge. Everyone knew when it had been a rough night for him—or should I say a rough morning. Everyone could see. Hell, some days you could smell the booze on him.

Let's just say people could tell.

See, folks, whenever Josh wore his dark sunglasses inside—OD'ing on Fahrenheit and violently chompin' gum—others knew he was tryin' to hide up the scent of a too much beer and Crown Royal night.

"Don't say shit to me, Old Man, no lectures today," he used to growl at me so many times in the past, before sliding into a chair next to me in the teacher's lounge. I'd smile or smirk or wink or chuckle, just to show him I was on his side, just to show a little love. Yeah, my dawgs, Josh may've hit the bottle harder than most, but like I said before, he was a born teacher. Like I said before, Joshua Moriel—hungover and at fifty percent—is better than most of the other faculty at one hundred.

That just a fact, folks.

Like I said, people, I was there.

I'd seen it.

But still, I saw that void there, too.

Sittin' in my crib that day, drinkin' and thinkin' 'bout Josh, my gall bladder barking, I decided to give him a shout-out. I could tell by his slurrin' he was doin' the same as me, but had a helluva head start.

"Shwit, Old Man, if you drinkin' at home wit your frucked up bladder, you should've came up anyways and we could've done drinkin' togwether."

"How you doin', cowboy? You good?"

"Yeah, yeah, but forget thwat. When you comin' to shee me?"

"Soon, my friend, soon."

And I meant it, folks. I needed to visit Josh as much for my peace of mind, as for his. After continuing to talk about nothin', I said goodbye and hung the phone up. Damn, I missed him that day.

I was just hopin' he was goin' to be alright.

I was hopin' we were *all* goin' to be alright.

As I stared at the clock hung over my kitchen sink, I

wondered if we were too late for life. Me, Josh, One Shoe, Solly, and 'specially our boy, Rev.

I wondered if we were too late.

If we were runnin' out of time

God, I hoped it wasn't too late.

God, I hoped we weren't runnin' out of time.

Let's just say I was hopin' on hope, people.

But shit, since I was stuck in the hood, let me get back to the hood.

There'll be plenty of time to tell y'all 'bout Josh, later in the story.

I hope.

Yeah, folks, I hope.

Hopin' on hope.

Chapter 11
Heat Wave

Man, the weather was hot!

One of them blazin' summer days when tar boils and oozes like tiny volcanoes on the pavement.

Straight up fire!

No ballers on the courts, everyone takin' it slow, even the fiends seemed to be losin' a step in their unending hunt to feed their jones'. Hell, corner boys were workin' harder at stayin' cool than making paper. Stick-up kids? Naw, man, even they were too hot to work. Dogs didn't howl, alley cats didn't screech, even five-o was laying low.

A heat wave, for sure.

A heat tsunami, for real.

Word.

WILLIAM TEETS

I was lampin' under the awning outside Yakabu's Bodega, sending One Shoe inside for tall boys and loosies. The damn A/C in Arthur's Bar was broken and a straight up hood brownout had the A/C in Pacheco's Pool Hall clicking on and off, offerin' no *real* heat relief.

Big titty mommas were hangin' out second story windows or loungin' on fire-escapes—pulling their wife-beaters down low—airing out those ample round and browns. At least that was a nice show and little distraction from the hotness. Wild-child street urchins were vandalin' the fire hydrants tryin' to unleash cold water hidden underground.

Everyone was feeling the heat.

But after people accepted their lot and accepted being more miserable, than usual, everything was status quo.

Copasetic.

As chill—no pun intended—as could be expected.

Hood people are an adaptive breed.

Believe dat.

But like I said, people, it was blazin' outside.

The sun was too hot.

The sun is too hot!

REVEREND WENT WALKING

Fall, Icarus, fall. I told you not to fly so high.

I had a funny feelin' on that day somethin' was gonna hit the roof, blowup. Felt funny in my gut. I could feel a storm brewin'. Something evil, something wicked. The motherfucker of all storms. Bad times comin'. Some kind of biblical tempest in the making.

And that's when I saw Rev—walkin' hard—towards No Neck's corner.

Let me fill you in, folks. Give you an update. Reverend was fifteen now, his birthday back in March, and he was on summer break from Saint Peter's School. He was still feelin' fucked-up inside about Luke, but still not admittin' his sorrow to himself or wantin' to share his pain with anyone else.

All I knew, from speakin' with Solly and keepin' my ear low to the street, was that Rev was goin' around kickin' some *free will* type shit he'd read about in some philosopher's book. Can't remember the philosopher's name now, one of those deep brothers, though, and Rev was layin' it down like some g-code for living. You know that boy was always into reading books and such. Always kickin' more book smarts than the rest of us down here. I just didn't know if this was clickin' for him now or not. I never would've thought all his reading might hurt him. Hell, as far as he was concerned, his readin' and self-taught education made him stronger.

I wasn't so sure, now.

Reverend was different.

Constantine was beside herself. Rev talkin' some hot-shit that he wasn't goin' back to Saint Pete's in the fall, but to public school with *real* brothers and sisters, and that he could do what he wanted.

That new free will idea bein' shouted loud and proud.

Solly was about to bust his ass and show Rev if he thought he was a man, he could take a man's ass-whoopin', but Constantine, surprisingly, said no. Even her huffin' hoof-cloved herd told her that to spare the rod was to spoil the child, but she held firm that if anyone was going to lay a hand on Reverend or set him straight, it would be her. And we all know, folks, 'bout Constantine's heavy hand and that she was scared up by no one.

"That boy ain't runnin' nothin' 'round here. Lord, no! It's the Devil I tell ya and the Devil is a lie. The same as our Savior being tempted by Lucifer's false light, that boy is temptin' me. Un-un, brothers and sisters, no child will be runnin' nothin' on me. Hallelujah! Can I get a witness?"

Myself, people, I think Constantine started recognizing age ain't nothing but a number. Her pride and ego, though,

REVEREND WENT WALKING

refused to let go of the fact that Rev was older now. That she was losin' control over him.

She could've used some help.

She needed some help.

Just me sayin' and all.

But Constantine—still bein' Constantine—listened to no one. She wasn't havin' no advice from anyone or anything. And believe me, y'all, she was frustrated as all get-out that none of her tried ass-whippings or Holy Roller Homilies worked on Rev anymore. You gotta understand too, people, Constantine had no back-up plan for dealing with Rev. No experience, no history, no nothin'. This was all new to her. And on top of that, Rev didn't have the trust confidence and respect for her like he'd had for Luke. That's what was missin'. That's why everything was fallin' apart, goin' to hell.

She just didn't know.

And, she just wouldn't listen.

She couldn't, folks.

She just couldn't help herself.

I wished she had asked me for advice. I would've told her to let Solly bust that boy's ass—get his attention—then have a heart-to-heart, but she didn't. Now, I'm no Dr. Phil or

WILLIAM TEETS

Oprah, but I raised two sons and been through the adolescent storm. I know what hardheaded teenage boys in the hood need.

Word.

See, with Rev becomin' a young man now, strong and tall and on his own trip, those threatenin' fire and brimstone sermons or a raised hand from Constance—or God Hisself—just wasn't goin' to work no more. With Constance not bein' able or willing to talk with Rev, all sincere-like, kinda man-to-man, her preachin' was nothin' more than unheard holy diatribes. More of those echoed muffled hymns whispering onto empty streets and lost on the intended masses. Heard only by those not needing to hear.

Remember, people, remember?

"Boy, I'm tellin' you like I told you before, your mother, my beautiful sister, may have brought you into this world, but I will take you out. The Devil is a lie! He is not welcome here! And if you denounce me, you denounce God, and you, are therefore a sinner, and not welcome. Not in my holy home. Not where God dwells. You will not stain holiness. What is my lovin' husband, Luke, thinkin' now, lookin' down at us from heaven? Ohh, we are bein' besieged by demons. Repent heathen; confess your sins to God almighty. I say again, boy, a sinner is not welcome to dwell in my house of holiness. Repent, evil one!"

REVEREND WENT WALKING

But, like I said, folks, all that rah-rah just didn't work no more.

Lost its teeth.

Lost its bite.

That whole falling on deaf ears type thing.

Reverend's mind stayed unchanged, unconvinced, non-believing.

He needed *real* salvation, *real* absolution, *real* love.

He needed Luke.

Now don't get it twisted, folks, Reverend also thought about what Luke might be thinkin'—if Luke was really up in the clouds somewhere, up in heaven—but as soon as he did, Rev convinced himself that heaven was nothin' more than a fairy tale. Nothin' more than another story, like a Baku comin' in the night to eat his dreams and nibble on his soul. He thought about how close Luke and him were to gettin' out of the hood—to mackin' a new life—but like always in the fucked-up hood, the crabs dragged him back into the bucket, just like before, just like always, just like now. That was Reverend's reality and he wasn't feelin' none of that shit.

Rev was done with everything.

Two tears in a bucket, fuck it.

Soundin' familiar again, brothers and sisters, soundin' familiar again?

Reverend blacked *most* thoughts from his mind. He refused to go to service at Saint Peter's anymore—man, did that make Constantine crazy—or pay any heed to Constantine, and that made her crazier. When the Holy Roller huffing herd of sisters came to the apartment for some kinda religious-lost lambhood intervention, he would push by them and book down the block. And if Constantine didn't want him stayin' in the apartment, she could keep the couch/bed/bedroom/living room/dining room/apartment for herself and Rev would move out. He thought that with his newly discovered credo of free will he had his life all figured out and was bullet proof.

What Rev didn't know—or didn't remember—is that bullets have no names.

Remember, folks?

Bullets have no names.

Not here in the hood.

Solly was still tryin' like a motherfucker to talk to our boy. Rev would listen all polite like—never showing his ass to Solly—Reverend wasn't stupid now, he knew Solly would lump him up in a New York minute if he became disrespectful, but again, nothin' was changed. Reverend held tight to his new philosophy of free will like a damn pit holdin' tight to a bone.

REVEREND WENT WALKING

Everyone was still hopin' that after the summer, though, Reverend would come to his senses and go back to Saint Peter's School. Hell, people, he was on the honor roll and already fillin' out college applications and all.

But no one knew for sure if *it* was going to happen.

No one knew for sure *what* was going to happen.

Rev's dreams and goals got blurred and fuzzy.

His wax *was* melting.

Life was gettin' in the way.

Reverend held firm to his new mantra.

Free will.

Do me.

Free will.

No one, people, knew what was going on inside that boy's head.

No one, that is, except Mighty Missy Brown.

Fall, Icarus, fall. I told you not to fly so high.

Chapter 12
Runnin' Out Of Time

So anyways, people, like I was sayin', on that blistering June day my eyes caught sight of Reverend walkin' hard over to No Neck's corner. Not Reverend's usual proud-soaring above it all-I know where I'm headin'-I got goals-I got dreams-walkin'-walk, but a different type of walk.

Didn't look right.

Didn't look like Rev.

Not the Rev I knew.

He started slinkying, pimp-rollin', just like all the other lost-fake-ass-wanna-be-down-thinkin' they're gangstas in the hood-frontin'-ass-niggas. I told One Shoe to get me two more tall boys and two more loosies from Yakabus. Like I said, I knew somethin' was about to go down. We was about to see somethin' bad. Somethin' I didn't wanna see. I knew it. I told you all about the feelin' in my gut, 'bout a storm rollin' in. I told y'all.

REVEREND WENT WALKING

Shit, now I had a courtside seat to watch whatever the storm was 'bout to bring.

Some supernatural, fucked-up, triple double.

Some evilness that lays our souls barren despite our cries for salvation.

Follow me, my peeps, this type of drama is never televised.

As Rev hard-trucked below 154th Street, No Neck pushed his cronies to each side, like Satan parting a sea of demons.

"Well, well, what do we 'ave here? What you doin' down here, church boy? Walkin' rough-shod like you gonna do sumptin'. You packin' more than this heat, church boy? You strapped? Yo, you got some beef? Sumptin' 'bout your unc? Sumptin' you need to prove, nigga? Tell me he ain't got beef, fellas, please *tell* me," No Neck sarcastically said to his crew.

And, oh, how No Neck's posse yipped and yapped like the pack of jackals they were. Their smiling, nasty stained teeth lookin' like dirty window panes, all their high-five, slappin' daps makin' them look like a troop of drunken baboons. My blood got hotter than the fire-ass weather. I tried to keep my dry mouth moist by sippin' my tall boys, spectin' the worst, and not sure what my old ass could do about somethin' bad comin', if somethin' bad came.

"Yo, church boy . . . Reverend . . . right? . . . you lost or sumptin'? Get your ass to barber man Solly's shop or back up to 163rd where you belong, nigga. Back with them church goin' folk. Don't come down here frontin', elses I'll have to put it on you. I done offered you once. You turned me down. I'm 'bout to take offense to why you here now. Maybe, like I said, this 'bout your unc. I'm a start feelin' threatened, nigga. I don't appreciate feelin' threatened. Might have to sick my dawgs on ya, woof-woof."

And the jackals and baboons yipped and yapped and screeched and screamed some more.

Rev kept walking—still hard—his eyes locked onto No Neck's eyes.

Shit, y'all, Lil' Stevie Wonder could see this wasn't gonna end good. Mad thoughts raced through my mind and I thought Rev was either goin' for some get-back at No Neck—just like that gorilla motherfucker said—tryin' to even some imaginary score for Luke, or Rev had some other insane thoughts running 'round his brain ain't none of us knew. Either way, my peeps, I couldn't let no foul shit go down and I jumped off my milk crate, but One Shoe armed me back when Rev said, "Naw, No Neck, no beef here. But I thought you told me to come see you whenever I wanted? Whenever I might be ready. Whenever is, might be now, depending on what you got to say."

And the corner got quiet.

Quiet like black space.

Quiet like calm water.

Quiet like death.

"Come here, little nigga, come here," No Neck said. "Hollywood, give me that bottle. Come here, church boy, drink this. A peace offerin', a bond, a trial, whatever. Let me see where ya at."

No Neck handed a pint of Wild Irish Rose White to Rev, and said, "Finish that if you can, show me what you made of, then maybe we talk."

Rev took the nearly full bottle of cheap wine with a steady hand and chugged it. Swallowed the whole shit. He thought for a moment his throat was on fire and loud alarms rang in his ears. But finish that cheap-ass wine he did. With watery eyes, he smashed the empty bottle onto the concrete sidewalk and coolly said, "Fuck you, No Neck. That all you got?"

And the corner erupted again into a cacophony of coot-calls yelps and howls.

A triumphant sound of death and decay masquerading as joy.

A sound that stung my ears, my peeps, I've heard them false truths before.

My heart sagged.

I was witnessin' another young brother being claimed by dead end urban streets. Streets that always fucking lie. Remember

WILLIAM TEETS

I told you that, people? Streets that have claimed too many youngbloods, but still want to claim more. Streets with an unending appetite. Streets that everyone and everything seems to have forgot. Religions, governments, that bullshit American Dream I've been tellin y'all about, how they all ignore the death on these streets. Streets that were now tryin' to strangle our boy, Rev. Just like I've been tellin' you all, all along. I told you, people, I told you what time it was, what happens in the hood, and now Reverend was close to becomin' just another statistic, another number in some report or a buried story in yesterday's news.

And no one *really* cares.

Do you?

What if that was your son?

What if that was your hood?

As always, I'm just sayin'.

Anyways, after Rev shattered the glass bottle, No Neck said, "Yeah, church boy, yeah, that's what I'm talkin' bout, nigga."

And Rev smiled.

I told Shoe, "Fuck the beer, let's go get some whiskey at Abdula's. Let's drink like tomorrow's another rumor."

"So you a gangsta now, huh, an OG, a baller, a big man? Think that makes you a man? Thinkin' you hard now? You think them kicks ice and ropes be where it's at?"

"Naw, Solly, it isn't even like that. You're trippin', looking into things too much."

"I'm trippin', Rev, I'm trippin'? Constantine said you ain't goin' to school, come home all hours highed-up and reeking of weed, disrespectful, and I'm trippin'?"

"She's exaggerating and all, you know how she is, word."

"But you part of No Neck's crew—ain't that right? A corner boy, a flunky, a circus clown? You tellin' me that ain't true?"

"Man, I'm just doing that on the side. Just to make a little paper. I'm just doing that to hang with Missy—she's like my girl now."

"First off, you can make paper at my shop. Second, I told you before that girl is bad news. She don't give a fuck about you, she don't care about no one but Missy. Fuckin' hood rat. And like I said, you ain't even goin' to school anymore. What's up with that?"

"Man, listen, I could pass the GED right now with a perfect score and get into community college tomorrow. School isn't like it was back in the day when you went. It's trash now. And you don't know Missy. No disrespect, Solly, but don't be talking about her like that. As far as money, no disrespect again, but I make a little more on the corner than I do at the shop."

"Yeah, that's true, but you also lookin' over your shoulder for PoPo or some other low-life gang member wantin' to take you out over some nonsense. And you're straight up frontin' 'bout school. Saint Pete's one of the best in the city. You know that. So stop feeding me all your bullshit. And Mighty Missy Brown, nigga, please. You like her tits and ass, not her."

"You're wrong, Solly. She listens to me. She understands what's inside me. We share stuff. Dreams and stuff. There's more to her then people see. She's my ride or die."

"Boy, you have truly lost your fucking mind. That corner, that ho, No Neck—you gonna end up dead or in jail. What makes you think you're different? You be thinkin' you're invincible? Look around, how many old slingers and gangstas you see hangin' on the block? How many? Answer me that, Rev. You don't. That's because they dead or in jail."

"You have it wrong, Solly. I *am* different."

"*You* got it wrong, little man. You *used* to be different. Now you're just like every other loser in the hood. Flushing your future down the sewer. You're better than that, Rev. Where's

REVEREND WENT WALKING

your self-respect, what happened to your dreams about goin' to school upstate, about leavin' this shit hole? What do you think Luke would say about all this, Rev? What would he say?"

"I have to bounce, Sol, I'll catch you later."

"What would Luke say, Rev?"

"Luke's dead."

Reverend rolled across the street and left Solly with balled up fists, shakin' on the corner. Just as Solly was about to head back to his shop, he caught outta the corner of his eye, Rev givin' dap to Crime Dog and Hollywood and pushin' up on Mighty Missy. Made Solly feel hollow inside. Made him feel sad. Made him feel more angry than the brother already was. But when Solly caught No Neck smilin' and blowin' kisses at him, it made him crazy angry. That type of angry I told y'all 'bout before. Anger that erases common sense as easy as white chalk from a blackboard. I'm so glad I was there, folks, so glad. I called out to Solly as he started walkin'—vexed—towards No Neck's corner.

"Not the time, Solly, not the time. Don't be stupid, brother, chill, we can still reach Rev, we still got time."

WILLIAM TEETS

"We're runnin' out of time, Old Man, we're runnin' out of time."

"Hold your head, Solly. Go back to your shop. Now's not the time."

"Like I said, Old Man, we're runnin' out of time."

"Solly!" I screamed.

Solly stopped—thank the Lord he stopped—two-stepped, shook his head, pounded his chest and spit. He started walkin' back to his shop. Him walkin' over into that pack of jackals wouldn't been no good for no one. He was right, though, people, he was right. We were runnin' out of time.

We're all runnin' out of time.

All of us down here in the hood.

All of us everywhere.

We're runnin' out of time, people.

Runnin' out of time.

Chapter 13
Blood Rent

"Yo, Rev, scrap, come here a minute. Let me talks to you 'bout sumptin, buzzin'."

"What's up, No Neck, what's poppin'?"

God, that street gang lingo, that gang mentality and talk. Don't even get me started on that. That's another fucked-up curse in the hood you don't want me rantin' 'bout. Cuzzin', 'buzzin', silly handshakes and what them fools call lessons. People, please. I'm not even goin' there. Bitch can tell you what roscoe means, learn mad gang signs, but can't tell you what eight times six is. Can't tell you the sixteenth president of the United States. It's a silly sideshow. I'll kick it 'bout that shit sometime later. Not now. I'm not givin' it credence. I've got a story to tell.

Oh, wait a sec.

I see the two of you with your tats and colors and fake tear drops cryin' down your wanna-be-down-faces, suckin' your teeth. Too bad.

Yeah, you youngbloods heard me correct.

Forget, y'all, and your weak 031 minds or blue folk bandanas or whatever. Go eat some bacon, y'all, on Halloween, playa. I'm not goin' there, so chill, dig the story I'm tellin' or step off. West Coast horseshit. We used to throw hands. We solved problems face-to-face like men, not with gats from a distance sprayin' innocents and ruinin' lives. Step off or stay. Don't matter to me. Let the facts be known how I feel though. You ain't intimidating this old head. I gots a story to tell. To those who wanta hear. To those who might learn.

Word.

What?

You flashin'?

For real?

Fuck you and your ratchet and your momma, too. That's right, you're all poison. Step off with your death. Tryin' to scare me up. Yeah, I'll be right here all night, brother. Ask your Uncle Chicky-Dee about me, young-un, yeah, I knows who you is. He'll let you know, too. Ask about Big Belly Bart and Old Man and the forty-ounce crew. Ask your people about Blue. You two come creepin' 'round here, y'all best come deep. Yeah, whatever, get to steppin'.

Sorry, folks.

Had to be said.

I'll say no more 'bout that inbred problem, now that them fugazy niggas gone.

Let's get back to the story, y'all.

For those who still wanta hear.

And there's still a lot of you, I see.

Let me rock on.

No Neck said to Rev, "I see that fuckin' barber man still all up in your grill. Hasslin' your ass like he's five-o or your pops. It's gettin' time we set that nigga straight, buzzin', know what I'm sayin'? He ain't real hood like me and you, dawg. He might break code, run to roscoe or some other kinda dumb shit. Put our news all up in the street. Know what I'm sayin', homie, you feel me?"

No Neck squinted his eyes after exhaling a weed cloud from his septic mouth and waved a blunt towards Reverend. Rev shook his head no—twice—and said, "I can deal with Solly. He's just talking that yin-yang. Shit, his shop is dirty, too. He isn't going to five-o. You don't have to sweat him, dawg."

Reverend changed his mind, nodded his head yes, and toked on the passed blunt from No Neck. In a held-breath suffocated voice, Rev said, "It's my crazy aunt who's blowing mine's all the time. She has me seriously stressed with her barking and lecturing and preaching."

Reverend exhaled his own weed cloud and continued, "I have to sneak in and out, day and night. The other day she slapped the shit out of me, dawg. I almost blacked, son, and violated her big ass, but I can't do that. I have to figure out something to do about her, though."

"I ain't treatin' you right? You ain't makin' enough cheddar?"

"Yeah, No Neck, I'm stacking, I'm good, why are you asking?"

"Pay her blood rent, son, that'll keep her quiet."

Reverend creased his brow and asked, "Blood rent? What's that? Blood rent?"

"Crime Dog, come here, tell church boy here what blood rent is."

"That's when you kick some benjis to your moms to keep her off your neck while you doin' your dirt. First few times she'll scream 'bout not takin' no blood money, but she'll take it, and then start spectin' it, and then you got her. Once mama dukes start takin' blood rent, she can't say shit 'bout nuttin'."

"I've never heard that before. Blood rent. Heard of blood money, but not blood rent."

"Just sumptin' me and Cool Breeze started callin' it back in the day and it stuck," No Neck, said. "And it works, dawg, start payin' your aunts some blood rent. She'll be chill then. Got it?"

"Yeah, man, I got it, but you don't know my aunt. She's loco. I mean crazy for *real*. I seriously doubt she'll be down with taking any blood rent."

"She will, homie, trust me, she will."

"What you doin' home so early in the afternoon, sinner boy?" Constantine asked Reverend. "Evilness walkin' in the sunlight amongst the righteous. Come to use my holy water to cleanse your dirty behind? Come to lay your heathen head on my couch to get some Devil rest? Not here unholy one, not here. You knows I will not stop denouncin' your sinful soul or be a flop house for Satan. As longs as I'm awake and there is air in my lungs, you best keep sneakin' and creepin' and only show your demon hide when I'm out or asleep. Hallelujah, praise be to the Holy Ghost and Jesus! Devil, get behind me. "

"No, Aunt Constantine, you're right."

"Hmmm, what you mean you know I'm right, demon boy?"

"Well, I do sleep here and do wash here and do keep my clothes here, so I was thinking I should help out with the bills and stuff. You know, chip in towards rent and stuff."

"And how, in God's mercy, will you do that, secret horned one?"

Reverend placed five crispy fifty dollar bills on the kitchen table. Constantine stared at the money and then squinted her eyes hard at Reverend before returning her gaze back to the Grants. Seconds felt like forever and Reverend backed up slowly. Best to be out of the big lady's reach and have a clear exit towards the door in case she flipped.

The room and air were still.

Quiet, like an empty church.

Ain't it crazy, folks, how long it takes seconds or minutes to pass when we're clockin'?

Rev's stomach was doin' flip-flops and he made sure to stay on high alert—DEFCON 5. There was no tellin' how this mighty holy heifer would react to such obvious bribery. She was an unpredictable beast. She might paw at the ground and charge at any second—nostrils flaring fire and smoke—the veracity of a pissed off she-bull leaving all in her wake in ruin and disaster. Or she might turn sideways and moo—docile like—and be passive and peaceful.

There was just no tellin'.

Such a magnificent beast she was.

Constantine began inhaling and exhaling and her heavy heaving bosom sucked all the air from the room and made the curtains flutter. Then, like someone slappin' a table top when everything is quiet, or shouting BOO! from behind your back, she lashed out in a holy diatribe that rattled the high heavens and startled the saints.

"You are truly a spawn from Satan, himself," she shouted. "Where have you hid your tail and horns? Tell me sinner boy, show me see your goat hooves. You, Devil child, were not born from my beautiful sister's loins. You were born of the beast! The Devil is roostin' in my home. Lord have mercy, the horned one is a lie! I denounce you, sinner child! Tryin' to buy absolution with blood money, a sack of silver coins. Tryin' to tempt me with the root of all evil. Bastard twin of Judas Iscariot, I denounce you and cast you from my holy abode. Be gone uncleansed one, leave me be. Amen! Glory to God in the Highest!"

And with that, Constantine picked up a cast iron skillet out of the drain board and began to take a step towards Reverend. He jetted out the apartment door and ran down the stairwell to the street, takin' three steps at a time.

Constantine hollered from high above, "That's right, wicked one, be gone Satan spawn. You have been vanquished, cast out. Return to your den of iniquity with your brethren beastly kin. You surely are marked with the number of the

WILLIAM TEETS

beast! Be gone, hallelujah, for even though I am an army of one, I am blessed with the strength of thousands, blessed by the Lord, our savior, Jesus Christ. I will not—cannot—be defeated! Can someone, anyone, give me an amen!"

And Constantine happily snorted at her triumph and her nostrils did flare. She majestically strutted and sashayed and shook her mammoth wooly head. She smiled to the high heavens. She felt victorious. After her conquest, standin' in the hallway, she heard someone shout through an adjacent apartment door, "Amen! Now shut the fuck up!"

She smiled.

Smiled like a hungry person eatin' tacos on Tuesdays. Fried fish on Fridays. One who basks in the light of the Lord on Sundays. She shook her mane and shouted a resounding, "Amen!"

The big lady loomed large, her girth swelling with pride. As she pranced back into her tiny apartment, into her tiny kitchen corral, returning the skillet to the drain board, she picked-up the crisp fifties from the table and studied them hard. She turned them over in her large, hairy, hoof-like hands and held them up to the white yellowish light above her small square sink.

She stuffed them into her bosom.

A tithe for Saint Peter's Church she thought to herself, a gift for the congregation, but at service the following morning, all the water buffalo women and collected cooing calves commented on her beautiful new Sunday hat and lovely designer shoes.

Hallelujah!

Amen!

Can I get a witness?

Shit was bad, people.

The whole hood was wildin' out even more then I could've ever imagined. Trust me, folks, I've seen some bad times. The riots and lootin' during blackouts. The murders and genocide of the crack wars. The black-on-black violence, the brutality and oppression of those sworn to protect and serve, and let's not forget that dishonest bitch—Justice—still peekin' an unfair racist look from behind her blindfold. Yeah, brother and sisters, I've done seen some bad times, but now things were badder. Worse things happenin' to folks in my hood. People I've known my whole life. Badder things happenin' on streets I walk every day. And everywhere I turned, everything kept getting darker.

The American Dream was becoming an even bigger farce. Brothers and sisters were killing or gettin' killed, just for wantin' to live. Just because they wanted a slice of that American lie that others enjoyed. Just because they wanted to live a little larger. The gap between those that have and those that have not was getting wider—if that's even possible. The poor wanted to hang the rich and the rich went about their biz—pretendin' the poor don't exist, thinkin' the poor were peasants. Kids were gettin' sliced up or gunned down in schools instead of gettin' an education and the PoPo were like a gestapo, allowed to stop common folk on the streets. Dressed like soldiers for war and driving armed Humvees, carryin' assault weapons, they asked for papers.

True story!

Like I said before, my people, no one seemed to give a fuck. Like I said, life in my hood was worse bad. Seems like ever since Luke's been dead, everyone's gone bananas.

Know what I'm sayin'?

Ya feel me?

Straight up fuckin' bananas.

The year was gettin' on towards late November. Nothin' had changed for the better, not since that crazy hot day in June where all this shit with Rev jumped off. Constantine was still

REVEREND WENT WALKING

holy rollin', now turnin' a blind eye towards Rev—as long as Grant was still her man—and the congregation continued to preach to those not needin' to hear the word. Congress was wagin' a war on the poor, instead of on poverty, and no one realized the difference. One Shoe was still drinking, I was doin' the same and gettin' older, and Josh was upstate doin' whatever he needed to do to keep on, keepin' on.

And Rev?

Well, let's just say Rev was headin' the wrong way down a one-way street.

I was gettin' a cut at Solly's on a late fall day, smokin' dukes and sippin' Canadian Club—damn, those Canucks make a good whiskey—y'all can keep your bourbons and Irish and Scotch blends, give me sweet rye any day. VO, Crown Royal, Canadian Club, it don't matter. Any day of the week—anytime—is a good time for rye, and with all the shit goin' down in the hood, trust me, folks, I was drinkin' mine's.

I was also feeling *real* bad for Solomon. See, my dudes, he was still tryin' like a champ to snap Reverend out of the curse Rev was under—from whatever witch cast him under the wicked spell to begin with—and, well, we all know who that might be.

One Shoe's drunk ass at least brought a little levity to the situation. He swore he had an aunt from the Islands, livin' uptown, who could sacrifice a chicken or goat or hog—sprinkle some blood, blow some smoke, spit some rum and cure Reverend of any spell he was under. For a small fee, of course. And a finder's fee for Shoe.

Me and Solly laughed a well-deserved laugh and told One Shoe we'd have just as much luck takin' Rev to a service at Holy Saint Pete's and sickin' the herd or Pastor Goodman-Brown on him for free. But don't get it twisted, brothers and sisters, Reverend was in a bad way. Don't get it twisted—shit was *real*.

"So Rev's been duckin' you, Sol? Won't even come around to say what's up?"

"Naw, Old Man, he knows I know what goes on down here and that he's gettin' his stupid ass in deeper and deeper. Shit, that DT—Schumacher—actually stopped in and asked me what's up with Rev. Said Rev's startin' to make a name for himself with the rollers."

Solly tilted my head up and then to one side, exhaled a breath of defeat, squared me up in the mirror, stared for a second and then continued cutting. He said, "Schu says he always respected Luke and me—knows about my nickel and dime shit, the boys ain't sweatin' that—but he wanted to know the lowdown on Rev. Says he doesn't want to see another young brother goin' upstate for a bid at the expense of some loser like No Neck."

"You tell him anything?"

REVEREND WENT WALKING

"Hell, no. I mean Schu's cool and the gang and all—went to school with him and all—but you know the rules, Old Timer. I can't be no snitch for the PoPo, even if they are tryin' to come correct. I can't trust them over my own. They got their rules, we got ours."

Solly stopped cuttin', lit up a loosie and poured a JD and ginger into a plastic cup. I could tell he was hurtin'. And confused. And frustrated. And angry. And I had no answers, folks. Wished I did, wished I could've pulled a Houdini and make all this bad shit go away, but I couldn't.

All I said was, "Sure you right, bro, sure you right. I hear you knockin'. Just don't know what to do about Rev. Like you said, I hear things too, and he's nowhere near up on his game as he thinks. And bein' led by No Neck? Lord, please."

"It's that bitty, Mighty Missy. She got his head—both heads—twisted," Solly gritted.

"I can dig that," I sighed.

As Solly continued my cut, I drifted through my menthol haze and faded out the barber shop banter. I closed my eyes and was young again. Just about Reverend's age. Her name was Tasha—before those types of names were common—before I found out Tasha's name was Russian for Christmas morning. How beautiful is that? Anyways, to me, Tasha's name was exotic and groovy soundin' and she was curvaceous and thick, just like Mighty Missy. She was my first—and pardon me, Barry—my last, my everything.

The first few times I made love to her I busted off like an out of control Uzi in the night—a hot rod creating fire and smoke between rubber and road—a Blue Spruce sheddin' piles of sleepin' snow from its boughs on the first day of Spring.

Yeah, people, my connect with Tasha was that lusty and romantic and *real*.

Man, listen, I was willin' the moon down to earth and fuckin' up the tides. Yeah, man, I remembered. I remembered for *real*. I swear I felt some heat in my loins just thinkin' 'bout it—crazy as that might sound—me being old and all. But I swear I felt it, folks, felt that hot rod feelin' of first love and first lust right there in Solly's chair.

I would have done anything for Tasha.

Anything.

My heart skipped a beat and my eyes opened wide.

I was back with the fellas in the shop.

"Reverend's in trouble, Solly, we need to talk to that boy, now! Rev's in deep trouble."

Fall, Icarus, fall. I told you not to fly so high.

Chapter 14
The Train Kept Rollin'

Doin' his own self-diagnosis, Josh took eighty-one milligram aspirins daily—for his blood flow—thinkin' them aspirins would stop him from havin' a heart attack or stroke. But they didn't do shit for a hangover. He'd have to swallow ten or twelve of them tiny pills to stop that rubber mallet from bouncin' off his brain. He'd think about a double Crown Royal making all his hassles go away, stop that mallet from bangin', but drinkin' wasn't viable, not at 6:18 a.m.

Not now, not yet.

Brotherman was gettin' close, though, to drownin' in a flood.

At least it was a Friday and there was a scheduled home visit for the students at the Hall. The school part of program would be closed after half a day. Most of the baby-jailin'-wanna-be- gangstas would be goin' home, and Josh knew he would only have two or three kids left behind in his first two classes. A nice, quiet, chill ending to his work week and he would have a few extra days off the followin' week.

Wake-up.

See, folks, at the Hall, the juvy teenage convicts, who the system calls court adjudicated male adolescents, got to visit their homes anywhere from three to seven days, every four to six weeks. The state and social workers called home visits therapeutic family intervention. The kids called the visits party time. The teachers called them mini-vacations. The families of the kids, well, they called home visits hell.

I called them crazy.

I never understood the logic of home visits. Follow this if you can, my people. The courts would sentence these teenage offenders—future convicts in trainin', some would say—to a place like Rutherford B. Hayes Haven Hall for all kinds of crimes and parole violations. Anywhere from twelve to eighteen months. Then the courts allowed these same cats home visits, and expected them to return back to the Hall, on their own recognizance to complete their sentence. If they didn't return, an AWOL warrant was issued for their arrest—another charge on their jacket—and they would be picked-up by local five-o and taken back to the Hall to start the whole process over again.

Sometimes.

PoPo didn't take the AWOL warrants too seriously.

Some kids came back, some didn't, and some weren't even OK'ed to go home in the first place. See, folks, so many of these broken-babies were wildin' out so bad at the Hall they couldn't be trusted goin' back to their communities. To raise hell and all. To hurt themselves or someone else.

Ain't no one takin' liability for these young-uns.

Shit, some of these baby-brothers were so battered and beaten down, they refused to go home even though they could've, because they knew they were better off where they were.

Naw, to me, a home visit was nothin' more than a bribe. Something to hold over the boys' heads to make sure they followed the rules.

Except for them lost kids.

I felt for them.

But the majority?

Like I said, crazy, right?

Hope that made sense to y'all.

Hope I explained it proper.

But like I said also, this home visit meant a short vacation for Joshua Moriel. With all the madness takin' place in the hood—what with Reverend and all—and everything goin' buck wild over the past few months, I decided to take a break and visit Josh. For *real* this time. After his Friday shift he was gonna pick me up at the train station and we were gonna catch up a bit. Man, I'm tellin' y'all, people, I needed a breather. Unfortunately, even though I left the hood, on the 12:47 north, the hood didn't leave me.

"If this kid, Reverend, is so smart and has so much potential, and has been doing so good for so long, why is he breaking so bad all of a sudden?"

"Like I told you, Josh, listen up. Rev's uncle, his foster pops, died unexpected-like and Rev's been buggin' ever since. His unc's best friend, Rev's godfather, Solly, been tryin' to hold him down but it ain't workin'. Rev's caught up in the game. I'm tellin' ya, happened that quick, right after Luke's death. Boy been walkin' round talkin' 'bout free will and shit. Talkin' 'bout he got the choice and right to do what he wants. Read it in some philosophy books. I can't remember the names he be throwing 'round, but they big time, I'd guess."

I swigged the rest of the CC in my glass and motioned to the bartender to refill mine and back up Josh. After sittin' quiet for a couple of minutes, I asked Josh what he knew about this free will noise that Rev's been spoutin'.

REVEREND WENT WALKING

Joshua leaned back against his bar stool and dragged his hand over his face. He sighed, shook his head and sighed again. "Christ, Old Man, why not just ask me to solve all the questions of the Universe? The concept of free will has been debated forever. Hell, I got a minor in philosophy and don't understand half of it. I've read William James, Kant . . . I don't know. But I have a hard time believing some fifteen-year-old slinger from the hood is reading William James' two-stage model or even Rene Descartes, for that matter."

"Descartes? That's the dude in the oven, right?"

"Yeah, Old Man, that's one way to describe him," Josh chuckled.

We stepped outside the bar for a smoke and continued our talk, "I'm tellin' you, Josh, Reverend's that smart, that deep. Kid reads everything he can get his hands on. Hell, he's been turnin' me onto books, just like you have over the years. He's done had me read Thoreau, Vonnegut, Orwell, just like you. He used to live in the library. Trust me, he's mad smart. He's a special type of different."

Josh chuckled again and said, "He ain't that smart, brother, because if he keeps doing what he's doing, he's going to be reading books in my class, at the Hall, with an eighteen-month bid. He's going to be wishing he had the chance to choose free will again. The courts and system will gladly impose their free will on him, taking his away in the process, and do it all for free, for *real*."

Back inside the bar, Josh signaled the bartender for two more beers and two more doubles. "Anything you leaving out, Old Timer? Anything else going on with this kid, Rev?"

"Well, yeah, there this bitty, see. Got his head all twisted up."

"Oh, shit, Old Man, let me guess, she's sixteen going on twenty-five. And better than that, I bet she's his first."

"Yeah, his first, and yeah, she's bangin'."

"Well now, that's a problem times three, isn't it? Not long until a little Reverend is riding a Big Wheel around the hood in a white tee covered in chocolate milk stains. You know about that song and dance and outcome."

"Christ, don't say that, please. That will surely seal the deal to Dead End Street for Rev. Keep that fucked-up vicious hood-cycle goin' strong. Rev's gonna break that curse. Break that cycle. But you know what, Josh, you know what I was thinkin' on the train? Maybe you could come down and meet Solly, meet Reverend, and kick some righteousness. Tell Rev what time it is. About his smarts and all. You'd be like a neutral country, like Switzerland or somethin'. Do some more of your positive, like you always done. Know what I'm sayin'?"

Josh's eyes went all wide for a sec, before he said, "Old Man, I'm about to have the bartender cut you off. Are you crazy? I'm not riding into the hood like some great white hunter to save the natives from themselves. Hell, I deal with enough of this shit and enough of these knucklehead kids at my job. I got my own damn problems with my own students."

"Exactly, Josh, that's why this plan would work. You always goin' above and beyond with the kids at the Hall and helpin' them out. You could do the same for Rev."

Josh raised his hands above his head, dropped them on his lap, and said, "Naw, trust me, brother, whatever you think about me—whatever I used to be—that me is long gone. I don't have much left to offer anyone, anymore. I'm burnt. New administration has seriously screwed program up at the Hall. You remember me telling you about that. Hell, I feel so old I'm catching up to you. I'm running on empty and starting not to give a damn like everyone else at the job. Just the way it is, Old Man, just the way it is."

"You are wrong, Joshua Moriel. I know you. I've seen you in action. You're a natural . . . you got a gift in dealin' with cats like Rev. You're selling yourself short. Ain't that what you always tellin' them kids? That they selling themselves short? Shit, besides, it couldn't hurt matters much."

"Don't know, brother, and not about to find out. Besides, someone has to be raising him. He doesn't have his own place, does he? He's not ballin' like that at fifteen, is he? Who's the adult he lives with? Who's holding the fort down?"

"That'd be Constantine. Luke's widow. Reverend's aunt. Fine lady back in the day, but she went a little crazy after her sister—Rev's mom—was killed in a car crash. Since Luke died, she's been even more bat-shit crazy, if you know what I mean. Holy Roller—preachin' to the choir—and now she's turning a blind eye to Reverend's doings because he's layin' a little paper on her. Never would've thought it, but Constantine's takin' blood money and turnin' her eye."

"She sounds like a *real* fucking saint."

After spendin' a few more days with Josh and tryin' to convince him to meet and talk with Reverend and Solly—to no avail—it was time for me to go. After a too many Bloody Mary mornin', Josh dropped me off at the train station to catch the 11:35 back to the hood. There was snow on the tracks and the trees were bare. No birds sang. The world felt so cold. I was brick—standing on the platform, waitin' for the train—and I zippered my Carhartt all the way to the top.

A cold chill still found my innards and I shivered.

My eyes wept.

A loud horn that warned the train's arrival to the station—so unlike the lonesome whistle wails you read about in books or hear in Country-and-Western songs—almost made me fall onto the tracks. I felt like the loneliest man in the Universe. I was dizzy or drunk or both and stepped carefully. I knew if

I fell into the gap I would be swallowed up by blackness and float through some dark infinite space forever. I thought of Descartes never leaving his oven.

Infinite Darkness.

Safely seated on the train, I stared out the window as the cars bounced, braked and bounced again. I saw a dead deer beside the tracks at one of the small town stops. Tongue lolling, lying in blood-spotted snow, the carcass was bein' eaten by a murder of big black crows. My grandmother, God rest her soul, would've told me seeing somethin' like that was a bad omen. Shit, people, where this train was takin' me was filled with nothin' but bad omens. Bad omens that come to be.

I looked away from the window and saw a young mother, across the aisle, holding a three or four-year-old in her lap. She ran her fingers through his golden blond hair. His big blues eyes caught mine and he smiled. I smiled back and asked God to make sure he was gettin' off this train with his mother anywhere before the last stop, which was mine.

They did.

In a town called Mount Pleasant.

I shivered again.

The train kept rollin'.

Chapter 15
The Letter

"I'm not going to touch Crime Dog. He hasn't done shit to me. Besides, he's a little ass nigga. Naw, man, you're all trippin'."

"Fuck that littl' ass nigga. He been shiesty. Been skimmin' off the top. Puttin' his hands in my pockets. Need to reminds him what time it is, break him down and then take him back in the fold all righteous and shit. Hell, he's my nephew. I can't dog him out, buzzin'. And besides, who you to question me, church boy?"

"I told you, No Neck, stop calling me church boy. And if you got beef with Crime Dog, he's your fam, touch him yourself."

"Better talk to your boy, Mighty Miss, he's gettin' all loud and insubordinate like. Soundin' like he don't wanta roll no more. Sound like he gonna have to bite, to back up all his barkin' if he keeps poppin' off at the grill. Woof-woof."

REVEREND WENT WALKING

Reverend's muscles tensed.

"Boo, it ain't nothing. Relax, baby. All No Neck sayin' is scare Crime Dog up, slap him up a littl'. It ain't nothing like touchin' him. Just scare him up. Do it for me, baby, do it 'cause I want you to."

"You think I should?"

"I know you should. Besides, it might turn me on. We'll cuddle and you can tell me more 'bout them stories later. 'Bout them mysteries. Share our secrets, you know, boo? Know what I'm sayin', my baby boy homie?"

Rev said to No Neck, "All right, No Neck, I'll rap with Crime Dog, but nothing off the hook. A couple bitch slaps, a little warning, and then we let him live and see if he comes correct."

"That's all I'm sayin', gangsta, that's all I'm sayin."

After gettin' back home from visiting Joshua, and ridin' the four, I took a dollar van downtown and cut through two empty lots to Solly's shop. Even though I enjoyed gettin' away and spendin' time with Josh, I was thirsty to find out what was happenin' in the hood. As I walked the last cross-street to Solly's, though, I can't lie, people, I had that funny fucked-up feelin' in my gut again. That feelin' of something not being right. That feelin' that another storm was coming—rumbling, raging, blowin' full force gales—bringing more grief. A storm that was becomin' way too common. I was hopin' things were better, but expectin' the worst. I even daydreamed like a child, hoping for some superheroes to arrive and save the day.

Save us from these streets.

Save us from ourselves.

But, shit, people, I knew better.

Wasn't I the one who told y'all superheroes don't *really* exist?

That heroes fail.

That we all ain't but a step away from our own kind of kryptonite.

Believe dat.

True story.

Hang on tight now, here's what took place next.

"Rev did what, now?" I asked Solly.

"Listen up, while I break it down. Hollywood's punk-ass was in here gettin' a cut the other day and runnin' off at the mouth 'bout how Reverend was supposed to press that Griffin boy—what they call him, McGruff or Crime Dog, or some silly shit like that—'bout him bein' short with money from his work. From what I could figure, this lil' nigga, Griffin, spazzed out, got all scared and shit when confronted by Rev, and started hookin' off. Rev fucked him up. Broke his nose and eye socket, lumped him up good, and now the kid's mother is screamin' at Constantine 'bout how she wants to get paid or she's going to PoPo."

"Shit, Constance got involved?" I asked.

Solly shook his head yes, poured us both Dickels in paper Dixie Cups, and continued.

"Constantine—herself—came down here wildin'. Hell, when's the last time you saw Constance down here? She's all screamin' and askin' me if I knew what the fuck was going on—used the word fuck, too—imagine that, Constantine cursing. Said she had enough, said she's done with Reverend, done with the hood. Said we're all about to drown in the harbor, whatever the hell that means, but that she'll be going with half the Saint Peter's congregation down south, whatever the fuck that means. I'm tellin' you Old Man, Crazy Constantine was talkin' in riddles."

I went to ask a question, but Solly raised his hand in the air and shook his head for me to be quiet. The brother was on a roll.

"Wait, Old Man, it gets better. She told me she'd sign over guardianship papers for Reverend—devil boy, she called him—to me. For all she cares he can go upstate to juvy. Said she was outtie and can't no one change her mind. I ain't got a clue, Old Man. I'm not sure what's goin' on."

I took a long swig—I mean a long one—and drained my paper cup. I didn't say a word, just held my empty out and Solly refilled it. This shit was gettin' crazier by the minute, folks. This shit's about to kill me, people. I mean Constantine, below 154th Street and cursing—that's off the charts enough—but leavin' the hood, signin' guardianship papers for Rev over to Solomon? The Griffin boy all banged-up? Rev becomin' straight up gangsta? Naw, folks, my head was swimmin' and sure enough drownin'. I took another long swig of Mr. George Dickel.

Can you all believe this?

Y'all still with me?

I walked outside Solly's shop and blew menthol smoke rings into the cold. The blue metallic rings danced collided and then condensed with the early evening air. They became unrecognizable scowls in the early dusk. Nothing more than huffs of lost dreams. Nothing more than imaginary gargoyles, dragons, bakus, or giant crab claws. Images we think we see—sometimes—in puffy white clouds.

I shook my head.

REVEREND WENT WALKING

Ain't shit was real.

Back in the shop, I asked Solly if he had heard everything right. Shit was too stupid, folks, too much trauma drama. I asked him again if he was clear on what he'd heard. If Constantine was for *real* with what she'd been sayin'.

"She's really buggin', Old Man, she's really serious. Talkin' 'bout she's OT. Talkin' 'bout if I don't accept guardianship of Rev, she's filin' a PINS petition and she's done with him. Says it's a definite Rev will be sent upstate. Says she knows a councilman, or minister, or pastor, or some fucking Holy Roller with mad juice. Talkin' that crazy shit 'bout her and the congregation leavin' for the south. Sayin' it's God's grace. Screaming about all of us being agents of darkness. I'm tellin' ya, Old Timer, Constantine's gone straight up fruit."

"What about the paper Reverend's been layin' on her?"

"Nothing, my brother, nothing. I'm tellin' you, she's ghost."

"What's Reverend sayin' 'bout all this? Does he know?"

"Of course he knows. He don't give a fuck about her, 'specially now that she's more loco than ever. He's thinkin' life gonna be all cool and the gang, livin' with me upstairs from the shop. Hell, I didn't even tell Donna. You know she stays over more than half the time. Rev's talkin' like we're boys. How the hell can I raise a child twenty-four-seven? I told him if this insanity happens—by a million to one chance

— 149 —

this madness happens—he's done with all that corner shit, told him it's back to school with his ass."

"And?"

"And, Reverend said a'ight. Said he's gettin' sick of No Neck and all the corner bullshit, anyways. Don't know if he's comin' correct or he's tryin' to play me to stay out of juvy or to stay with that hood rat, Missy. I feel like I owe it to Luke to at least try. I mean I am Rev's godfather and all. And, Christ, Old Man, Rev's like a little brother to me and he's definitely worth the gamble. Hell, me and you both know the system ain't no good for no one, but my head's boxed right now."

"Sure you right, brother, but . . ."

"But I'll fuck Rev up, Old Man, if he plays me. Don't get it twisted. If I sign those papers, I'm in for the long haul. For doin' the right thing. Reverend's gotta understand that. Constance is so crazy, though, I can't figure out what end is up. But if this happens, Rev has got to know what time it is."

"Well, Solly, let's make sure he does."

A few days later, I was lampin' on the block.

REVEREND WENT WALKING

I got word from Solly he needed to see me. And fast. I sighed deeply into the early evening air, wonderin' what could be up now, and noticed I didn't see my breath. With all the ruckus happenin' every other day, I didn't even realize winter was passin' and spring was knockin' at the door.

It was March fifteenth.

When I got to Solly's, my face rammed into the unexpected locked door. The OPEN neon sign was off. Solly let me in, locked the door behind us, said nothin', and fell back into one of his barber chairs. His large, let go exhale—which was becomin' an all too familiar reflex for all of us—sounded like a faded trumpet blowin' retreat from my old army days. I exhaled, too. Solly was holdin' one of those big, official-lookin', yellow envelopes on his lap and motioned me to sit down.

"What's up, brother? What's so urgent? Why you close shop so early?"

"Got this envelope today. Had to sign for it. Thought it was a subpoena or sealed indictment or some shit. I was goin' to refuse, but the mail dude says it's nothin' bad, says it's from some lawyer in VA couriered especially for me. Brother seemed official, so I took it."

Solly lit a duke and stared at the nicotine and water-stained ceiling tiles for a few seconds before saying, "Inside the big envelope is two regular envelopes. One addressed to me, the other to Rev. A fancy cover letter says they're to be opened only by the people they're addressed to. I can open mine upon receipt and Reverend can open his on the twentieth."

"That's Rev's birthday, ain't it?"

"Yeah."

"You open yours?"

"Yeah."

"Well, what's up? What'd say?"

Solly handed me a couple sheets of paper. I took my specs outta of my pocket and put them on. Before reading, I lit a loosie and had Solly pour me a straight strong one in a coffee mug. I leaned back into my chair and blew out another full-sized exhale. The date on the letter was from eleven years earlier.

I read the letter.

Homeboy,

If we're not reading this together, by now you know why. What I'm about to write in this letter, is something I've been carrying hard now for five years. I set this mailing up with Billy Jackson, a lawyer-friend of mine from the army, who's good money (trust him). If anything was to happen to me, he was to courier this package to you, five days before Reverend's sixteenth birthday.

I hope it's found you and Reverend well.

REVEREND WENT WALKING

It's about a secret I've kept and shared with no one. Not even you, my brother. I'm not proud about what you are about to find out, but I'm damn sure not ashamed either. My only regret is that I'm not with you now to share this secret with Rev.

After reading your letter, give Reverend his letter on his sixteenth birthday and please be there with him when he reads it. I'm not sure if he's going to flip out or not, or even care, or even if you are all still together. Just be there to have his back and make sure he can handle the news correct if you all are. You are his godfather for a reason. You are my brother from another mother. No jokes. I really mean that. I love you, Solly, and you have always been fam. After reading the news below, I can only hope that you'll take on the responsibility of helping out and checking up on Rev as much as you can. I don't want him to become a statistic to the streets like so many others. There is no one else I would've chosen but you. I Love that boy more than anything in this world, or after. Feel that, my brother.

Six years ago, me and Constance were visiting Thomasina and Eric upstate. Me and Thomasina were up late, drinking too much, but I'm not using that as an excuse. I've come to terms with what happened and don't need an excuse. Anyways, Thomasina starts saying how her and Eric's marriage is falling apart, they're going to be getting a divorce, things aren't working anymore, etc., on and on. One thing led to another and we ended up making love. I say making love, because Reverend was conceived that night.

I am Reverend's father.

WILLIAM TEETS

Like I said, no one but me and Thomasina ever knew. I always wanted to tell Reverend, but couldn't lay that heavy shit on him with me being away and all, and him being so young. I decided this was one time when honesty would not be the best policy. Maybe it wasn't the best decision by me, but what is, is. I planned to tell Reverend on his 16th *birthday, but with the danger I was in, with my job and all, I set this up in case something happened to me. I guess something did if I'm not reading this with you now.*

Solly, Reverend needs to know. Please carry this out and try to keep Reverend righteous. As far as Constantine knowing . . . I addressed that in Rev's letter.

Peace,

Luke

"Holy, shit."

"Who you tellin', Old Man?"

"I always said that boy looked like Luke."

"Fuck outta here. You ain't never said that."

"I did, I did, but what now?"

"Time to talk this through and then get Rev."

"Bet."

Chapter 16
Balls Said The Queen, If I Had Them I'd Be King

Some heavy shit, I know, my peeps.

Me and Solly banged our heads and ideas together and were tempted to damn-near read Rev's letter and reseal the envelope again, but that just wouldn't be right. And besides, folks, if you all remember, I told y'all awhile back, secrets can be real complicated—can cause harm and crush souls—that whole Latin, derived from secretus . . . well . . . you remember.

But this secret was a motherfucker.

Crazy good and kinda bad at the same time.

Not too often in life we get served both chocolate and vanilla, right answers to wrong questions, somethin' good born from somethin' bad. But this secret had all that.

WILLIAM TEETS

No doubt.

I just didn't know what the hell to do, though, folks. It was one of those times you just roll with the punches and hope you're still standin' at the bell. Solly felt the same. We thought it best to just let Rev read his letter—both of us with him—and play the rest by ear. Damn, what else was there?

See, I was never a man who put much stock in what-ifs and the like—to complain about a shitty hand. I always played mine's and tried to win the pot regardless—sometimes successful, other times not so much. An outcome either way. See, folks, the forgotten people of America in the ghetto, we learn young in life there's no safety nets to catch your ass when you fall, and you need to make your owns. Learned early on no one *really* cares. Understood life on the street ain't so sweet.

Hell, I don't have no juice with the Man's machine. A congressman or senator. Not even repped by one. That whole false American Dream shit I spoke about earlier? About how that golden dream is advertised on a regular, but denied sale to so many? And the good word—the religions saving the unwashed masses—people, please, don't even get me started. We black folks were left holdin' Bibles and chanting hymns in churches—churches on every corner of every block, along with liquor lotto grocery stores and broken OTB's. Just like Brother Malcolm said. The word, and the presses that printed the word, the buildings and businesses that sold the word, were *all* owned by the Man. Sold to keep us down. And remember

I told y'all about public housing homes for poor folk, built on landfills and chemical dumps while contractors and politicians get their palms greased, make mad loot, and . . . oh . . . OK . . . right, folks . . . I'm goin' on a ramble again. Y'all want to hear about Rev. Alright, I'll chill now, but you will hear me speak later, and you will learn.

Five days after Solly received the letters—Reverend's birthday—me and Solly put word out on the street that we needed to see him urgent like. We chilled at Solly's shop waitin' for Rev and waitin' to see what would come next.

I'm not gonna front, people, I was feelin' a bit tense and uptight when I saw Rev bouncin' his special, Reverend walk towards the shop and I swigged a little CC. Again, for medicinal purposes only. My nerves were buggin'. Reverend sprang into the shop with his million dollar smile, all iced out and polite like, and gave both me and Solly dap.

"What's up, fellas? Heard you wanted to see me with the quickness. Why you closed early, Sol? What's up? This got something to do about them guardianship papers? Aunt Constantine? My birthday? Please don't lecture me about Missy and the corner, that scene's played. So what's going on? What's up?"

Solly explained about receiving the envelope from the lawyer in VA and that what Reverend was about to read was goin' to be some *real*, deep, emotional shit. Told him we were there for him, but then Solly just stopped talkin' and handed Rev his letter.

WILLIAM TEETS

That whole crazy come-what-may.

Reverend read his letter, a little longer than Solly's—'til this day none of us has ever laid eyes on what Luke wrote to Rev—and when done, Reverend dropped the papers in his lap and tears welled up in his eyes. The shop was mad quiet. The three of us sat in silence for a few minutes, or hell, maybe hours, and then a few tears ran down Rev's face, softly.

"Rev, you a'ight? I know this is heavy, bro. It's OK to cry, little brother. We're here for you. Damn, I hate to see you sad and cryin'. 'Specially on your birthday and . . ."

And folks, as God is my witness, Reverend went into some Shakespearean type soliloquy that stunned me and Solly.

"I'm crying because I'm happy, Solly, not because I'm sad. I knew it. I knew Luke was my father. You feel a connection like that. That electricity. That true love. You guys know I never knew my folks. It killed me not having a mother or father. Never knowing a parent's love. And even though I yearned for that love my whole life it was only a dream I made up in my mind. Some fantasy I could never have. But I tried to make it *real* with make-believe."

Reverend stood up and wiped his tears on his sleeve. He lifted his damp eyes toward the ceiling, let go of his own long-winded exhale, and turned and faced Solly and me.

"Even though I couldn't remember my parents, Luke showed me so much love—like a father—it made me happy, but guilty, too. Guilty that I couldn't return the amount of love that man gave to me. I always wanted love like that—a parent's love—love so real you can't ever give back as much as you get, but I felt guilty not being able to give Luke the amount of love he gave me. And now I know why. Luke's my father. He shared a parent's love with me. That's why. Now I know. Knowing Luke is my father, knowing that bond is *real*, it will be *real* forever . . . And yeah, man, it hurts he's gone, but I know, I know now I knew my father. I touched him, hugged him, smelled him, and can still love him. You feel me? I can't hug dreams or ghosts or make-believe, but I can love memories and touch angels, and Luke is an angel. My angel. My father. You feel me, fellas?

"I feel you, Rev. I feel you all too much," Solly said.

The two of them hugged and cried tears for a man they both loved. Brother love and son love. *Real* love. Everything they held back, denied, or failed to admit to themselves or others—regarding Luke's death—was released that night. Released to the heavens. Released to the stars. There was nothin' between them but righteousness and truth and honor and glory and courage and trust and love and respect and any other Godly transcendental quality you could think of.

Plato would've been proud.

My peeps, let me tell you, that whole letter-readin' secret-sharin' experience between Luke and Rev and Solly and me turned into a cryin' love fest.

WILLIAM TEETS

We cried like babies.

Man, it was so fuckin' beautiful.

We sat back and shared stories about Luke late into the night. Rev sayin' how this birthday was his best birthday ever and how he was done with the game and was gonna honor Luke by leaving the block alone and gettin' back to school. Solly said he was gonna sign them guardianship papers as quick as can be, and be there for Rev, always.

My brothers and sisters, that March night was the wildest end to a cold-ass winter I ever seened. And Constantine wasn't frontin'. She signed legal guardianship of Reverend over to Solomon and it became all official like—believe that or not—right after the beginnin' of spring. A motherfuckin' rebirth. Reverend gave Crime Dog's moms five Franklin's and a bindle and the whole fight scene—Crime Dog's broken nose, eye socket and all—was forgotten. Crime Dog—who suffered blurry vision in his eye ever since—was back workin' the corner for No Neck, who was none too happy about Rev leaving his crew and No Neck threatened payback on a regular. Mighty Missy Brown was still in town and Solly was a hot mess regardin' his new found responsibilities. Reverend made the transition easy on Solly, though, by honoring his word about quittin' the streets and returnin' to school.

Everything was groovy.

I wish I could end the story here, folks, and tell y'all everyone lived happily ever after, but I can't. I wish I could tell y'all Reverend rode off into the sunset—victorious—on a magnificent steed, as trumpets blared and crowds cheered, but I can't.

Still too much trauma drama, still too many crabs in the bucket.

Even in good times, even when storms subside, you best believe something bad is lurking. You best believe fate's not that easy to escape. A life that no one else recognizes but you. Most of America never sees shit like this. Remember I said how this drama is never televised? Remember what I said about superheroes and Casper and the streets and such? How I told you all earlier about the hot-ass sun melting wax wings and Bakus stealin' dreams in the night?

Remember?

Fall, Icarus, fall. I told you not to fly so high.

Chapter 17
Is Miss Jones On The Bus?

Gather 'round now, people, listen-up. Y'all know from earlier in the story when I told y'all what time it was, how I had lots more stories from the hood to share with you? Well, people, I still do. We ain't done yet. This story ain't through. Not by a long shot. Don't get all happy 'bout Reverend and happy with yourselves. Don't go off holdin' hands, plantin' flowers and singin' Kumbaya. Don't be fooled, folks, don't get caught slippin'.

I still gots so much more to tell.

Lots more to share.

Believe it or not, though, brothers and sisters, happenings in the hood continued to take turns for the better. Solly found out through Luke's lawyer, Billy Jackson—the dude from VA—that Luke had set up a righteous trust fund for Reverend. Solly enrolled Rev back into Saint Pete's Parochial. Due to Rev's smarts and earlier success at the school, if he doubled up classes for the last six weeks of the spring semester and attended a full summer school schedule, he would be back on track for his normal graduation date.

Forget about a GED for my man.

He's gonna be the *real* deal!

I felt good inside.

Reverend, even with all his extra school work, put in hours at Solly's shop and was back to bein' the Reverend we all knew and loved. He was hittin' his books super hard and stayin' off the corner. Most everything was copasetic. I say most everything, folks, because besides these damn streets, there was still one distraction, one negative around. Yeah, you guessed it, people, Mighty Missy Brown.

"I still love her, Solly," Rev said with an innocence only the young can contrive. "I can't just turn my feelings on and off like a faucet."

"Well, she don't love you, homeboy, won't give you the time of day."

"That's because of No Neck. He's still heated I stepped off on him. Trying to scare me up and put fear in my heart when I walk by the block. Turning Missy against me. I swear, sometimes I feel like busting a bat across his big-ass head."

Solly laughed, "Shit, Rev, why you wanta ruin a perfectly good bat for?"

"I'm serious, Sol. He better stay out of my way and stop having his punk-ass crew trying to press me. Filling Missy's head with propaganda and lies. I'll violate, that's my word," Rev tried to convince Solly, or maybe himself.

"Listen, Rev, No Neck ain't no killer, but he's still bad news. Just keep your distance, stay up, and don't get caught slippin'. As far as Missy, I know it hurts, brother, but trust me, where you're headin' there's going to be a million Missy Browns. Those college shorties gonna be fighting over a brother like you—jockin' you—and the beauty is, unlike Missy, they'll be able to spell dog if you spot them the d and the g."

"Oh, you got jokes now."

"Naw, I hear you, Rev, just sayin', stay up and stay strong. Missy will fade, and that corner ain't got nothin' good for you. You above all that nonsense. You feel me?"

"Yeah, I feel you, Sol."

"Good, then go clean up the back room, hit your books, and I'll order in some Chinese."

"Cool."

Yeah, people, except for the normal dangers and traps and high jinks—what the hell does high jinks mean, anyway?—life was movin' forward on a positive tip for all of us. I hit a number for two grand, was kickin' it a lot more with Josh on a regular, Solly was keepin' it *real*, I already told y'all about

Rev, and Cool Breeze—No Neck's piece-of-shit lieutenant—was popped for a Glock and got a three year bid.

Yeah, folks, things were lookin' up.

I couldn't remember feelin' this good about the hood in a long, long time. But even though I felt good 'bout how Reverend was keepin' everything a hundred, and good about how Solly was steppin' up, I also saw how Reverend was bein' tested by No Neck and his crew on a regular. And like most everyone else, I recognized Rev's pining for Mighty Missy. Because of this, I kicked it with Rev as much as I could and filled in Solly with what I saw and ear-hustled from the street.

I kept my fingers crossed.

Feel me?

See, people, Reverend wasn't goin' through nothin' no other kid lookin' to break free from the hood was goin' through. But he was Rev, and he was special, and he was ours. We all didn't want to see him swallowed by the streets, taking a part of our souls with him. I done seen that dreadfulness too many times with too many other youngbloods. In a way, Rev was a ticket for all of us to get out of the hood. Without even knowin' it, Rev was beatin' back the crabs and soarin' for us all. And like I said, folks, life seemed to be movin' forward on a positive tip and everything appeared status quo. I called Josh and made plans to visit him over the Easter weekend that was less than a few days away, lookin' forward to a well-deserved rest from all the storms that so recently howled, but so recently subsided.

I was tryin' to explain to One Shoe everything that went and was goin' down, while we stood outside Abdula's on a beautiful spring morning, passing a fifth. Shit was weird, folks. Even though I knew—and was pretty much a part of everything that happened—when I told One Shoe all the stories and scenarios regarding Rev, they seemed to be somebody else's story. Like I was a spectator watchin' myself in a movie. Almost like my recollections didn't belong to me. You ever feel that way, people? I don't know why, like I said, weird, but all I could think was that all of us down here on the block weren't too used to sharin' happy endings. Didn't tell too many stories that ended with a smile. Seldom, if ever, did any of our tales end, *And they all lived happily ever after.*

Hell, the year was crazy for sure.

Believe that.

Word.

Anyways, on this warm spring day—not that lion and lamb shit that always confuses me—the block was quieter than usual. I almost dropped the fifth, though, when I was startled by a sight and sound that screeched around the corner.

REVEREND WENT WALKING

A loud lively sound like the crazy cheer of a crowd when the home team kicks a last-second winning field goal.

There before my eyes, brothers and sisters, I saw a yellow cheese-bus rollin' down the Ave. That bus was rockin' and swayin' side-to-side and I thought for sure that behemoth vehicle was goin' to topple over. I heard cow bells and tambourines, chants, cheers, and whistles, and I saw Constantine—standin' up front, by the opened accordion door—yell out to all the people clapping on the bus, "All right, sisters, let's sing loud and proud as we pass through these Satan streets. Let these heathens hear the word, let them hear the righteous. We are leavin' Sodom and Gomorrah. Let's sing so loud, sisters, we make the walls of Jericho fall again. Goodbye, sinners, for we is gone. The harbor has risen and cleansed the saved and will surely drown the wicked, but we is gone. Michael has rowed his boat ashore, hallelujah, and we have been delivered. Oh Lord, can I get a witness? We are leavin' the evil, leavin' the sinful, leavin' unholy creatures behind! Don't look back, sisters, you'll be turned into pillars of salt. The rapture is upon us. Amen, sisters, amen."

And the entire bus started singing *This Little Light of Mine*.

Loud.

I mean real loud.

The Holy Herd was leaving town.

Stampin' and snortin' and singin'.

WILLIAM TEETS

Beautiful beasts on a holy migration.

Searching for themselves or new born sinner lambs to save.

A crusade?

That part was muddled.

Always been.

I thought about Reverend.

I thought about Solly.

I thought about Joshua.

I thought about Luke.

I thought about what was goin' to happen next.

Hell, I even thought about Tasha.

I shook my head, took a big swig from the fifth, and said, "Well, I'll be goddamned."

Shoe asked me, "Is Miss Jones on the bus?"

I smiled.

Chapter 18
When You're Blessed The Sun Shines All The Time

As I walked to the four, I swear, people, if my old bones weren't so creaky and broke down, I would've skipped or danced—right there on the sidewalk, right in front of everyone. The Universe had granted one of those beautiful spring days that you're sure were created just for you. One of those days when people walk with their heads upright, noddin' and smilin' to each other. Everyone feelin' a positive groovy-like vibe. Crazy how weather can affect our moods and spirits, but believe me, lovely days can do that. I felt like reachin' up into the sky and grabbin' the sun, holdin' that magnificent shine in my hands, and then slidin' that treasure into my back pocket. Save the glory for a rainy day. Yeah, yeah, I know, you all thinkin' my ass would burn up—probably so—but I'm just sayin', that day I was walkin' to the four was damn near perfect.

I thought back to the cold winter. How everything was urgent and bleak and ominous—great word again, people, right, ominous?—and that thought made me smile more. Even though, deep in my soul, I knew wickedness could be around the next corner waitin' to pounce like some jungle predator. I blocked that idea from my mind, though, and shook my head and laughed—at least for now—at how great everything was turnin' out. I bought my round trip ticket for upstate and left the hood behind, ridin' the northbound to visit Josh for Easter. Call it slippin' if you want, folks. Call it sleepin' if you want, my dudes. But I really believed this day was a rebirth.

Another resurrection.

Resurrection, indeed, brothers and sisters, resurrection, indeed.

A Holy resurrection. A *real* resurrection.

Not some fake-ass, fabricated, man-made resurrection.

Just, resurrection!

Man, I was excited to visit Josh, to fill him in on all the good stuff that's happened since we last met up and talked. I was also hopin' that my visit would quiet some concerns I had about him and his drinkin'. Seemed like every damn time I kicked it with Josh on the jack, he was washed, I mean loaded. I knew he was havin' issues at the Hall with a new fucked-up administration, some money problems and all he was dealin' with, but like I said, I was hopin' my visit could ease him up some.

See, old friends or family can do that for people. Make them feel better inside. But, like I told y'all before, Josh didn't surround himself with too many people. Realized early in his life a wife, two-and-a-half-kids, and a white picket fence wasn't for him. Said he was too selfish. Too autocratic is what he'd say. Said if he was gonna share love, that love would be on his terms and because he wanted to, not because he had to. Said most people can't accept that honest truth and that's why so many families are torn up and scarred and don't never make it. Told me lots of people don't get married because they are in love, they get married because they love the idea of marriage, the idea of being in love. Wantin' to be loved and play house. Fulfill society's expectations. Not be left out of the norm. Then, the entire shit just becomes a job and all the horrors start. Deep different philosophy, I know, but I think Josh's thoughts make some kinda sense.

What do you think, people?

Just sayin'.

Just askin'.

Anyways, when I walked onto the platform from the train, I saw Josh leanin' over the roof of his car waitin' for me. He didn't see me and I stopped for a moment up in a cut to check him out on the low. I didn't like what I saw, folks. He was starin' off into space and payin' no attention to all the people about him. Like the commuters, and the taxis, the buses, and the loud-ass construction crew to his left wasn't even there. His face looked to be in a hurry. Like it was runnin' away from somethin' or maybe chasing somethin'. Not hang-dogged, not sad or melancholy, not worried, but like he was in a hurry. Like he was lookin' at his future being poured away into his past. I couldn't see his eyes—Josh wore sunglasses damn near twenty-four-seven—so that whole windows to the soul shit wasn't workin'. I think that's why he wore those damn shades so much in the first place. To hide up hangovers, but also to not expose his soul. I walked towards him and plastered a big Kool-Aid smile on my face nonetheless. Josh saw me and smiled back.

"What's up, Old Man, what's news?"

"Same old, same old, but I do got some goodness to share with you," I said, slidin' into the front seat of his car. "But that can wait 'til later. How you been, my brother?"

"Can't complain. When I do, no one listens anyway. You know how that old saying goes," Josh laughed.

"Sure you right, brother, sure you right."

I lit a smoke and me and Josh made some small talk. I felt relaxed and exhaled one of those big sighs that earlier in the year were being thrown around like hand grenades. Remember, folks, all those desperation exhales? Sure you do. This one felt good, though.

Real good.

Righteous.

Deserved.

Like I was sayin' earlier, ain't it crazy how when you visit with old friends—true friends—that no matter how much time has passed since you've seen each other last, you pick up where you left off and there's never no awkwardness? Never a skip? Everything just flows. You feel me, folks? That's how things are with me and Josh.

"I have to stop by the bar for a minute. You want to go or you want me to drop you off at the apartment."

"You have to stop at the bar?"

"Yeah. What are you, a parrot?"

"Of course you do. I'm down. Why'd you even ask?"

"Seemed proper and respectful."

"Yeah, dawg, whatever."

We stopped at one of Josh's local gin mills—that's what me and mine called bars back in the day—and grabbed a couple stools in the corner. I'm not sure why Josh said he had to stop. He didn't meet no one, pay no one, get paid by anyone, and besides sayin' hello to a few people, didn't talk to no one. I didn't ask him his reasons for havin' to go to the joint, though, but I did ask, "On a serious tip, Josh, you good? You lookin' a bit haggard and worn down, if I say so myself. I'm sure not one to talk, but you hittin' them too hard? I'm old and in the way, but you're too young, man, don't let that shit in the bottom of a glass start calling your name and you go runnin'."

"Naw, Old Man, I'm good, just tired. Got up early. When I'm off of work I get up like three-thirty, four a.m. and just sit quietly in the dark. I light a smoke, and I believe just before sunrise any dream can be fulfilled. Like I can touch God, become a part of the Universe. Know what I'm saying?"

"Yeah, I do. I feel that way sometimes, too."

I wondered to myself if that's a drunkard thing. Do any of you feel that way, people? Do any of you do what Josh was talkin' 'bout? Hell, I knew exactly what Josh was sayin'. How many of you do? Something about the darkness before dawn offering answers to those unasked questions I told y'all 'bout earlier. Waitin' to share a secret before sunrise. Becomin' one with the Universe.

Ah, hell, I don't know.

I told y'all before, drunkards are a strange breed.

Strange indeed.

We sat in silence.

See folks, I could dig where Josh was comin' from. He had

REVEREND WENT WALKING

something empty inside him he was tryin' to fill. Can't never say what it is. Everyone has their own square hole they tryin' to stick a circle in. We don't realize we all doin' the same in some kinda way or another. I just didn't want Josh fillin' his with whiskey and beer chasers. Not healthy. Some folks do fill their emptiness that way, though, or with drugs. Others fill their empty souls with work—Josh again—or doting too much on family, drivin' everyone nuts. Some try to fill their hole with material stuff, new cars and money and eye-candy on the arm, and all. Some people don't recognize nothin' and wander aimlessly fillin' nothin' with nothin'. I've seen crazy cats commit all kinds of violence and abuse and hurt to fill their hollowness and let's not forget the straight up liars who swear they ain't got no hole to fill to even start with.

Shit, look at Constantine and the Holy Herd. Religion's a big hole filler. They be sticking rectangles, circles, stars and stop signs into a square and tellin' you those shapes fit, and is righteous, and if you don't see them fit, if you don't believe them shapes are correct, you're a straight up sinner. Not that I don't believe in someone or something upstairs, but I've seen organized religions fuck people up just as bad as the rock on the corner. All that original sin shit, religious guilt, false fire and brimstone, people professin' they can talk to God so therefore they know what's right for the next brother. You've all heard me rant this prior. Hell, look at Reverend. His beauty, his golden innocence, his sweet soul breath was damn near destroyed and extinguished by all that crazy insanity.

WILLIAM TEETS

Naw, folks, there's a big difference between religion and spirituality. Between man and God. Who did Constantine and the herd *really* help in the hood before bookin' down south? Them kids on the corner? The homeless? The victims in public housing? No, they preached to and helped those who didn't need help in the first place. They helped themselves. Linin' their pockets with gold. Naw, folks, I didn't have the heart to tell One Shoe that Miss Jones wasn't on that crazy yellow cheese-bus. Couldn't tell him she just moved uptown to a different crack den, to suck dick for rock where no one knew her name.

Cheers to that, motherfuckers.

Where's the NBC sitcom for that, people?

What God has joined together let no man tear asunder . . . my ass.

Jesus is a long ways away from religion if you want my take on it.

I ain't no Holy Man, I'm just sayin'.

Sorry, brothers and sisters, I done went off the rails again, didn't I? Went fruit, again, huh? Ain't tellin' the story?

Just think about my words, though.

How we don't even feed our poor or house our homeless.

Take care of our children.

But sing hymns on Sundays.

Don't get it twisted.

Believe in the good and the love and the compassion.

Just not all that rhetorical ritualistic babble only practiced on Sundays.

OK, OK, I got you, my dudes.

Loud and clear.

Let's get back to Joshua.

I filled Josh in on all the recent good news regarding Rev and Solly and Luke's letter. Told him about crazy Constantine—damn, he got a good laugh out of that—and how everything was lookin' up. I left my concerns about his drinking alone and listened quietly to his bitching about how the Hall was sinkin' fast. You can't tell someone they need to put a fire out when you're throwin' gasoline on your own. I figured my talk could wait until tomorrow over breakfast.

Sober.

Maybe.

We stayed a few more hours at the bar—I still wasn't sure

WILLIAM TEETS

why Josh needed to stop—but I think I knew, and we headed home with a dozen wings and two burgers to go. I asked him if he was OK to drive and he told me he was. As we pulled out of the parking lot, just to mess with him, I asked Josh why he was still wearin' his sunglasses; it was dusk and gettin' on dark.

He said, "When you're blessed, Old Man, the sun shines all the time."

I smiled.

I also felt a strange and knowing twinge inside me.

Like someone tryin' to put a square peg in a round hole.

Like someone hidin' a secret from the soul, which the soul already knows.

What God has joined together . . . well, you know the rest.

Chapter 19
Just The Way It Is

"Yo, sleepy boy, let's go. It's damn near openin' time. This is the day the Lord has made. Let us rejoice and be glad in it. Just heard that on the radio. Dope, right?"

"Psalms 118:24."

"Damn, Rev, how the hell you know that? You too damn smart for your own good. I'm gonna get your ass on Jeopardy."

"Hell, Solly, Aunt Constantine made some lasting impressions on me, I guess. Just the way it is."

"Sure you right, bro, sure you right. Listen up, man. When you get yourself ready, go down to Charlie Ching's Sub Shop and grab us a couple Philly cheesesteaks with jalapenos. Here's thirty bucks. Give the change to One Shoe if you see him and be sure to tell him to get something to eat. I'm about to open."

"Gotcha, Solly.

WILLIAM TEETS

"Make sure Shoe eats, if you see him."

"I got you, Sol. Damn."

"Right on, brother, right on. Today is going to be a good day. Let us rejoice."

I woke up to Bob Dylan singin' about painting some masterpiece and Van Morrison sayin' somethin' about some stairway, over and over again. Loud. I mean real loud. I staggered out my room and said, "Damn, Josh, you ain't got no Chi-Lites or Nina, something a little more conducive for an early morning?"

"Naw, Old Man, this music is a religious experience."

"For pagans maybe."

I turned the music down.

It was time for me to leave Josh and return to the hood. Our visit went good—real good—but at nine in the morn', Josh was already into one.

"What's up with drinkin' the sunrise away?" I asked.

"Just sad to see you go, I guess, just the way it is," Josh laughed.

"Whatever, homeboy, whatever."

"People talkin'. You feel me, shortie? Nigga dissin' me in public and shit, thinkin' he can step off with no static. Him and that barber man holdin' court like they run the block. Pussy-ass motherfuckers. Time they learned a lesson. It's time to violate. I gots a plan. You down, homegirl? I'll pay you lovely. Believe dat."

"What you got in mind, No Neck?"

"Simple. Simple and easy, Missy. I tends to use you for bait, to violate church boy. You know he's still sweatin' you. You knows he's still hot for your ass. I've gots a plan. Listen up now. It's gonna fuck up Reverend, and our hands won't even be dirty. They'll all be cryin' like the bitches they are. Ain't no one mess with No Neck. No one. "

"How much cheddar you talkin' for my services?"

"More than enough, Mighty Miss, more than enough. Word."

I showered and packed my bag and told Josh—over objections from him—that I would walk to the train station. The station was close enough to do so and besides, brotherman was in no condition to drive. He promised me he wouldn't leave his apartment, except by cab, and I hugged him goodbye. I hugged him *real* tight and told him he wasn't alone and I'd be back soon. Told him to recognize the good, the light in all of us, and to focus on the positive. Just words, people, I know, just sayings we're supposed to say, but I didn't know what else to do. Those words were all I had. I didn't have no bag of tricks, no verses for the wise. I wished I had some, a magic glass slipper, some magical beans, some fairy tale ending to tell Josh that we would all live happily ever after, but I didn't have none of that shit, folks. I only hugged him—*real* tight—again.

Hell, I learned a long time ago, as harsh as it may sound, sometimes you have to leave those willin' to wreck themselves to their own demise. They'll overcome their demons or destroy themselves. Just the way it is. Even if leavin' breaks our hearts. Even if walkin' away leaves us questioning if we could've done more. Even if what we do don't seem right, it's just the way it is.

I left Josh's apartment with a bag of Scooby snacks he'd made up for me, a flask of rye he slid into my windbreaker pocket, my bag strapped over my shoulder, and a lie from him that he was fine. I headed towards the train. Halfway down the block—Josh done turned up the music again—I heard Van crooning about a Bible. I prayed Josh was *really* gettin' a religious experience. An awakening. For *real*. Some kind of key to unlock the lock holdin' his soul from bein' free. I ain't gonna front, people, my eyes watered a little bit.

I felt for the brother.

"Solly, you ever think about why we buy our Philly cheesesteaks from a Chinaman, our liquor from an Arab, drink at white Arthur's Bar and most of our bodegas are owned by everyone but us. I know America is a melting pot and diversified, but seems like you're the only black owned business in the hood besides the churches. And, well, the service they provide can be questioned, right?"

"You going all Malcolm on me, Rev? We recognize, we talk about the injustice, but nothing changes, does it? Just the way it is."

"Not right, Sol. Not right to accept things just the way they are."

"Well, you're a brother that can change all that. Make a difference. The world needs educated brothers like you. Your smarts can transform the future. Show the injustice of everything to the world. Word. I believe that, Rev. Rallying minds to see what's correct is up to educated youngbloods like you. To expose the inequalities, the racism, the lies. Follow the paths of our great minds and leaders. Dr. King, Nat Turner, Frederick Douglass, Sister Rosa, Harriet Tubman, Baldwin, Maya, Langston Hughes, Ali, Malcolm himself, dig? Only education can change the world. Dig?"

"Yeah, Sol, I dig. Didn't know you were so up on the topic."

"I'm up on it, Rev, but now get your Malcolm-ass to sweepin' the sidewalk."

Reverend laughed.

"You see him, Missy? Look at him sweepin' like a Toby. Do your thing, baby, I'll makes the call now. Remember, I'll makes the call, wait 'til you hear the sirens, then make the move, make the drop. Got it, homegirl, you straight?"

Mighty Missy rolled and fluttered her eyes, looking up towards No Neck, "Damn, son, Reverend's so sweet, so innocent, so fine. I hate to do him grimy like this."

"Oh, you extorting me now? Make it an even G. What you say now, bitch?"

"Let's do this then."

"Yeah, I thought so. Greedy-ass."

While I was ridin' home on the train, my phone started blowin' up. Ringin' every few seconds then cuttin' off. I couldn't get no reception. I thought for sure Josh had done something stupid after me leavin' and I almost got off the local, half way down the line, and returned north, before a text came through to my phone.

911. Call when u can.

The text was from Solly and I thought to myself, what the fuck now? I tried callin' him, but couldn't get through. I was about fifty minutes outside the city and was sweatin' what I might hear. I tried to text back, but didn't know how. Shit, folks, when I left the hood, everything was groovy. My mind raced mad bad thoughts through my head. Was Solly in trouble? Did something happen to Rev? Did One Shoe finally blow his liver out? I kept redialing Solly's phone, but gettin' no connect. I was scared and worried and all I got was the lady next to me on the train askin' if I wanted a doughnut. I politely refused. Instead, I sipped the flask Josh slid in my pocket and was mad happy he did so. The rye was golden. The doughnut lady frowned.

Missy called Reverend's name and slapped her ass. Shook her titties like an old time showgirl and shouted from across the corner for Rev to join her. Reverend laid the broom he'd been sweepin' the walk with against Solly's shop window and with the quickness, like Odysseus bein' attracted to a Siren's call in one of them big old books Rev read—remember, folks?—he zig-zagged between traffic and ended up face-to-face with Mighty Missy Brown.

"Hey, playa, what's up? Why ain't you come by to see me, lover?"

"I did . . . but you said . . . I thought . . . I mean, I thought . . ."

Two blue-and-whites and a Crown Vic barreled around the block, tires squealin', sirens blarin'. They rolled up on the corner where Rev and Missy were standin' and five-o jumped out deep.

"Here, lover boy, hold this."

Missy shoved a ripped, brown, paper bag into Reverend's hands and screamed, "He's got a gun!"

The cops surrounded Rev as the torn bag fell away and he was left standin' alone with a deuce-deuce.

"Drop the gun, nigger, on the ground, now!"

Missy ran away.

A beer-belly hillbilly-looking DT shouted, "Drop the gun now! On the ground, brother!"

Reverend got his thoughts in order—quick—and placed the twenty-two caliber on the pavement with one hand while holdin' his other above his head—instinctual survival actions learned and known by any still-alive-black man-in the hood. Rev was tackled to the sidewalk and knocked unconscious. He was cuffed and dragged and thrown into the back of a cruiser. He got a free ride downtown, courtesy of the boys.

REVEREND WENT WALKING

No Neck stood across the street howling.

Mighty Missy counted her Benjamin's.

Another young black man was headin' to jail.

People stopped and looked and murmured about themselves.

Barkers didn't bark and hawkers didn't hawk.

Stick-up boys laid low.

Someone got brave and yelled, "Two for twenty, two for twenty, five-o gone, I got da red tops."

Business returned to normal.

The stoplight changed.

Cars drove.

People walked.

Another young black man headed to jail.

Just another day in the ghetto.

No need for excitement.

Just the way it is.

Chapter 20
A Win For The Good Guys

And y'all thought I was lying, you all thought my crazy old ass be exaggerating about crabs in a bucket and Bakus runnin' wild in the night. Well, what do y'all think now? Tell me this damn hood ain't cursed, that misery don't love company. Can't none of you do it, can't none of you say shit. But inside yourselves y'all see the truth. Y'all seein' everything exposed—ripped apart and raw—and left bleeding right there on Main Street. Y'all catching a glimpse of the remains that the sucking vampire government used up and then forgot about. Y'all seeing Ms. Justice in an early mornin' alley before dawn, gettin' sexed up by those sworn to protect and serve.

Do I have any believers now?

Still think I be goin' off the rails for no reason?

Yeah, I see some heads shakin', denying, but not walkin' away. I see y'all stayin'. All right then, if y'all ready to continue, let me tell you the story a little more. About Solly, about Joshua, but mostly about our main man, Reverend.

Sit back and relax.

And be advised.

HBO will show this feature only at night.

"If everyone—the cops, the DA, the legal aide—believes our story, how in the hell can they still move forward in prosecuting Rev?" Solly asked Billy Jackson over the phone.

"Because it's a slam dunk. Reverend was seen in broad daylight holding a handgun. Your only proof that it wasn't his is his word and people vouching for his character. Neither hold any weight in the courtroom. I spoke with the DA and she said the best she could do was charge Reverend as a youthful offender and recommend the judge sentence him to a residential treatment center for twelve to eighteen months. Trust me, Solomon, she's doing us a favor. It's better than a one-to-three and a felony on his record for the rest of his life."

"Yeah, but it just ain't right. It messes up his school plans, college, everything that brother can be. And who's to say he comes out on the other end the same. You know as well as I do, counselor, the system ain't no good for no one. This is a kid, with the exception of a bad few months, a few bad choices, has been on the up-and-up and avoidin' all the grime on the streets for all his life."

"Goes to show what a few bad choices can do to someone's life," Billy Jackson said.

"You know what I'm sayin'."

"And you know what *I'm* saying."

"Well, is there anything else we can do? Luke wrote in his letter you're a solid brother and trustworthy. Can you think of anything we can do to get Rev cleared?

"I've read over everything and your only possible chance of acquittal is to have that girl . . . what's her name . . . Melissa Brown . . . have her give a sworn deposition to the DA that she was coerced into doing what she did. That she felt threatened by that Thaddeus McGee character. Do that and you'll have a good chance of exonerating Reverend."

"And then what the hell we gonna do when pigs are flyin' all around the ghetto? She ain't gonna say shit, excuse my French."

"It's your only shot, Solomon, your only play. Give me a call if you need anything else. I'll ride this out until the end with you. No charge. Luke was the finest brother I ever knew."

"I will, Mr. Jackson. Good lookin', but I can't see that hood rat helpin' out anyone but herself."

REVEREND WENT WALKING

The sheets weren't white; they were dull forty watt beige. The pillow was flat and had yellow drool or piss stains or both soaked into the fabric. The pillow case was no better. The mattress reminded Reverend of a worn-out wrestling mat at Saint Pete's and the twelve bed dorm room Rev would be calling home for the next eighteen months smelled moldy and stale. The tattered carpet that covered the floor had duct tape repaired rips and pock marks of hurry-up extinguished cigarette butts. The windows were painted shut.

Home sweet home.

Far from where the buffalo roam.

Far from the dreams and plans Rev and Luke had not so long ago. Far from Luke teaching at West Point and Rev coming home from college on holidays and breaks to their country home. Far away from Nathaniel Hawthorne Library and all the books atlases and poets' dreams. Far from Solly's shop and Charlie Chings and Yakabu's and far away from where Reverend expected to be. But unfortunately, not far enough away from where clowns think they can wear crowns and thus become kings.

"Where you from, New Jack?" asked a dark-skinned Haitian called Too Bad.

"My home," Rev answered.

"Who you down with? What set? Be smart, New Jack, we'll find out. This dorm is YG or you're OD," Too Bad laughed, thinking he was clever.

"No G, nigga, now you don't have to find out nothing," Rev said.

Too Bad's smile turned into a scrunched up snarl and he went to step towards Reverend. Rev dropped the clothes in his hands onto his bed and squared up.

"Is there a problem here?" asked the house leader, who appeared at the dorm door. "I know motherfuckers ain't showin' their ass on my shift. Line it up—now—for dinner! Too Bad, you ain't actin' the fool on my time, are you?"

"No, Mr. T, not at all."

"Good. Like I said, get it lined up and move it out for dinner."

Too Bad grilled Reverend hard.

"That hood rat ho be duckin' down alleys and disappearin' around corners like fuckin' Cat Woman. Won't let me talk with her," Solly told me over a couple of whiskeys at his shop.

"I asked Shoe to have Blue talk to her, but it didn't help, yet," I said.

"Blue? Jamaican Blue? What's he got to do with this?"

"Blue is Missy's uncle."

"Get out of town. I didn't know that shit. Luke and Blue were close. I'm gonna look him up."

"We already did, Solly. Blue will do what he can do. Don't go stressin', Blue."

"Tramp. What about your boy, Joshua? Can he do anything?"

"Well, that's why I stopped by."

See, folks, Reverend was given an eighteen month bid at Rutherford B. Hayes Haven Hall for the handgun Mighty Missy and No Neck planted on him. In case y'all don't remember, the Hall is where I used to work and where Josh still does. Josh informed me that Reverend was holdin' his own, but was being pressed—like most new kids in placement—and Josh was tryin' to get Rev transferred into his English class in order to offer a little support and hope. And Lord knows that boy needed some hope.

We were all sick to our stomachs with the way shit played out. There was no doubt that Rev was set up. Hell, everyone knew he was. The hood, five-o, even the fuckin' District Attorney. But like Billy Jackson said, with no proof suitable for the powers that be, Lady Justice covered her eyes with her blindfold, dropped her scale, and forgot about another young black man from the ghetto.

And just when everything was goin' so good.

Just when everything was workin' out.

You all know how Rev was back on track, folks. Gettin' caught up in school, sending out those college apps and stayin' off the corner, but now none of that meant nothin'. His best plan for success now was to get a GED at the Hall and attend a local community college. Not that anything is wrong with all that, but with his smarts, Reverend could've gone to one of those big Ivy schools and not been made to settle for less. Too many young folks from the hood are forced to settle for less. Naw, people, the sky was the limit for Reverend, but now the sky was taken away.

Taken away from all of us.

Plus, I didn't like the look, the vibe Rev was giving off, when he was remanded at court. I understood. I knew Rev had to switch to jailin' mode, that whole when in Rome do what the Romans do, but I still didn't like the look. I know that look too well, and I'd seen it too many times. I also know bein' locked away can change a brother, and most times not for the better.

I told Solly that Josh had promised to call me on a regular

with updates about Rev and promised to try and hold Rev down. In the meantime we were goin' to keep tryin' to get Mighty Missy Brown to come clean and Blue said he would continue kickin' it with her too.

I just couldn't stop thinkin' 'bout what must've been going through Rev's mind, though. The amount of disappointment and pain that boy's been through in the past year was enough to break the strongest of men, let alone an adolescent. The whole Luke scene, Rev goin' all gangsta for a minute, all that craziness with Constantine, and finally being set-up and endin' up jailed because of his first love. Naw, man, shit was too much.

I left Solly's shop and headed up to Saint Peter's. I'm not even sure why. I didn't go in; just stood outside those big massive missive doors I told y'all about earlier. I closed my eyes and strained my ears to hear one of those muffled hallowed hymns from inside the church whisper onto the street. Remember I told y'all about them, earlier? A voice that would tell us everything was goin' to be all right, that someone was listenin'.

Well, brothers and sisters, I didn't hear no voice.

Didn't hear no whisper.

All I heard was Pastor Goodman-Brown ask me from the top of the granite stairs if I needed something, needed some help.

WILLIAM TEETS

"Just an even break, Parson, a win for the good guys. A win for the good guys," I replied.

I turned and walked back downtown.

Fall, Icarus, fall. I told you not to fly so high.

Chapter 21
We All Pay In The End

"Two fights in two weeks. Not bad. How's the eye?" Joshua asked Reverend.

"You should see the other guy," Rev smiled.

"Yeah, man, I bet. Anyways, Rev, I called you in to let you know you'll be in my class starting Monday. I wanted to kick it with you for a minute though, if you don't mind."

"Sure thing. I don't have much, but I do have time."

Both Josh and Rev laughed.

"You know I know Old Man and all and he asked me to hold you down—to look out the best I can—and to let you know I'm here for you if you need anything. He's like family to me, and you're like family to him, so I guess that makes us cousins or something."

Reverend and Josh laughed again and for the first time in a long time, Reverend exhaled.

"Also, Rev, I want you to know you aced the intake testing. Scored 12.9 across the boards. College level everything. You're not going to get half of what you need academically in this school, but if you're up to the task, I'd be willing to write independent study lessons for you. They won't count towards grades or credits, but Old Man said you were special, and well, your intake testing says that, too. I think it's important for you to keep challenging yourself."

"Yeah, Mr. M, I'd like that. Give me something to do besides fighting."

Reverend and Josh laughed a third time.

"Good, I'll see you on Monday then."

"Bet."

As Rev was leaving the classroom, Josh asked, "Hey, Rev, did you read William James' Two-Stage Model?"

"Yeah."

Joshua smiled and shook his head.

"You been here two weeks and been in two fights. What's *your* problem? That shit don't fly in my house, money. You either get with the program or you gonna get the fuck up outta here. I'll recommend you for Modification. Send your punk ass to a lockup where you'll get beat down every day. Too Bad don't get in trouble. He's one of my leaders. You join the house and he's in two fights. What's up with that? What you gotta say for yourself?"

"With all due respect, Mr. R, Too Bad sucker punched *me*. And he doesn't have problems with the other kids because they're scared of him and more scared to say something. You don't see the stuff he's doing on the low."

"Oh, so now you tellin' me hows to do my job. I don't like you, money. Let's get that shit outta the way, right now. You a problem maker. Well you'll find out, yes sir, you'll find out, we gotta way of solvin' problems around here. Mark my words, money, mark my words."

"Can I leave now?"

"Get the fuck out the office."

After using the bathroom, Reverend walked back into his dorm.

The room was quiet.

Mad quiet.

Too quiet.

Rev knew right away something was up. He played it off,

though, and sat on the end of his bed, sure not to have his back turned towards no one. Too Bad was scheming with two other residents of the house called Crazytown and Lou-Lou—remember them stupid-ass nicknames I've done told y'all 'bout before, folks, need I say more?—when Mr. R entered the dorm and said, "Y'all move it up front for study period."

Eight boys gathered up their books and pads and pencils and scurried to the front of the house. Too Bad, Crazytown, and Lou-Lou stayed behind. Reverend went to move up front, but Mr. R blocked his exit and closed the dorm room door.

"New Jack here been talkin' shit 'bout you Too Bad. What you gonna do 'bout that?"

Too Bad took his shirt off and twisted his face into one of those wrinkled up snarls. "You ain't learned your lesson, New Jack. Now I'm gonna have to put it on you."

"We already fought twice after you snuck me. I'll shoot a third, but a fair one," Reverend said.

"I don't need no help with your pussy-ass," Too Bad hissed.

Rev squared up and as Too Bad walked up on him, all huffin' and puffin' and swelled up like, his hands were by his side as he kept hikin' up his sweats and sayin', "So what's up now, nigga? What you gonna . . ."

And before Too Bad could finish his sentence, Rev took a

step and laced Too Bad flush on the chin with a right cross. Too Bad's knees buckled once, then twice and he fell sideways onto a bed.

Knocked out!

The dorm got quiet, again.

Reverend kept his eyes on Crazytown and Lou-Lou and started backin' up towards the door to leave the dorm when he was hemmed up from behind by Mr. R, who said, "Get this nigga, you two pussies. That's why your dumb asses are here."

And with that, folks, Crazytown and Lou-Lou charged Rev. Mr. R held Reverend in a yoke, but Rev managed to kick at Lou-Lou, keepin' him at bay. Crazytown punched Rev hard on the side of his head and Mr. R tightened his hold.

Rev was dazed.

"Snitches get stitches, bitch," said Lou-Lou and he landed a combination to Reverend's ribs. Rev groaned. Just as Mr. R was about to call the group assault off, thinkin' he had taught Reverend what needed to be learned, Too Bad came out of nowhere and hit Reverend on the top of his head with an iron.

"Oh, shit! Nigga, is you crazy?" Mr. R said as he released his hold on Reverend.

Reverend's body slumped to the floor.

A dark pool of red-black blood leaked from a gash on top of Reverend's head. Mr. R, Crazytown, and Lou-Lou stared at Too Bad with that *what the fuck* look and then stared at Rev, lifeless on the carpet, red-black blood pooling some more.

"Naw, nigga, you buggin'. I'm not goin' down for this. This is on you, you dumb fuck," Mr. R said. "Crazytown, Lou-Lou, go get T."

The two boys ran to the front of the house.

"You OD'ed, Too Bad," Mr. R said, and he hurriedly ran and tackled Too Bad, holdin' him down on the floor.

Mr. T ran into the dorm.

"What the fuck?"

He directed Daniels, another staff member, to call the crisis response team and the infirmary and tell them to respond stat. Mr. T took his shirt off and pressed it on Rev's gash, trying to stop the blood flow.

"I got him, T. I saw the whole shit. I walked in and saw Too Bad hit that boy with that there iron."

"You lyin' motherfucker. You told us to," Too Bad foamed under Mr. R's body.

"Shut up, boy. I seened it all. You tried to kill that kid. Good thing me and Crazytown and Lou-Lou came by when we did. Ain't that right, boys?" Mr. R said.

Crazytown and Lou-Lou nodded their heads yes, eyes wide open.

"You rat bastards. You sellin' me out? I'll kill you all," shouted Too Bad.

"See, T, the boy's crazy, but I got him. I got here just in time."

"Everyone shut the fuck up!" Mr. T shouted.

He held Reverend's head in his cradled arms. The red-black blood soaked into T's clothes and the dirty stained carpet. Like looking at fire, everyone's eyes were fixed on the blood.

All were captivated.

They stared like they were a part of some ancient ritual, some primeval ceremony that was sacred and holy.

That only blood or fire or raging storms can command.

They smelled the blood, saw fire, and felt pelted by hurricane winds and water, and damn near danced and screamed.

They didn't.

WILLIAM TEETS

They watched.

Almost envious.

The stillness of the sacred ceremony was shattered, when Daniels yelled, "They're coming now. Everybody get out of the way."

The nurse from the infirmary told Mr. T to call an ambulance as soon as she saw Rev. Too Bad struggled to break free from Mr. R's restraint but couldn't. The crisis team moved all of the other kids into the opposite dorm as the nurse began to shake and said, "This is bad."

With time slowed to stillness, the medics finally arrived. With the quickness, the EMT crew bandaged Rev's head, loaded him onto a stretcher, and wheeled him outside to the waiting ambulance.

Red-black blood soaked through virgin white gauze.

"All right, get ready to lift him. One, two, three . . ."

One two three, Rev, hot damn, cee-lo, baby boy.

Shoe? Is that you, Shoe?

Yeah, Rev, it's me, little bruh.

Where am I, Shoe? Am I dead?

Hell no, Rev, you're on 123rd street. You done hit the jackpot, baby boy. Cee-lo. Roll again, Rev. You gots to roll again.

"Break it down, roll it in, secure him. Check his vitals."

What's that light? Where's that bright light coming from? One Shoe? One Shoe, you there?

That old, sinful, sinnin' wino ain't here.

Aunt Constantine? Is that you? Where am I? My head hurts, damn, I'm hurting. What's that bright light? Aunt Constantine?

That's the light of the Lord tryin' to save your heathen soul, devil boy.

The pain, what's with the pain?

That's the horned one tryin' to keep your soul from the Lord. Why you still fightin' for, Reverend? Let the sin go, lost lamb, go to the light. Why didn't you listen, baby lamb, why didn't you heed the Good Word? I told you the Devil would come home to roost. I told you He was a lie. Hallelujah! Can I get a witness? Why didn't you hear, Devil child? Why didn't you listen? Why did you break the eggs? I told you we can't make no angel cake without the eggs. Look at all the broken eggs. Look at all the broken eggs.

"He's vomiting. Turn his head. Clear his mouth. Clean off that puke. Clear the puke!"

Luke. Luke. You here, Luke?

WILLIAM TEETS

I'm always here, Rev. I'm always with you.

I gave away my self-respect, Luke. You told me not to, but I did. I was bad, Luke.

No, Reverend. You made a mistake. It's OK, we all do. You got your self-respect back. You fought and earned your honor back. You never quit. I'm proud of you, Rev. You never quit.

I was in a fight, Luke. What happened?

Keep fighting now, Rev. Keep fighting. You're going to be fine, my son.

"Pick up the pace, he's starting to convulse. Run. Run. Pick it up, run!"

He's got a gun. He's got a gun.

Missy? Missy, why did you do that to me?

Really, playa, really? I did it for the cheddar. You know the rules on the block. Earn that cheddar.

I stopped, Missy. I left the corner. I was doing right, I was doing good.

Shit, lover boy, you can't just step off. The DJ still gots to be paid. You can't dance and not pay the DJ. How can you dance with the Devil and not pay his DJ, Rev? Crime Dog paid. Cool breeze paid. Why you think you different?

REVEREND WENT WALKING

How come you don't pay, Missy? How come No Neck don't pay?

We will, homie, we will. We all pay in the end. Each and every one of us.

We all pay in the end.

Chapter 22
No Do Overs

Hold on, people, hold on. I know y'all worried about Reverend and you should be, but let me tell the story. Don't start buggin' out and trippin'. Everyone settle down and listen up now. I know what happened, let me tell the tale proper. Let me tell y'all what went down.

When Solly got the call from the Hall sayin' what happened to Rev, me and him and One Shoe drove upstate in Solly's car to the hospital where Rev was at. Shit was crazy, folks, and mad scary. I couldn't believe all the bad luck that been happenin' to Rev, again. Can you, people? Remember I was just talkin' 'bout that? Remember? One Shoe was convinced another witch or warlock was at work and had hexed Reverend again, and Christ, with all the shit that poor boy been goin' through, he started makin' a believer out of me.

I mean how many curve balls can life throw at us before we want to quit playin' the game? And hell, we all know the game is rigged to start with. Naw, folks, this tragedy with

Rev made me think, and I'll pull your coat to this—life ain't fair, folks. Why should this tragedy be any different?

Y'all already heard me kick it about the unlevel playin' field in the hood, how that game is rigged from jump street, and here's the proof being shoved in our faces again like a dog havin' his nose shoved in his own shit for not followin' house rules. What was gettin' my goat, though, was that Rev was playin' by the rules. As best he could. Naw, my peeps, the game bein' rigged was makin' losers out of all of us. What's fucked-up, though, is that hood people lose faster, and more, than most others.

Leave us asking if America *really* is beautiful.

And for who?

Know what I'm sayin'?

But I couldn't cry and moan and bitch about life bein' unfair. Neither could Solly. Rev was in a bad way and we had to push by all the pushin' back life was doin' or none of nothin' would be worth a dime. Yeah, I know this scene was off the hook more than normal, but there was no time for feelin' sorry. We needed to get our minds right and do everything we could for Rev. Nothin' or no one else was givin' a good goddamn and I mean nothin' or no one. We had to go hard or go home.

No doubt.

As I sat staring at Rev, all those tubes in his body, all those TV screens beeping and bleating, I said a little prayer to the man upstairs. An echoed voice in my head kept tellin' me saviors don't save us, only we can save ourselves. I closed my eyes tighter and prayed a little harder, but like Saint Peter's Church bell's ringing, travelin' the streets from uptown to down, I still heard the echo—saviors don't save us, only we can save ourselves.

"Reverend obviously has a major concussion, but his skull is not fractured. That is good news. His brain is swollen, however, and he's lost a lot of blood. This is a concern. We therefore medically-induced a coma in order to keep him quiet and calm in hopes the swelling in the brain subsides. I'm estimating it will be at least another two or three days until Reverend is conscious. He also suffered two fractured ribs, but that is minimal in relation to his cerebral injuries," a hospital doctor said.

"When he wakes up, Doc, will there be any brain damage or memory loss or anything? Will he be any different?" Solly asked.

"Too early to tell."

"What about his speech? Ya know he's real smart too, will that be affected? His coordination?"

REVEREND WENT WALKING

"As I said, sir, we will know more in a few days."

The doctor's smart-ass, pompous smile—you know the one, people, that smile used by those who think they are smarter than others—pissed me off. That doctor's smile reminded me of some snub-nosed monkey, some condescending motherfucker. I was gonna lace him. Damn, I hate silver-spoon-fed people born on third base, goin' through life swearin' they hit a triple.

Y'all feel me, folks?

This was the kinda shit-head doctor we were dealin' with.

I had to speak up for Solly, had to speak up for Rev.

"What he's askin', Doc, are the chances, the odds, are they in our favor of Rev wakin' up normal or not?" I asked.

"I do not deal in odds, sir. I am not . . . what *you* people would call . . . a bookie, I believe. As I have stated, we will know more in two or three days. You can come back then," the doctor said, as he started walking away. He stopped and turned, "You keep saying how smart this Reverend is. Didn't this incident occur at Rutherford B. Hayes Haven Hall for juvenile delinquents?"

"So what you sayin', Doc?" Solly asked.

"Never mind. No further questions? Good then," the pompous-ass said, as he stalked from the room.

WILLIAM TEETS

"Asshole," said One Shoe.

"Big asshole," I confirmed.

As me, Solly, and Shoe cruised down the interstate in Solly's car, we were all quiet and lost in our thoughts. I don't know what they were thinkin', but I was still heated over how that doctor talked to us and acted. I didn't say anything to the fellas 'cause I didn't want to upset them more than they already were, but I found out later, they were thinkin' the same as me.

Hell, folks, we didn't know any more about Rev's condition than we knew before. I was mad as all get-out. Mad at Mighty Missy Brown and No Neck, mad at the streets, mad at the Hall and supposed justice system, and really mad at that arrogant monkey doctor. Where was the compassion? Where was the kindness? Where was that Hippocratic Oath *they* be talkin' 'bout?

More like hypocritical if you askin' me.

That prick doctor dismissed us like we didn't matter and Rev didn't matter. Like we was no better than shit in a sewer. His condescending crack about Rev bein' in the Hall gnawed at my insides. See, my peeps, to him we were just gangsta hood niggas. Not worthy to be treated respectful like. I mean I know the world can be a rough place and like I said, life ain't fair—I can accept that—but what was killing me is that Rev wasn't the only young brother from a hood laid up like he was. They're so many Reverends from so many ghettos from so many cities and no one gives a good goddamn. Especially people like that doctor. They're worse than the money changin' bastards in the Bible.

To that doctor, and so many more people in society, Rev was nothin' more than a thug black teen who got beat down in a fight. They didn't know him. They didn't care to know him. They didn't know his goodness and light, his beauty and potential. As long as Reverend didn't show up on their manicured lawns or in their coffee shops or in their kids' school, they don't think twice about him. And the result is special young folk like Reverend are left off on the side of the road like so much road kill, so much carnage, just because their skin is the wrong color and they live in the wrong zip code.

Let what happened to Rev happen to a white boy from Mister Rogers' neighborhood or some money spendin' tourist in the city or some rich politician's kid in private school, and see what kinda holy hell goes down. Man, listen! That doctor would be giving up-to-date press conferences on news channels and the daily papers' headlines would scream about what an atrocity had befallen us.

Like I said, I was heated.

WILLIAM TEETS

Sorry, my peeps, I had to get that shit off my chest or I would've exploded.

But my words are true.

I hope y'all starting to pick-up what I'm layin' down.

What I've been talkin' 'bout.

That whole false American Dream fable.

The lies and inequalities.

How the more things change the more they stay the same.

That's why I go off the rails sometimes.

Shit just drives me crazy and beats me down.

Just sayin'.

Just kickin' some knowledge to you.

But I know, yeah, yeah, I know, I promised to tell you the story and update y'all about Rev. Let me get back on track.

After two-and-a-half days, Rev was taken out of his coma. He was sore and banged up, but out of critical condition. I ain't gonna front, folks, I thought we were gonna lose the brother. Thankfully, that didn't happen, and Rev was in good health, all things considered.

REVEREND WENT WALKING

"We want to keep him here for another few days for observation, but everything appears to be coming along fine. When Reverend is returned to Rutherford Hayes, as a delinquent, I have advised that he spends a week in their infirmary for further observation and rest. If all goes well, there should be no lasting ill effects," the doctor said.

"What about . . ."

"No questions? Good then. Take care, folks," the doctor said as he exited the room.

"What an asshole," Rev said.

We all shook our heads and laughed.

Rev was back to bein' Rev—and like only the young can do—he shrugged the entire incident off and was ready to keep on keepin' on. I was mad impressed by Rev's strength and character. What he'd been through in his young life would've ended most folks. Rev was the poster boy for keep on keepin' on, for never giving up. He told me later, he was shook up and scared, but thoughts of Luke and Luke's love kept him strong.

I smiled.

Rev is one deep brother and Luke was savin' the day again.

I guess there is still some righteous beauty in the world.

A little, anyways.

As far as a follow-up to everything that happened, Solly contacted Billy Jackson about the whole affair. Jackson presented a supposition or deposition or some such shit to the court, to have Rev's sentence vacated, but the motion was denied. Jackson also told Solly that he was slapping a lawsuit on the Hall for negligence or endangerment or somethin' like that and there was a good chance Rev was gonna get a nice chunk of change for whatever that's worth.

And just like the Good Book says, brothers and sisters, and I'm paraphrasing here—Constantine could quote the scripture better—but what is hidden in darkness will be brought to the light. And that's exactly what happened to that Mr. R cat and those coward-ass kids who violated Reverend. The only good thing—and I mean the *only* good thing—to come out of Rev gettin' jumped, is that it put Mr. R on front street for the piece of shit he is. All the kids in the house told the authorities about how Mr. R and Too Bad and Crazytown and Lou-Lou were strong-arming them on the low. They also stated that none of the other staff in the house were down with the shadiness.

R was arrested, tried, and convicted and got a two year bid, upstate with the big boys. Enough bad shit can't happen to that nigga, far as I'm concerned. Crazytown and Lou-Lou were Modified to a Title II lock-up, and Too Bad, who was seventeen at the time, was charged as an adult and got a one-to-three year joint.

Now I know I done told y'all jail ain't no good for no one, but if y'all remember, I also said sometimes some cats still need

REVEREND WENT WALKING

to go. Well R and Too Bad fall into that category. Fuck them. They got what they deserved if you askin' me. Hell, they in the same boat as Rev, from the same mean streets, but want to set him up and jump him for no reason. For bullshit. And that R cat bein' a staff and all? S'pose to be lookin' out for the youngbloods? Naw, my people. Like I said. Fuck them.

Me, Solly, and Shoe returned back home to the hood, and Rev was back at the Hall. I was wiped out, folks. About everything. About all I'd seen in just the past eighteen months alone. It was like the more I learned from life, the less I knew. As I sat on a crate in front of Yakabus, nursin' a forty, I felt so damn defeated. So much like givin' up. And then I heard a whisper in my ear, a lilting voice on the wind. I trembled thinkin' it was some kinda Holy Word or hymn from Saint Peter's sharing wisdom or the Good Word with me—my own road to Damascus type shit—but it wasn't.

It was One Shoe asking to borrow a Hamilton.

I laughed so loud and long I damn near pissed myself. At least Shoe had me smilin' again. I lit a duke and blew lost rings into the early September night. Yeah, folks, I realized life can be messed up at times and seem like it just ain't worth livin', but don't forget, people, it's the only one we get. Life ain't no kickball game, ain't no game of two-hand-touch, ain't no tag. As much as you may want there to be, remember my peeps, there ain't no do overs—never—you get what you get the first time around.

Word.

Chapter 23
Pie In The Sky

"I'm telling you, Old Man, that kid's a regular superstar. He came back to the Hall like he was an MVP Super Bowl winner going to Disneyland. Everyone loves him. The faculty, the students, everyone."

"No shit, Josh. Man, that's cool and the gang. I'll let Solly and the boys at the shop know, but what was that other thing you had to talk to me about? That surprise, you said?"

Josh motioned to the bartender for a round and smiled. "Sit back, brother, and listen up. I know a guy who knows a guy who . . ."

I spent Thanksgiving morning at the shelter on 134th downtown, serving soup and such to the homeless and less fortunate families—hell, I try and give back when I can—and

REVEREND WENT WALKING

then a group of us wayward lost souls gathered at Solly's for a pot-luck dinner and drinks. Deep fried turkey wings, sweet potatoes, greens, whiting, cold beer, Canadian Club—well, you get the picture—but anyways, the next day I was mad happy to be ridin' the northbound to meet up with Josh. We had made plans earlier in the month to get together during the holidays and I was hype. I ain't seen my brother in a minute.

Of course—our first stop—after Josh scooped me up at the train station, was to go to his local watering hole and knock back a few. He seemed better, though. Not as haggard. Had a little more light in his eyes. A little more purpose. After kickin' the customary catching up talk, the conversation turned to Reverend.

"He's disappointed he couldn't go on the home visit for Thanksgiving, the court order and all, but he handled the bad news like a trouper. I stopped by and saw him the other day. He said to say, 'What's up,' to you and Solly and everyone else."

"Yeah, man, it was rough not havin' Rev home, but Solly and me got to kick it with him last week on one of those ten-minute calls they be gettin'. He sounded good. Said you holdin' him down. But the surprise, Josh, what's up with your surprise?"

Josh went on to say how he was blown away by Rev's smarts and personality from the genesis. How he gave him mad special lesson plans and books to read as promised and how he enrolled Rev in the GED program at the Hall. Said Rev was the first student to ever get a perfect score on the GED practice test. Told me Rev was smarter than even me and Solly knew.

"You have no idea how smart this kid is. How advanced. His writing skills, his reading, his comprehension, his overall knowledge. Christ, I've been asking for a student like Rev in my prayers."

"I told you, Josh. Rev's mad smart."

"It's more than that, Old Timer. His analytical thinking, his creativity, it's gun smoke, man. Unmitigated gun smoke. You hear me, brother?"

"Yeah, I hear what you're sayin', but what's the surprise you've been talkin' 'bout? This news 'bout Rev ain't no new news to me."

"Well, brace yourself now. I'm good friends with this professor at William Rodgers, one of the best liberal arts colleges in the country—hell, in the world—who works with another professor who's some genius or some shit. This genius professor has developed an exam and curriculum for inner city students who show academic promise and potential. If they score high enough on an entrance exam, meet certain criteria, they have the opportunity to attend Rodgers on a full scholarship."

"So what are you sayin'? What does all that mean? Is Rev right to go there?"

"That's just it. This professor is accepting twenty-four at-risk students into the program who pass the entrance exam with the highest scores. The scholarship winners get a great education and this professor sees how they perform at Rodgers. He tracks their progress, the way they adapt, their social interactions, all kinds of stuff for a study he's doing. It's a win-win. The professor gets his data for his study while the kids get a free top-notch education."

"And?"

"And, like I said, I have an in with my friend and got Rev on the list to take the test and Rev aced it. Was eighth highest out of almost a thousand applicants. He scored off the charts."

"Shit, that is gun smoke, Josh. Smith and Wesson, forty-four caliber gun smoke. Man, this is good news."

"But."

Oh hell, folks, here we go, Yo. Those damn crabs gettin' ready to snatch-a-brother-back-in-the- bucket-but.

I didn't like the sound of that.

My heart sank a bit.

WILLIAM TEETS

I don't like the word but.

"What's the but, Josh?"

"Well, this professor refuses to accept any kid with a crime, an arrest, any contact with the justice system. Wants only at-risk youth who have managed to stay out of trouble with the law, even though the deck's been stacked against them. Kids who have *survived the savage streets, temptations and maladies of an impoverished environment, yet maintain their educational focus and self-worth, while surrounded by chaos created from a socio-economic maelstrom* is how he put it or something like that. I'm paraphrasing. This dude is wild. Anyways, even family court convictions or sealed records like Reverend's would disqualify him, though."

"Well hell, Josh, why tell me all this and then drop that knowledge on me? Damn, you know Rev has that charge. Bullshit or not, man, it's real as rain, as far as the courts are concerned."

"That's just it, Old Man, it's a bogus charge. If that girl Missy or that No Neck character will vouch they set Reverend up and his charges are dropped like the DA said she'd do, he'll be eligible to be accepted. Remember the District Attorney said she'd drop the charges if that happens?"

My blood started risin' to my head, people. I was gettin' vexed. I didn't like what I was hearin' and finished my double in a gulp so I wouldn't go ballistic.

Josh kept talkin'.

"And, the best part, Old Timer, is the program doesn't start until the September semester next year. That gives us plenty of time to work things out. My boy at Rodgers said we have until the end of the spring semester to clear all this nonsense up and then Reverend will be a go. Gives him plenty of time to take and pass the GED, too. My boy said there's no problem with a GED. You follow?"

I tried, people, believe me I tried, but I couldn't hold back any longer. I had to let go. I was burnt and didn't care how Josh took what I was about to bark. Didn't care if I hurt his feelings. This shit he was kickin' was the king of crazy.

"Have you lost your mind, white boy? What, I'm just gonna stroll down to the corner and say, 'Excuse me, Mr. No Neck, excuse me Missy Brown, will you all mind turnin' yourselves in to the PoPo—takin' a rap for a felony—so Reverend can go to college, thank you very much.' What the fuck, Josh? What the fuck? You know we been tryin' that from the start with no success before we even heard of this school, Rodgers."

"Hear me out now, Old Timer. Reverend has told me that Missy might do it. He said they're in love and shit. He said she might flip on No Neck. Get immunity for herself and clear Rev's name. Said they've been writing letters to each other. Do you understand this opportunity, brother?"

"Do you understand the hood, Josh? You already told Rev about this? Already got his hopes high? Love and shit? Nigga, please. What are you fifteen? Do you understand Mighty Missy is a rattlesnake, a viper, that scorpion that stings the frog halfway across the pond? Damn, Josh, come on man, be *real*. You know better than this."

"Listen, my brother, it's worth a try. Have that girl's Uncle Blue talk to her again. I'll have Rev write a letter again. Make a call from my phone if we can track down Missy's number. We *all* have to try."

"You don't know shit about how the hood works. How folks don't mess with five-o for nothin'. That whole fucked-up snitches get stitches code. Blue? Jamaican Blue? Hell, he can make anyone do or say anything, but he ain't about to put that pain on his niece. You shouldn't even know his name, let alone speak it. And you tellin' Rev, you fucked-up, big man. You sold him dreams from *your* world. In *our* world dreams turn to nightmares with the quickness. I love you, Josh, and you're down with a lot, but this time you done stepped out of bounds. Saw things only from *your* world."

"Well, I'm not quitting, fuck you very much. I believe in Reverend and believe we can make this work. With or without you."

This made me even more hotter than I already was, brothers and sisters. I waved at the bartender to bring another round. Josh was seriously lost in some fairy tale land, when I had a thought, when I understood. "Who you doin' this for, Josh, you or Reverend? You're too smart, you know this whole idea is off the meat rack. You bein' blinded by what you want to happen? Have you asked yourself that? Who you tryin' to help—to save—you or Rev? Don't think savin' others will save you, brother. You gotta save yourself first before you start savin' someone else."

"To hell with you, Old Man. This is one race in my life that I'm going to run and win."

"Ah, fuck, Josh. Don't try to be no hero now. You're too late. Where me and Rev from the race has already started, been run and lost. It's been rigged before the starter pistol ever even fired. It doesn't matter who crosses the finish line first. The race is rigged, Josh, it's fixed. Just like the game is hustled on the corners, son. The winner has already been chosen. The last is first and if the first brother is wrong, then he's last too. Let it go, big man, let it go. Don't even run. You're wishin' on dreams, and sellin' dreams, 'specially to Rev, and just like the race, my man, that ain't fair either."

"But, listen, Old . . ."

"Listen, my ass! I would love for this whole college scene to happen. You know that. But what's the chance, really? What's the odds of getting that hood rat Missy to flip? Naw, brother, get your sense back, keep it a hundred. You know this is some pie in the sky shit."

WILLIAM TEETS

Me and Josh sat on our bar stools in silence. It's not like I wouldn't want this to go down for Rev, folks, you all know that, but where I'm from you got to deal in reality. I know Josh meant good, but all he did was muddy up the unclean water even more. Kicked-up more mud and muck. Made the damn nightmare cloudier than ever. And I was so pissed he told Rev about this whole school plan without sayin' anything to me or Solly first. I mean Josh is fam and all, but he dropped the ball on this one.

Rev's been through so many ups and downs in his young life, it's like he's ridin' an unending roller coaster, dig? He's already had too many bad things happen to him and bounced back strong. How much can you ask of a brother before he breaks bad? Really? How many times have I asked you all that question already? Don't get it twisted, I believe most times, no one should never give up, no matter how bad the struggle be seemin', but sometimes you gotta take an L. Naw, folks, the way I sees it is Rev takes the loss and does his bid at juvy. After he gets out, he's still a prospect, can still go to college. Maybe not this Rodgers' joint, but college nonetheless. I don't want to cut no one down, but like I said prior, people, where me and Rev from, you have to deal in cold hard reality. That's just facts.

Neither me or Josh knew what else to say so we said nothin'. We stayed chillin' on our stools with the loud-ass silence all about us. You know that sound, folks, right? You've heard it scream in your ears, haven't you? Silence that shouts so loud you be thinkin' you might never hear right again.

REVEREND WENT WALKING

This had the beginnings of bein' an ugly visit.

I sighed sadly.

I motioned to the bartender for another round.

Fall, Icarus, fall. I told you not to fly so high.

Chapter 24
We Are Where We Are

Me and Josh finished our last round at the bar in silence. We paid our tab and Josh drove us back to his apartment in silence. No Billy Preston, no Marley, no Bill Withers, no nothin' like he used to play for me, back in the day.

No sound.

Just silent conversation.

Once inside Josh's crib, I dropped my bag and took a seat in his worn-out recliner. Josh poured two doubles and handed one to me.

In silence.

Hell, I went first.

"Listen, brother, I didn't mean to come down on you so hard, but you shouldn't of told Rev about that college. I mean I know you meanin' well and lookin' out for Rev and all, but damn, Josh, for real? With everything that kid's been through? How much can he handle before he breaks for good?"

Then Josh opened up. I mean he let go, people. Blew me away, but I picked up on what he was puttin' down. "You're right, Old Man. I got caught up in the hype. And as much as I want to help Rev, you're right again about what you said. A part of me *is* doing this for me. Hell, Old Timer, I don't know. It's just that I've been so empty, for so long, I've been tryin' to fill that hollowness inside me with the job, my students, anything that's positive. Something that doesn't pour from a bottle. Getting Rev into that program at Rodgers is a shot at redemption for him, but I guess for me too. You understand?"

"I feel you, son, believe me I feel you, that's what's up, but like I told you before, that job ain't your life. It's a part of your life. You can't replace your being with it. And you can't help others if you're hurtin' yourself. And the booze, well damn, Josh, we both know that's just suicide on an installment plan."

"Yeah, man, with a shit-load of interest."

Now I don't know if it was the alcohol—you all know that stuff's like truth serum—but me and Josh talked long into the night 'bout all kinds of crazy stuff. Spilled our guts about what is, what was, and what could've and should've been. Not that cryin'-in-your-beer-country-and-western-type-talk, but deep, serious, lookin'-in-your-soul-type-talk.

WILLIAM TEETS

And talk we did.

We talked, we drank, we talked, and then we drank some more.

Lots more, people.

I'm tellin' you all, don't try this shit at home.

This is for professionals only.

Anyways, I woke up early the next mornin' in the chair I'd been sittin' in the night before—guess my legs weren't workin' good enough to make it to my bed—with a Mets' blanket half wrapped around me, a wild wolf howlin' in my brain, and an ashtray for a mouth. I recollected best I could what me and Josh kicked it about, but like talkin' on the jack when you half asleep at three a.m., bits and pieces of mine and Josh's sharin' played hide and seek in my head.

I'm tellin' you, people, I lost big parts of our conversation—or at least assumed I did—into the ether.

Blackout city.

What I did recall, though, was some honest inner-lookin' on Josh's part. And I felt for the brother, folks.

Word I did.

I mean he laid himself raw to me and to hisself, and that ain't easy for no one to do.

I hoped the purging helped.

I was still missin' that somethin', though. That somethin' in my brain like a long-ago forgotten face you can see so clear, but then it gets so damn blurry. A trivia answer dancin' on the tip of my tongue. An old phone number—hell, remember when we had to remember phone numbers, people?—well that's what last night's talk between me and Josh was like. Answers floatin' so close in my brain I coulda up and grabbed them, but when I tried, they laughed at my foolishness and slipped away again.

Know what I'm sayin'?

Oh, hell, I don't know.

I lost parts of mine and Josh's talk so bad I knew I couldn't corral them ever again.

Let's just leave it at that, folks.

Let's just say blackouts are a motherfucker.

Let's just say we ain't half the shit we think we are.

"How you feelin', Old Timer?" Josh asked, as he walked into the room.

"Like I need a breakfast of champions."

"One Bloody Mary Special coming up."

WILLIAM TEETS

As Josh played mad scientist in his kitchen, mixin' up a concoction that would've made a coven of witches proud, I tried to brush my teeth and wash my face, but sat my old ass back down with the quickness.

Sittin' down worked.

The room stopped spinnin' and the clouds in my eyes cleared.

Hygiene could wait for now.

I kept on tryin' to piece together last night—tried and true—but the evening stayed lost in an alcohol haze. You see, folks, even though the booze is a truth serum, that same serum makes you believe and say things that aren't honest or believed, too.

Believe that!

My head continued swimmin' in confusion and Josh handed me a Bloody Mary none too soon.

My phone rang.

Solly.

My stomach clenched, thinkin' what now—seemed lately, any news was bad news—and I answered as fast as I could to see what was up, but just as fast to stop that torturous sound on my celly, frontin' as a ring.

REVEREND WENT WALKING

Damn, y'all, whatever happened to *real* bells ringin'? You know, folks, bells. *Real* bells. Bells that meant somethin' back in the day. School bells, church bells, dinner bells, phone ringin' bells, *real* bells. Ain't shit clean no more, *real* no more, anywhere, nowhere.

Know what I'm sayin'?

Bells ring silent now, ya feel me? Ah, hell, let me stop, 'less I go on a rant again, y'all don't wanta hear 'bout bells.

I answered the torturous tone.

"Solly, what's good, my brother?"

"Just following up on last night's convo. You told me to call you in the mornin'. I didn't wake you, did I? You sound a little rough, Old Man. A little better than last night, but still a little rough."

Last night's convo? What the hell was he talkin' 'bout? Folks, I'm tellin' y'all, I didn't have a clue about rappin' with Solly last night. Not an inkling—'nother one of them strange words, inkling, right?—and I didn't even try to play it off.

"Listen, Solly, 'bout last night. Me and Josh got a snoot full and to be straight up with you, I don't remember kickin' it with you at all."

"I figured. You were slurrin' and carryin' on pretty good. You were talkin' about some big college program Rev could get into, if we could convince Jamaican Blue to get Mighty Missy—that hooker bitch ho—to cop to her scam about Rev and No Neck and the gun. Hell, Old Timer, you were all over the grid. Talkin' crazy. What's up? What's good?"

I sighed.

One of those goddamn knowing-your-beat-down-sighs I done told y'all 'bout so many times before in this story.

My head hurt.

So did my soul.

I briefly thought 'bout Jesus.

Don't ask me why.

Hell, even Constantine entered my mind.

Ain't that scary, my people?

I talked on.

"Listen, Solly, it's a long, mixed-up, far-out story. I'll be home tomorrow afternoon. Don't say nothin' to Blue or anyone else 'til I get home. I'll stop by the shop first thing and fill you in. Cool, my brother?"

"Cool."

When I shut my phone, Josh was starin' at me with that

what's up look. I swilled my drink, lettin' it burn my insides, burn my brain, burn me, burn my soul.

Some sort of ghetto penance, I guess.

I said nothin'.

My eyes watered and I held my empty glass out to Josh for a refill. I lit a stogie and laid my head back with my eyes closed. I heard Josh shakin' the shaker like a villain. I thought about me, I thought about Tasha—ain't that crazy, folks, how I keeps thinkin' 'bout her?—but mostly, I thought about Rev. It was time for me and Josh to put together the puzzle of our talk from last night.

Time for reality.

Time for the truth.

Shit, my peeps, I sometimes wonder if those two entities even *really* exist anymore.

Know what I'm sayin'?

Right?

Josh remembered a lot more about the night before than I did. Seems that after we had our fill of sharin' our deepest thoughts, spillin' our guts and sharin' our spirits, we talked more about Rev and the program at Rodgers. How we could *all* make that college dream work. I must've been boxed, folks, 'cause Josh said I convinced *him* we could make things right regardin' Rev's bootleg arrest. Could do that and lead Rev into Rodgers. Opposite from the stance I'd done took at the bar. Josh said, that I said, we could come up with a good enough plan so Rev could get off and get into that fine-ass school.

What the fuck was I thinkin'?

"More pipe dreams, Josh. Listen, I'm not sure what my drunk-ass might've said or agreed to last night, but I still don't see it happenin'. What I said at the bar is my bond."

"Is it, Old Man? You kicked some heavy knowledge last night and made some real good sense."

"Humor me. What words of wisdom did I so gracefully impart?" I asked sarcastically.

"That whole corny shit about missing all the shots we don't take, but then you said something *real* deep, about how there is nothing but darkness and light and that the darkness and light don't choose us, but that we choose them."

"I said that?"

"Yeah. And you also said we have to try and make this whole Reverend situation work out because it's in *all* of our best interests. Rev's first, obviously, but that it's also a part of the goodness that comes with all the light. The Universe. That we're *all* invested in the light—in Rev—*all* of us."

"Said that too, huh?"

"You sure did, man. And you said a lot more that made a lot of sense, even quoted some writers I had no idea you even read. You picked up our spirits, got us out of the doldrums we were in, and hell, I know your new position made me feel good."

"You know I was shit-faced, right?"

"Still made sense."

I sat quietly and processed the words I didn't remember sayin'. I knew better, people, but after a few minutes I said anyways, "Well, I guess we can try. I'll kick it with Blue again, but no promises, Josh, and no gettin' Reverend hyped up or anyone else for that matter. This venture is still a shot in the dark, but I'll see what I can do when I get home tomorrow afternoon. But, remember, Josh, nothin' to no one. Now give me another one of those concoctions of yours."

"Right on, my brother, right on. That's what I'm talking about."

Josh mixed up another remedy.

I'm tellin' you folks, I had to be hammered to say what I said. Not only didn't I believe gettin' Rev cleared of his charges could happen, but the more I thought about the whole issue at hand, the more I felt that Reverend couldn't take too many more setbacks in his young life.

WILLIAM TEETS

Too many more body shots to the soul.

That's what was really botherin' me, and like I told y'all before, so many times, and like you all seened, that boy's been through the ringer and it's amazin' he done came out in one piece. We can't keep expectin' him to rebound all righteous and strong, but hell, if he was game and Josh was game and if Solly would be willing, I guess I could too.

See, people, a part of me has always believed in those old sayins' like honesty bein' the best policy and two wrongs not makin' a right, the one about the bird in the hand and the bush and such. They have to be *true* to last so long. I'm talkin' two thousand years long *true*. I decided that *it couldn't hurt to try* was another one of them sayin's worth believin' in for the time bein'. I just wasn't so sure that that last old sayin' was goin' to ring true—just like old-ass bells I done told y'all 'bout—without some bad bein' done to someone.

The next mornin'—sayin' goodbye to Josh at the train station—I reminded him not to get his hopes, or Reverends, up too high. Told him not to go all hog-wild with happiness just because I said I'd work on findin' a solution.

Talk to Blue again.

Hell, Blue can be a bad brother.

Reminded Josh that not many stories *really* end up happily ever after.

Honestly, my peeps, I still didn't know what the hell I was thinkin', but stranger shit has happened. I thought about another one of them old-ass truths, the one about nothin' ever bein' impossible, and I smiled and frowned at the same time.

Just sayin'.

I was real mixed-up inside.

Before walkin' to the platform, I said to Josh, "Funny how sometimes in life we look at ourselves and don't know how we got where we are."

He said, "Yeah, Old Timer, but I heard a wise man say we are where we are."

"Yeah, who said that?" I asked.

"You did, the other night."

Chapter 25
And A Child Shall Lead Them

After gettin' back to the city, I met up with Solly at the shop. I filled him in 'bout my visit with Josh, the whole Rodgers' calamity—that's what I called it, people, a calamity—and we put our heads together to see what more we could do to help Reverend in beatin' his charge and gettin' him into that good-ass college.

There was nothin', though. At least not nothin' we already tried.

But we labored on.

Labored on like Hercules and his twelve feats.

Shit, my dudes, our burden felt like that kinda colossus undertakin'.

Know what I'm sayin'?

"I just don't feel too good 'bout askin' Blue again, Solly."

REVEREND WENT WALKING

"I hear ya, Old Man, but you told Josh you were gonna kick it with Blue again, right?"

"Yeah, but I need a plan for that. You just don't keep walkin' up to a man like Blue and keep askin' favors, even more so now since Shoe and me asked him a couple times already."

"Yeah, Old Man, but you got to try."

"Fuck you, my brother, why don't you try?"

"Let's think of a different solution, a different way to help Rev," Solly said with the quickness. He didn't want to even think about talkin' wit' Blue.

And think we did, folks, about other solutions.

Long and hard.

Unfortunately nothin' came.

Nothin', people, nothin'.

Zero.

Nada.

Nil.

Squadoosh.

Everything boiled down to me, Solly, us, askin' Blue for help again. But, to ask him again could be seen as disrespectful. Let me explain to y'all, once more, Blue was not a man to be trifled with. He was noise with a capital N. But I'd promised Josh I would ask and Solly agreed.

We would try.

Damn, how the hell did I get myself into this mess?

I wanted to up and quit right then and there.

But, folks, don't misconstrue what I be sayin'. I was now a hundred percent on board in understandin' we had to get Rev into that school. That college was his ticket, man, his way out, our way out; one for the good guys, and all that other rah-rah shit. The crabs couldn't win again. Me and Solly agreed on that. We just weren't sure who or how we were goin' to buck up to Blue again. And let's get somethin' crystal, folks, I ain't no pussy, known Blue for years, but Blue could put fear in Hades' heart.

Just sayin'.

Just tellin', y'all.

And with mine and Solly's thoughts and arguin' bouncin' off the walls of Solly's shop, pourin' drinks and stressin', we didn't even recognize, in some great cosmic irony—Jamaican Blue, his motherfuckin' self—walkin' in the shop for a cut.

Just like that.

Solly's shop door bells rang loud, and there stood, Blue.

Well, I'll be good and goddamned.

Solly looked at me, I looked at Solly, and the whole scenario was some kinda sign from above, one of those omens my grandma, bless her soul, was always tellin' me about—remember the train, folks, omens, my grandma, sure you do—but me and Solly didn't say nothin'. Like I said prior, Jamaican Blue was not a man to be trifled with.

There was an awkward silence in the shop, and Blue picked up on the loudness. He said, "Yuh two bredda's 'ave sumpting to seh to Blue, nuh?"

His voice sounded like thunder.

Blue always spoke in the third person.

Made his demeanor more menacing.

Made his presence more felt.

Being a bad-ass brother—good heart and all, but still a bad-ass—Blue didn't need much help in commanding a presence. Not as far as I was concerned.

"Sumpting 'bout da bwoy, Reverend? How is 'im doin' da jail wit' babylon?" asked Blue.

"Ah, no, Blue, we don't want to bother you with that again, but it's just . . . ah, never mind," Solly stammered.

"Don't yuh lie, Solomon. One Shoe buck up Blue t'is morn'. Bwoy 'ave 'imself good 'ting wit' jerusalem if Blue's wicked niece turn 'erself in, or zutapong No Neck, nuh?"

"Well, yeah, but what is, is, right?"

"Yuh, mon, but Blue try again. She 'ardeaded', truss Blue, mon."

"Well anything, Blue, anything you could do is greatly appreciated. You know that."

"Yuh, mon, Blue, truss. Luke was Blue's key, mon. Blue 'as much respect for Luke and bwoy called Reverend. Blue see wicked niece Satday. Try again. Yuh 'ave some acid for Blue, Solomon? Blue wit' gettin' red today."

"Yeah, brother, let me get you a cup."

"Tenk yuh, Solomon."

And that was it, folks. Jamaican Blue sat still and quiet through the rest of his cut, sipped the rum Solomon gave him—five refills worth and five different times said thank you, or should I say tenk yuh—damn, that Caribbean patois is a bitch to understand sometimes, and then Blue was gone.

Problem solved.

REVEREND WENT WALKING

Or was it?

Upstate at the Hall, Josh and Rev were onto their own trip unbeknownst to me and Solly.

"You're going too hard, Rev. AWOL is out of the question. Too dangerous. There are other solutions. Old Man is going to talk to Jamaican Blue again. Going AWOL isn't going to look good to the courts either. It's a slap in their face, you feel me?"

"Yeah, Mr. M, I feel you, but it's my only recourse. I've got to speak to Missy face-to-face. I have no home visit for six months due to the court order. That's too late to solve this issue. Mr. Blue tried talking with Missy already and it didn't work. It's my future, know what I'm saying? Everything I've read, everything I've learned, everything I know, hell, everything you've taught me is telling me to take this gamble. It's my only play. Look at the poster behind you, even that says if you don't take a chance, you don't stand a chance."

"Yeah, Rev, but . . ."

"But nothing, Mr. M. All those great books you gave me that I never heard of or read on my own, *Steppenwolf*, *The Ginger Man*, hell, *The Drifters*, they were all about the hero's journey, isn't that right? What about *The Odyssey*, all of the classics, Kerouac's *On the Road*, weren't they all about taking chances, living life, and experiencing life's all? Was *Narcissus and Goldmund* a lie? I need my heart to burn. I can't regret. I can't be Goldmund on my death bed. I saw your passion and belief—those writings are like a religion for you—and when you shared those books with me, they're a religion I can believe in, too. You taught me that. Was it all a lie?"

"No, Rev, but you're young. You still think life's answers can be found in books, in stories, they're not *real* life, Rev. Not *real* life."

"So everything is a lie."

Now, folks, I had no idea 'bout this talk between Rev and Josh at the time. I done found out later, way later. If I had known then, I would've told Josh to tell Rev to shut the hell up. That youngsters are foolish. That's why adults are adults and children, children, right? We're supposed to save them from pipe dreams and such, right? But, shit, Josh still had a lot of child in him. Regardless of what he said to Rev, Josh still believed in fairy tales and books and superheroes. Still thought the day could be saved by some righteous Calvary.

Ask Custer how that shit worked out for his ass.

See, people, Josh loved hearin' music and readin' lyrics and poetry, like most folks do, but he took them arts to heart. Didn't make him a bad person—I'm just sayin'—but he was a dreamer in a *real* man's world. I loved him for that, but hated him at the same time. Maybe 'cause I couldn't hear the bells in the French Quarter, maybe 'cause I couldn't smell the ocean spray with Ulysses, maybe 'cause I disagreed with him, or maybe 'cause I did agree. I don't know, folks, I just knew I could never be him.

Maybe that bothered me too.

Josh needed to be an adult, though.

'Specially then.

'Specially with Rev.

Like I said, though, folks, Josh and Rev were upstate goin' at each other hard.

"Look, Rev, books can give you a foundation for ideas or philosophies or principles, but they're not scripture, they're not absolute. They're ideas, fiction, man, that's why they're called fiction. You can't base your existence, your life, on ideas from some writer. You have to be grounded in reality. Remember how messed-up in the head most of those writers were? Drunk and drug addled. Straight up crazy. Remember we talked about that, too? You have to be grounded in reality, Rev. Hell, I learned that from Old Man. Still am."

"I am, Mr. M. I am grounded in reality. My reality. Not what society says, not what the masses say—I learned that from *you*. I need to see Missy in person, to convince her to tell the DA what time it is. I need this phony charge dropped. I need to get into Rodgers. Hell, I scored eighth on a test out of like hundreds. Me. I did that. I need this. I *earned* this. And besides, this sounds like Old Man talking, not you."

"I agree. And I like you saying *need* instead of *want*, but that doesn't mean going AWOL is the answer. Write Missy a letter again. We'll call her on my phone if you can get her number. It might work. But AWOL is out of the question. You probably wouldn't even make it to the train station before the State Troopers caught you."

"I talked with Ralph. He's AWOLed before and he gave me the MO on how to make it."

"Black Ralph or White Ralph?"

"Black Ralph. White Ralph lives in Buffalo. Anyways, Black Ralph has made it twice. Says where everyone gets caught is in the woods by Brick Hill Road. Said if you stay in the woods the whole time the cops send in a K-9 and then you're dog food. Said he left the woods when he first heard the cops and dog and chilled at the A&P across the street from the firehouse. Right before Brick Hill. Went into the store like a shopper. Pushed a carriage and everything. Once the cops cooled their search after an hour or so he ducked off to the train station on the low and made it home. Said the second time, he got a ride to the station from some nice old lady."

Josh rubbed his face in his hands and looked towards the ceiling. Neither Josh nor Rev said nothin' for several minutes.

Silence.

That silence I done told y'all about so many times before, remember?

Sure you do.

"I can't cosign this Rev, I just can't. I got a job. I have to look out for you even if you don't understand that. I've got a responsibility to the agency. To you. To me."

"Do what you've got to do Mr. M. Turn me in. I don't care. No disrespect, but I'm going to do me regardless. If not tonight, next week, next month, can't keep me on AWOL risk forever."

"So you're planning this tonight? After eleven I presume? After the house staff switches to night security?"

"That's how AWOL's are done. You going to turn me in? Notify the SOD?"

"I don't know, Rev. I don't know. Christ, Rev, I just don't know."

WILLIAM TEETS

And Josh really didn't know, people. He was all confused about the whole conversation with Rev. Like I told y'all, he was a dreamer and found some cheap romanticism in Rev's plan. Saw him like a present day Siddhartha, some Huckleberry Finn on some fantasy journey, was persuaded by Rev's adolescent angst and logic. Like I told y'all, people, Josh was still an adolescent in a way.

He went home that night—well, not right home, he stopped at a juke-joint—and thought hard about the dilemma. Turn Rev in, call the Supervisor on Duty, put Rev on the AWOL risk sheet, or let fate play itself out like some bullshit novel.

Problem being, folks, life's no novel.

A novel is fiction.

Like Josh said.

This was *real* life.

Wasn't no raft or river in this story.

Problem being—in *real* life—the Big Bad Wolf huffs and puffs and blows *all* the piggy's houses down, even the brick one. Eats all them hogs. True story, brothers and sisters, true story. Hansel and Gretel didn't have no bread crumbs. They were gobbled up by the old hag hidin' out in the woods. The three bears had more than porridge for dinner after findin' Goldi snoozin' in their beds and you best believe Snow White never woke up after eatin' no poisoned apple.

That's truth, y'all.

Truth in the hood at least.

Just sayin' and all.

Just sayin'.

Fall, Icarus, fall. I told you not to fly so high.

Chapter 26
AWOL

I'm sorry, folks, don't want to sound like no curmudgeon—another great word, people, curmudgeon, right?—but Josh was upstate thinkin' too hard 'bout what to do in regards with Rev. Any adult person—sane adult person—would've let the Hall know Rev was plannin' an AWOL, right?

Not Josh.

No, not Joshua Moriel.

Like I said people, I didn't know about none of this when this craziness was happenin', zilch, nada, oh, hell, we've been through that already. No, folks, Josh was sittin' hard and thinkin'. Thinkin' and drinkin' 'bout the merits of lettin' Rev AWOL. Of sayin' nuttin' to the powers that be, or sayin' somethin' to them. Doin' the right thing—in my opinion—was puttin' Rev on the AWOL risk list.

Easy choice, right, folks?

REVEREND WENT WALKING

No, my peeps, not for Joshua Moriel.

He had to be the consummate rebel, had to down double whiskeys, play the martyr, quote Shakespeare or some Tom Waits song, believe Mother Goose was alive and well, smoke Marlboro Reds and then make a decision. Couldn't just make the correct call like us simple folk. Make the right one, see right from wrong. No, my peeps, he had to make this decision a Broadway Production, a best seller on the Times' list, a motherfuckin' Academy Award winner. Had to make everything bat-shit crazy.

And that's what Joshua did.

Let's see how that worked out for the brother.

Let's see if they're unicorns and two-headed llamas.

I don't believe there are, folks.

I'm just sayin'.

I could be wrong, though.

Again, I'm just sayin'.

Reverend laid in his bed keepin' his eyes on the night watchman sittin' in the middle of the dorms. He knew Mr.

WILLIAM TEETS

Robinson's routine. Do a head count at eleven, eat a sandwich of sardines and mustard at eleven-fifteen, and fall asleep by eleven-forty-five. You could set your watch on the brother.

And Rev did.

By eleven-forty-five, Mr. Robinson was snoozin'.

Rev quietly got out of his bed, put on his black sweats and black hoody and gingerly slipped by the sleepin' night watchman. Once outside the house, Reverend made sure no cars were passin' on the county road and he hopped the low stone wall that surrounded the Hall. He jetted into the woods across the street and crouched down behind some spruces. His heart was poundin' in his chest. You all know how that cliché feels people, right? Feels like you might self-combust and explode on the spot. Feels like your heart might rip through your ribs leavin' carnage and waste all about ya. You know that stressful feelin', folks, an alarmed heart on high alert?

Well, that's how our boy, Reverend, was feelin'.

Rev was surprised he had sweat on his brow in the cold November night.

After settlin' his jangled nerves, Rev knew he had about a thirty to forty minute head start to the train station before he would be discovered missin' at the Hall. The train station was about an hour away. Not much time. He replayed in his head what Black Ralph had told him, *stay in the woods 'til you hear the dog or voices or sirens, then turn left before Brick Hill Road and chill at the A&P 'til things cool off. Don't go as far as Brick Hill. You'll be caught then.*

Brotherman was shook.

The night and woods were dark.

He couldn't see.

He was runnin' on adrenaline and instinct and ignorance.

Reverend tried to jog, but overgrown thickets and barren branches pushed him back.

Slowed him down.

A lot.

He cursed Black Ralph under his breath for leavin' so many side details out and thought of the tree branches becomin' alive like arms and grabbin' him like in the *Wizard of Oz*.

He chuckled to himself.

To relieve his fear.

Didn't work.

He plowed ahead for another half-an-hour, bein' slapped up and slapped down by thorns and more branches and such.

WILLIAM TEETS

That's when he heard the dog.

A baying hound, hot on his trail.

Straight out of a Robert Johnson Delta Blue's song.

Least that's how I heard the scene when Rev told me his story later on.

Anyways, Rev heard a distant faint voice over a State Trooper's car speaker sayin' to come out of the woods and give up. Damn, that was quick, Rev thought.

He started to panic and knew he was close to Brick Hill Road.

Close to goin' too far.

Close to bein' captured.

The hound was gainin' ground.

The audio voice became louder and clearer.

Where was the fire house?

Where was the A&P?

Had Black Ralph lied?

Rev was in a panic.

REVEREND WENT WALKING

He knew he had to find the fire house and then cut into the A&P before the dog or five-o nabbed him. Deep inside, and I swear Rev told me this later, folks, he said he felt a primeval fear stir in his soul. A feelin' of a dormant instinct wakin' up was the way he put it, of slave runnin' ancestors chased by white men with dogs in the south not too long ago.

Felt a kinship and fear in his innards.

Somethin' right out of *Roots*.

Y'all remember *Roots*, people?

Sure you do.

Reverend was terrified.

Felt like a fuckin' present day Kunta Kinte.

Toby on the run.

He then remembered stories told by other boys who were caught tryin' to AWOL. 'Bout how them boys got beat downs from the Troopers who were mighty pissed off that they were made to chase down baby-delinquents in the cold weather, late at night.

Rev heard the K-9 hound gettin' closer.

Rev knew he was gettin' close to Brick Hill Road.

WILLIAM TEETS

Close to bein' caught.

Close to the end of the line.

Close to gettin' a beat down.

Then he saw the fire house, people, heard the heavy traffic on Route 138, knew the A&P was right across that route, knew he was near to makin' it.

He heard the hellhound breakin' brush behind him.

He slid down an embankment of frozen mud and roots and stone and saw the lights of the A&P.

Sanctuary.

He waited nervously for enough traffic to slow so he could cross Route 138 into the parking lot of the A&P.

There was mad traffic.

He looked up and down the route and saw no flashin' lights, no patrol cars, he was so fuckin' close.

Then the dog.

That damn hound, sprung to life from Simon Legree's wolf pack. That fuckin' hound was chasin' down another black man.

Too close.

Too bayin'.

Man's best friend, my ass.

Reverend zigged and zagged and heard car horns blow and brakes screech as he dashed across Route 138, crazily, into the A&P parking lot. He bent over, hands on his knees and head bowed, and breathed more heavy then he could ever remember doin' so before.

Reverend smiled.

Then Reverend laughed.

He was good money.

He had made it.

As he sucked fresh air into his expanding lungs, relaxing, Reverend heard again and then saw that damned K-9 hound from hell barking at him from across Route 138. White canines flashin' in the night and dog spit flyin' freely into the air. Two State Trooper vehicles pulled up and one of the cops leashed the dog.

The hound continued to howl.

The Stateys looked across the road to see what their dog was so anxious about and saw Reverend standin' there.

Breathin' hard.

WILLIAM TEETS

Now almost beaten.

Busted.

Five-o got their dog, hopped into their SUV's, and lit up their lights and sirens, tryin' to cross Route 138.

Reverend ran towards the A&P.

His lungs were fire again and goin' to explode.

He sucked air harder.

The police eventually stopped traffic on Route 138 and the Troopers wheeled their wagons into the entrance of the shopping center.

Reverend knew if he ducked into the store he would be discovered by five-o. If he jetted back into the woods or stayed outside the store, the K-9 would make quick work of him.

He was done, folks.

He was defeated.

Reverend lost.

Goodbye, William Rodgers, goodbye future.

Hello City College, hello ghetto education.

REVEREND WENT WALKING

Reverend stood in his spot—soul crushed—and watched the wailing police cars meander through stopped traffic on Route 138 and begin their way into the A&P lot.

They too knew they were soon to be victorious.

They too knew a beat down reward was close at hand.

How close?

Close enough?

"Yo, Rev, get in," Reverend heard from somewhere that seemed surreal.

"Now, damnit!"

Reverend jumped in the front seat of a beat-up convertible.

He laid down low and the driver pulled out of the parkin' lot like Morgan Freeman drivin' Miss Daisy.

All calm and cool like.

Drove right past the incomin' Troopers and their wild dog in tow.

The driver of the beat-up convertible headed south on Route 138.

Rev was saved by the proverbial fucking bell.

WILLIAM TEETS

You remember bells, people, right?

Sure you do.

I'd done told you about them, earlier.

Josh said, "Damn, Rev, that was close."

Chapter 27
The Best Laid Schemes Of . . .

The rain stopped. The streets puddled and smelled of summer. Fog was laden in the air and great huffs of steam hissed. An internal combustion engine, acted upon by pressure from expanded gases, rifled the night with sound. A girl, a beautiful dark-skinned girl, walked strong and straight. She announced her presence with the clack of her high-heeled shoes, which sparked flames against the pavement.

Reverend was lost. Lost in catacombs of back streets and alleys, all encased in concrete. His walk, his bounce, his magical step gone. He staggered and waded against an unseen tide of nothingness. He called out to the beautiful girl. His voice unheard. The great combustion engine roared on. Smoky steam spewed towards heaven.

Reverend stood on a dock. A dock vined by thick frayed ropes knotted to huge metal cleats. The opposite ends of the mighty ropes were lashed to nothing. They held only infinity. An ancient wizard's spell or a witches' wild coven enchanted the ropes into snakes. Huge, thick, undulated serpents slithered across Reverend's feet. The snakes fell over the sides of the worn wooden dock and made loud splashes into the water below.

Reverend jumped back and screamed. A hollow scream. A strangled scream which could not be heard over the echoed slaps of the snakes that fell into the river. The wooden pilings of the dock morphed into large crucifixes silhouetted against the dank night. They began to sway, and they too fell over; over the dock, over the beach, and into the water. The fallen crucifixes left anything and anyone crushed in their wake.

Joshua was there, too. Off to the side. An afterthought of impotence, he was denied true creation. He called to Reverend, told him to run, but his screams too went unheard. Shackled by impalpable manacles, Joshua was unable to move, unable to assist, unable to offer salvation to Reverend.

Reverend walked a dirt road. Huts and hovels lined either side of his path. Great oil drums offered fire flames to pagan gods. Unclean men and women with rotted stained teeth, blotched bloody skin and soiled threadbare clothes pointed at Reverend. Pointed at him with crooked fingers and overgrown fingernails. They heckled him, denounced him and accused him of not being worthy. Cur dogs growled and babies played in their own feces. Large black flies circled and flew into unsuspecting eyes, noses and mouths. A shanty town constructed by a madman developer. Reverend looked for, but could not find, the beautiful dark-skinned girl.

REVEREND WENT WALKING

She was gone.

Joshua was there, too. Still paralyzed, he could not move. He called out to Reverend once more, his scream stifled by the raucous laughter of the unholy denizens of the bastardized unchaste parish. The mongrel dogs surrounded Joshua—ears laid low, tails held high—they gnashed their teeth. The babies' faces contorted into demonic apparitions of twists and snarls and evilness. They cursed Joshua with depraved vulgarities and vile profanities. They flung their feces at him. Joshua screamed. His scream again, unheard.

In a vestibule beneath an awning, Joshua looked onto an empty street. No cars, no pedestrians, no sound. He saw Reverend on the opposite side. Reverend trailed, chased, pursued a beautiful dark-skinned girl. Reverend could not catch her, could not close the distance between him and the girl. Joshua shouted for Reverend to run.

Reverend ran and got closer to the girl. As he drew nearer to her, Joshua felt exalted, grand and noble. Joshua's thoughts controlled Reverend. He wished Reverend closer to the girl and it was so. They were both together now, Joshua and Reverend. They both got closer to the girl. Her high-heeled shoes clacked again against the pavement and more sparks illuminated the night. Joshua stopped and watched, filled with awe and joy at the brilliant and delightful sight. He smiled ideally and the street became a splendid spectacular universe created and commanded by his will.

Reverend was a step away from the beautiful girl. He reached out and placed his hand softly on her shoulder. She stopped her walk. Sparks from her shoes stopped, too. The girl stood still. Josh was next to Reverend. The beautiful dark-skinned girl turned around. Her eyes shone spectacular and her smile was calm. Joshua had never seen such beauty. He wanted to brush her cheeks with his fingertips. He wanted to feel her wet lips with his. She threw her head back and laughed. Her bosom heaved and her hair whipped. Josh reached to touch—to touch the angel he had fashioned greater than any god had before him.

The beautiful dark-skinned girl looked into Joshua's eyes. She slashed Reverend's throat with an athame. She howled. The quick slice poured Reverend's blood onto the street. Reverend wrapped his hands around his throat. His blood spurted from between his fingers. He looked at Joshua with a chilled hopeless plead. An expression of angst and want. Joshua cringed and screamed once more. He could do nothing, now.

Josh jerked awake. He quickly sat up and turned the nightstand light on. He sweated heavily. The nightmare dissipated, but not before Josh thought if what he had done, assisting Reverend, was a terrible mistake. He could not fall back asleep. The clock read four-eleven in the morning. Josh lit a cigarette with shaking hands and poured a double. He called the Hall's main office and left a message he would not be reporting to work as scheduled.

He was ill.

Chapter 28
A Nickel In The Well

Yeah, folks, yeah.

Josh had one hell of a nightmare. Scared the shit out of him. Deserved him right if you're askin' me. Just sayin' of course, just throwin' my nickel in the well. Lucky for him he didn't see rattlesnake eyes like I did, with Usman Buhari. Remember, folks, remember Usman? Sure you do.

But do y'all feel me, now?

Could you have even imagined what that fool, Josh, done did?

Still blows my mind, brothers and sisters. Blows my mind like Marvin singin'. It was that kinda stupid real. That kinda dumbness. That loss of somethin' wicked this way comin'.

Hell, burn them books.

Y'all dig?

WILLIAM TEETS

Hear me now, though.

Let me take y'all back to that night. Let me tell y'all what went down. And don't get it twisted, my people, remember, I was still in the dark about what was takin' place. I was countin' sheep and such, hopefully dreamin' 'bout Tasha—just sayin', just wishin'—while Josh and Rev were doin' their great escape. Not like Steve McQueen's great escape, no, not that, but more like *Hogan's Heroes*, if you know what I mean, again.

As always, just me sayin'.

Just me tellin'.

Let me rock on.

Give me a swig of that, my brother.

Give an old man a light, youngblood.

Yeah.

Righteous.

Good lookin'.

Got an old man right.

An old man correct.

An old man who ain't that old.

REVEREND WENT WALKING

Believe dat.

Don't let this silver top fool ya, now.

Word.

But let's keep on truckin'.

As Josh drove out of the A&P parking lot, south on Route 138, headin' towards the train station, Rev said, "Mr. M, what the fuck?"

"There's strings attached, Rev. Rules. I'm not sure why I'm doing what I'm doing, but you see Missy, try your approach, and then high-tail your ass back to the Hall. Understand? No ifs-ands- or-buts. Got it?"

"Got it, Mr. M. Got it *real*. You been drinking?"

"Not enough, son, not enough."

Josh's ass, thinkin' he was slick and all, drove Reverend to the next train station south of the one by the Hall. Just in case PoPo was waitin' at the first one. Lucky that brother didn't get a DUI or kill himself and that kid. I'm still kinda pissed about the whole thing even now. Josh drivin' himself and Rev, drunk. What the hell was that madman thinkin'? He'll deny he was boxed, but I know better. What about you folks? What do y'all think?

Anyways, Josh kept on givin' edicts—love that word too, people, edicts—to Rev about returnin' to the Hall in twenty-four hours, not breaking *Joshua's* rules in regards to the AWOL, makin' a pact, keepin' it real, rememberin' the guidelines, rememberin' the rules, and on and on. Ain't that some shit, folks? Hell, Reverend going AWOL and Josh helpin', done broke all the rules in the first place.

Big Time!

Ya feel me, folks?

The classic two wrongs tryin' to make a right.

Shit, that music don't play in any Universe.

Y'all best believe that.

Anyways, as I was tellin', Josh dropped Rev off at the Willoughby train station, south of Silver Bridge station—the one closest to the Hall. Josh gave Rev his last forty-three bucks, reviewed the rules and their agreement and told Rev to take care of business with Missy, and then get his ass back to Silver Bridge. Pronto.

Made Rev promise.

Yeah, right.

Sending Rev, seventeen, no phone, no heads up to anyone, a measly forty-three bucks in Rev's sweatpants pocket, to speak with a viper in a viper's nest.

Brilliant!

Not.

Right, folks, right?

But that was Josh doin' his best Falstaff.

Leading a prince astray.

And don't dare get it crossed up in your domes, my people. Reverend is a prince. Better, as far as I'm concerned. He's a king! I love that boy, y'all. Love him righteous. Love him for the hero he is.

A real hero.

Dig that, folks.

Not those Sunday's papers' heroes. No, not them.

Give me another swig, young-un.

Now I know I done told y'all superheroes don't exist—I still stand by that—but think outside the box on this if you can. Forget your Hulks and Wolverines, your Captain Americas and Iron Men. Forget John Wayne and fuck Josey Wales. Hell, I just wish America could *realize all* the *real* lost superheroes like Rev. The lost superhero children in our midst. The one's bein' destroyed not by some Dr. Evil or Lex Luthor, but by under-financed schools and racism, by crime and corruption and savage inequalities. Look up *Savage Inequalities*, folks. Stole that from my man, Jon Kozol. But like I was sayin', superhero kids bein' ravaged by drugs and the Man and that seeing-eyed, bitch, Lady Justice, by . . . oh, hell I could rant forever . . . let me stop.

But let me ask just one more question, my peeps.

Where's Marvel for that shit?

Where's Disney for tellin' *real* stories?

Not some Cinderella get-down.

I want to see *real* life.

I want a black or brown superhero.

A Black Savior. A Black Santa. A Black Batman. Where have you gone, Joe . . . oh, fuck that fake- ass song . . . where have you gone Willie Mays? Jackie Robinson? Satchel Paige?

Say Hey to that, America.

Say Hey to that, people.

OK, sorry . . . sorry . . . I was about to start one of my rants again wasn't I?

What?

I already did?

REVEREND WENT WALKING

OK, then back to the story, but, damn, people, y'all need to understand—if you ain't done so by now—what a talented and special being Rev *is*, and that America's filled with them.

In Detroit, in Chicago, in New Orleans, hell, on some Indian reservation in East Bumfuck, North Dakota.

Y'all know what I'm sayin'?

Beauty in its finest form.

Simple.

Innocent breath waitin' to exhale.

But, y'all are right, let me get ya back to the story.

To Rev ridin' the train.

Back to the ghetto.

Back to the streets.

Back to Mighty Missy.

Follow this shit, now.

I'm about to ramp this story up.

Solly got a call from the Hall regardin' Rev's AWOL 'bout one-thirty in the mornin' or so, when the Hall realized Rev had made his AWOL work. Realized Rev beat the Troopers, the hound from Hades—not sure how—just that he did. The Hall also informed Solly they called the 72nd Precinct to issue an AWOL warrant for Reverend, which, like I touched on earlier, them cops take about as serious as a missing cat report.

Then Solly called me.

"I don't know, Old Man, hell, it's two in the mornin' or something. They said Rev is AWOL. Gone. Where'd he go, Old Timer? Tell me where he went? That ain't Rev. He was doin' so well up there. So solid. Can you call your man, Josh?"

And I called Josh.

No answer.

Another lost nickel in the well.

Chapter 29
On A Road

I got nowhere tryin' to connect with Josh on the jack.

I called Solly back and said we'd have to try talkin' with Josh later.

And don't forget, people, I can't say it enough, folks, I was still in the dark 'bout everything goin' down. Still snookered. But don't fret none, my peeps, the real story ya need to hear is not me buggin' out on Josh when I learned of his stupidity, you'll hear that commotion later on, but of Rev's AWOL.

That's where this story gets crazy.

What?

What's that you say?

Didn't think the story could get any crazier?

Well sit right back and you'll hear a tale.

WILLIAM TEETS

And again, brothers and sisters, you won't find this shit televised nowhere.

This is real life for too many.

Reverend bought a round trip fare from the conductor and stuck the return ticket in his sock. That boy's always thinkin' ahead, always planning for the future, and he sat back in his seat and gave a mighty exhale.

Yeah, people, one of those again.

See, brothers and sisters, Rev's way of calculating in his noggin' is to process everything, cross all those t's, dot all those i's, all thorough-like, and have a fool proof plan, but this time he was flyin' blind.

The old whiskey bottle wing and a prayer deal.

He knew where he was going, knew what he needed to do when he got there, just wasn't so sure how to go about the doin' part. He had to first find Missy—that crazy girl could be anywhere in the hood—then Rev had to convince her to talk with him. If Missy agreed to talk, Reverend still had to convert her to flip on No Neck and save Rev's ass and ultimately his dream. He was hopin' hard she'd be sympathetic to his situation 'bout gettin' into Rodgers, but hood people like Missy don't put much value on a proper education. Not when they're graduates from that old school of hard knocks, but Rev *had* to make this plan work.

REVEREND WENT WALKING

And don't get it twisted my people, he had to do all this while ducking five-o, Solly, me and One Shoe, and anyone else in the hood who knows Rev should be upstate in juvy, but most of all, folks, Rev didn't want to run in to that goon motherfucker, No Neck.

Tall order for our boy.

Yes, indeed, tall order.

Between the forty-three ducats Josh gave Rev and the couple of bucks Rev had of his own, he had a total of seventeen dollars left after buyin' his train tickets. Enough for a couple roundtrip subway rides and maybe something to eat. Definitely not enough to buy Mighty Missy Brown. He had to tighten his plan—his game—way up. He had to snake charm that viper into bein' something other than an asp. Rev had to change the spots of a leopard, the stripes of a zebra and come out in one piece.

Talk about heavy?

Lord, I wished I never heard of Rodgers University or that damn test Josh had Reverend take. This was too much for our boy—for anyone for that matter—just me sayin' and all, just me sayin'.

Anyways, Rev's train pulled in around two a.m. He caught a couple of connects then the six uptown and walked from underground about two-twenty-five.

WILLIAM TEETS

It was cloudy and cold.

Not too many brothers or sisters outside, 'cept for the hustlers and the fiends and don't forget unfriendly ghosts and ghouls in the darkness.

Rev did not need to see no ghouls. No Baku's in the night.

All them myths Rev done read about, Ulysses and Hercules and Perseus, well, let's just say those folks ain't had shit on Rev's trials and tribulations and hero's journey now.

For *real*, y'all.

Word.

Believe that!

Rev pulled his hoody tight and hiked up his sweats. The cold cut him like barbed-wire strung across the prairies. Remember the prairies, y'all? Where the deer and the antelope play? Right. Rev focused his mind even more. Focused hard on his task. That whole mind over matter bullshit we be hearin' 'bout. Hell, when it's cold, it's cold, but if anyone could make his mind triumph the matter, it was definitely our main man, Rev.

Damn, I love that boy. Did I say that already? Well, if I did, I'm sayin' again, I love that boy. Feel mad bad for him, too. I knows I keep repeatin' myself, but Rev didn't deserve none of this, but I'm a firm believer in when you ask the Lord why me, the Universe answers, why not you?

Feel me, people?

Ask that brother, Job.

Hear what I'm sayin'?

Let me tell you all again, life ain't fair.

Favor ain't fair.

Fair ain't fair.

All right, y'all.

Settle down.

I ain't 'bout to go off the rails.

Chill, y'all, chill.

Listen up, now.

Rev walked up towards 138th, hugging the buildings and keepin' an eye out on the low, just in case he had to duck up in a cut. He saw a couple fiends staggering 'round up ahead when he felt a hand on his shoulder. Rev's muscles tensed, he clenched his fist, and swung around. Shit, folks, he knew no one was touchin' him to say *good mornin'*. When Rev spun around, some crackhead crouched and said, "Chill, nigga, chill. Don't wallop me. Suck your dick for a hit."

WILLIAM TEETS

Rev felt even colder.

He dipped his head and walked past the two toothless fiends sermoning to him, "Hey, brother, I got ten and this here toaster. What you got for us?"

Made Rev damn near sick to his stomach. Made him think of Rodgers and escaping this hell for sure. Made his quest to find Mighty Medusa Brown that much more important. Made him want to take flight right then and there, and soar into the brick November night, and never land again, until he was far, far, away.

Feel me, folks, y'all feel me?

Rev walked on.

At 140th and Franklin—there's another one of them streets bein' named after an old dead white man—Rev saw GoJohnny and Czar workin' the corner. GoJohnny and Czar, two more crazy nicknames you'll find only in the hood, were low-level workers that Rev knew from back in the day. GoJohnny was a piano prodigy and Czar an all-city tailback over at Lincoln— even the damn school is named after . . . well, you all got the picture by now. Both of them boys were superheroes in their own right just a few years ago. Recruited by major universities. But now, they were slingin' 'cause they couldn't believe there was a whole world outside the hood, couldn't escape all them crabs in the bucket. Didn't believe the world wanted to hear beautiful symphonies or see a ballet on a football field.

Still believed in Bakus.

Couldn't believe in their dreams.

What's that line from Vonnegut?

Right, my sister.

So it goes.

"Yo, GoJo, Czar, what's good?" Rev asked.

"Who dat? Rev, is that you?" Czar asked.

"Yeah, man, it's Rev. What's good, y'all?"

"What you doin' here, Rev? Heard you were locked. You lookin' for work?" GoJohnny asked.

"Naw, man, it's all good. I'm lookin' for Mighty Missy. You see her?"

"Naw, bro, and don't want to see that crazy bitch. She's the bad lead story on the evening news. Bitch got a serious attitude problem," GoJohnny said.

"I seened her earlier. Yesterday up on 145th. Talkin' some shit with crazy Danijah 'bout how Missy headin' back to Philly, gonna run her own block and end up a female Scarface," Czar said.

"Word?"

"That's what I heard, son. Don't know if it's true or not, but that's what I heard. Just sayin'."

Rev got colder.

"Weren't you hittin' that crazy ho, Rev? Back in the day? I'll admit she's a fine piece of ass. And those titties, man, yo, son, feel me?" GoJohnny laughed.

"I gotta jet, y'all. Catch you all later. Peace," Rev said.

"Don't be like that, Rev. I'm just sayin'."

"Naw, man, it's cool, I just gotta book, son."

"Peace, brother," GoJohnny said.

"Peace out, Rev," Czar said.

"Hey, Yo, if youse ever need some work . . ."

And our boy Rev walked away dazed.

If Missy went back to Philly, well, y'all fill in the blanks.

On 143rd and McKinley, Rev realized his whole AWOL plan might've been for naught.

Might be worth less than the now twelve bucks in his pocket.

Rev felt like he was walking on a road to nowhere.

Dig it, my people.

Our boy was twisted up.

Feel for him.

For real.

Rev's head starting spinnin' again and his stomach muscles knotted up all tight and like. His eyes watered, his mouth was dry.

Reverend was on a road to salvation—or a road to perdition—but either fucking way, folks, he was on a road.

Yeah, man, he was on a road.

Chapter 30
Fickle

As Rev's feets pounded the pavement he kept tellin' himself to be cool and think. Fact was, folks, Rev was all thought out. He done hit every hot spot he could think where that tawdry Missy might be, but he done come up empty.

Philadelphia kept banging against Rev's brain. What if what Czar said he'd heard was true? What if Missy really did jet back to Philly? Well, y'all know the answer to that one, right? If that was indeed the case, then it was goodbye Rodgers, goodbye scholarship, hello ghetto, hello City College. Hell, I'm gettin' mad tired and pissed off of sayin' them words. Y'all got to be tired of hearin' them. But the truth can be hard.

Let's stay on Rev's journey.

Rev shivered again, as he continued to walk. He knew his whole future, his existence, was all on the line.

On both fire and ice.

Reverend knew if he didn't succeed, he would he be just another failed prodigy, just another superhero kid from the hood whose light was snuffed out too soon and too suddenly. All too often. Left sellin' dope on the corner, drinkin' a forty, smokin' a spliff, and sayin', "Yeah, man, one time I was . . ."

The only place Reverend didn't check out was Missy's mom's apartment. That's where Missy laid her head and chilled when she wasn't out causing havoc—which was rarely—but Rev wasn't too keen on going there because that crib was right in the middle of No Neck's territory and mad close to Solly's shop. Rev was certain he'd be found out. Better by Solly than No Neck, but Reverend knew an ass-whuppin' was comin' to him either which way if he was caught.

Rev thought about Josh.

How Josh had *saved* him.

The promise he made.

Thought about time runnin' out and the night gettin' ready to break day, and Rev thought about givin' up.

Sellin' the farm.

WILLIAM TEETS

Packin' it in and returning to the Hall.

Hell, at least he gave his situation an honest effort.

His best shot.

Wasn't that enough?

Rev wasn't so sure.

Then, people, and I shit you not, this is what Rev told me happened. When he was about ready to head back upstate, all defeated and whatnot, said he heard plain as vanilla pudding, words on the wind. Words floating on the November cold air. Said he heard Luke's voice clearer than shined silver tellin' him not to give up. Tellin' him to check out Missy's mom's crib before goin' back north on the train. Not in his head, folks, not in his soul or his thoughts, but real auditory words spoken by Luke. Carried by angel's wings to his ears. As if Luke was there, in the flesh, livin' and talkin' and offering guidance to our boy.

That's what Rev told me, people, later on.

Still says it to this day.

Who am I to doubt?

Who am I to say shit didn't happen that way?

Remember, my people, I don't judge.

And if Reverend said that's how his journey went down, I believe him.

Hell, y'all, I knows how this story ends.

What about you, folks?

Do you believe?

Do you have any faith that craziness happens in this world that is unworldly?

Miracles?

Spirits?

Angels?

God?

Just sayin'.

Just askin', is all.

Well, my dudes, that's what happened according to our main man, Rev. Convinced him on the spot to head uptown and check out Missy's crib.

His love for Luke.

His trust in Luke.

WILLIAM TEETS

Only problem was, if angels and God can speak to us, can't demons and the Devil do so, too?

Think 'bout that, people.

Rev didn't.

Didn't think about the Devil disguised as a false savior. Remember what I said about saviors, y'all? Remember? How saviors save those who save themselves. Remember? Sure you do.

Sure you do.

Reverend didn't think about none of that, though, and was certain the lilting words on the wind he heard were truth, and Reverend went walking to 148th Street, South Nazarene End. He figured he would walk behind the fish market, creep up to Missy's mom's house, and check out if Missy was lampin' in her first floor bedroom. He'd been to that bedroom window many times, sneakin' in and out under the cover of darkness, but now so much more was at stake.

It was around three-thirty a.m.

Only 'bout three hours of dark left, before Reverend would be exposed by the sun, his dreams burned up, his wax melted again, before he had to get out of town, out of the hood, and back to the Hall.

Folks, take a sec. and think about how many times our futures, our lives, have been altered by the smallest of things.

Think about it.

If you didn't go back into your crib to take a piss or double-check you done turned the stove off for real, changing your timeline but by only a few seconds or minutes, you would have walked into a bullet on the boulevard. A bullet with no name. Would a big-ass delivery truck have mowed you down as you stepped off the curb if you were at that spot forty-five seconds earlier?

Hell, maybe you missed meeting your soul mate 'cause you went back inside to take that leak. Maybe you didn't stop at the bodega and buy a winning Lottery ticket 'cause you wanted to wear a different pair of kicks and was runnin' late for a job interview. Maybe because you *did* go back inside your crib and arrived at the corner of Fate and Future later, you *were* flattened out on the street by that delivery truck. Hell, maybe, if . . . what . . . what's that you say? Right, the story, back to the story. Sorry, y'all, just tryin' to make a point about how fickle—'nother great word, people, fickle—life can be.

But, right, back to Reverend.

Son, give an old man another taste, would ya?

Alright then.

WILLIAM TEETS

So, like I was sayin', Rev headed uptown to check out Missy's mom's place. He moved cut to cut, keepin' a lookout for any danger. No Neck and Solly were probably snoozin' in their warm beds, or so Rev convinced himself, and the only threat he needed to be aware of was any ghouls out ghouling. And let's not forget five-o ready to stop and frisk and ask for papers from any black youngblood out on the streets just before dawn.

'Nother no *good morning, sir*, there.

Rev was bein' stealthy, cats, stealthy.

Slick, sly, smart.

Careful.

Correct.

He entered South Nazarene End and creeped up to Missy's bedroom window.

It was mad dark.

Reverend tapped on Missy's window pane.

He tapped a little harder.

It was so cold he thought the glass might shatter.

His breath—my people, Reverend was breathin' heavy—made clouds on the pane.

REVEREND WENT WALKING

He almost saw a Baku, a ghoulie, in the condensation clouds.

Or so he thought.

He got his shit together and cleared his mind.

Reverend went to tap again.

Then he felt it.

A vice-like grip from behind him.

On his shoulder.

On the base of his neck.

Not like that crack whore's touch on his shoulder earlier in the morning, but a strong, Mr. Spock, Vulcan-like grip.

Sent the worst shiver through his blood since this whole road journey started.

He wanted to spin around and swing.

Wanted to run like a brother bein' chased by the police.

Fight or flight.

Reverend couldn't do either.

The grip had him wincing and leaning to one side.

WILLIAM TEETS

Brought instant tears to his eyes.

He couldn't move.

Paralyzed.

Rev was helpless.

Luke had given bad advice.

The angels had told a lie.

Or the Devil had tricked, like the trickster he is.

Gotten his due.

Time to collect.

Two wrongs never make a right.

Remember I told y'all that earlier?

Remember Constantine: The Devil will collect his dues?

Rev was at someone or something else's mercy.

Of this world or not of this world.

Anyways, Rev was fucked.

Fall, Icarus, fall. I told you not to fly so high.

Chapter 31
Checkers

Who or what had Rev paralyzed, you ask?

Relax, people, settle down.

Let me keep tellin' y'all the story.

Ya ever had something happen to you, folks, like a car wreck, or gettin' sucker punched? Robbed by a stick-up kid on a Sunday night? Something real quick and out of the obvious? Somethin' that sends nothin' but shudder and fear and hopelessness through ya? Well, that's what Rev was feelin'. Hopeless and fearful and afraid.

Mad thoughts, random thoughts, raced through Reverend's mind.

The pain of the grip was pure agony.

Rev was powerless.

Hell, Rev thought back to that time when Luke touched No Neck's shoulder on the corner and brought the big man to his knees. How No Neck was so helpless to do anything. Rev thought 'bout playin' the dozens with Luke and breakin' bad on folks, all for fun. Thought about Nathaniel Hawthorne Library and the zoo and campin' upstate. Thought 'bout Solly's shop and Constantine sayin' *Don't break the eggs*. Seventeen years young whirled by in seven seconds.

Ain't it amazin', folks, how whole scenes of our lives can run through our minds in a few seconds when we think we're dyin'? I mean years and years of bullshit, inconsequential thoughts, or *real* ones, relived in a few precious moments. Kinda crazy, right?

Well, Rev thought for sure he was a goner. Sure he was gotten by a Baku, grabbed by a crab's claw. A pack of wild ghouls run amuck. Thought he was gonna die like so many other young brothers.

So many America never knows about.

So many America never cares about.

Extinguished before their flame could even ever be lit and allowed to burn.

Extinguished!

Yeah, folks, Reverend thought his life was done. Thought

REVEREND WENT WALKING

for sure he was gonna be a passing mention in Tuesday's obituaries.

And then someone spoke.

"Check it deep, at steppa, why jerusalem bwoy creepin' Blue's sis' yard? Yuh wanna catch a cutlass or tack, mon? Blue taught yuh a tief, mon"

Reverend knew the voice. He said, "No, Blue, it's me. Reverend. Luke's boy."

"Blue know. Ease up, yuh, undastan'? Truss Blue. Blue nuh realize who at steppa is, salt for bwoy. But Blue know all di while. Nuh true? Why Blue buck wit' at steppa jerusalem bwoy? Taint ya s'pose ta be wit' babylon?"

"I'm looking for Missy, Blue. I need to talk to her."

"For sum fuckery? Yuh tryin' ta get glamity, yuh, mon?"

"No, Blue, I came for *justice*. Not to get into Missy's pants. That's my word, Blue. I came to try and get Missy to tell the truth about No Neck. How they set me up. I've got to straighten a situation out for a scholarship I . . ."

And Jamaican Blue laughed loud like thunder.

Excuse the cliché, y'all, but his laugh was so bombastic. Damn near Devil laugh. Y'all remember, Blue, right? Remember, my dawgs and cats, how I told y'all Blue was a solid brother? Remember how I told y'all, too, he was no one to be trifled with? Well, sumptin' else I never told you about was that he was one of Usman Buhari's boys.

Never told y'all that, did I?

Well, I'm tellin' y'all now.

Why?

Cause the story in the hood was Blue merked Usman—his partner in crime—in cold blood. Murdered him with those bullet holes I'd done seen left in Usman's body. The blood on the concrete, the rattlesnake eyes that scared me to death, Usman's horrifyin' last breath—the beef between those two brothers was supposedly over who would get the last swig of a bottle of Wray & Nephew.

Word.

That just ain't some urban legend, neither.

That's the supposed truth.

I don't know, I'm just sayin'.

Can't always believe what you hear, y'all, but I know what I saw.

Blue is not a trifling-ass brother.

Done told y'all that, time and time again.

REVEREND WENT WALKING

I'd seened some of Blue's handiwork and heard about a lot worse.

I know Blue done took out 'bout nine people g-code street-legal style, another eight on contract. He tortured a hell of a lot more for various reasons and cheddar. That's how he makes his wampum—on the low—on the street, but you didn't hear that from me.

Just hope he ain't plannin' to go all Jamaican Blue on Rev's ass.

"Yuh serious, jerusalem bwoy? Yuh no jester, Blue?"

"No, Blue, I'm serious. I went AWOL from juvy to try to convince Missy to come correct."

Blue laughed again.

Just not as loud.

Then Blue got all serious and such.

"Listen, Reverend bwoy. Blue know yuh script. Old Man and Solly buck up Blue. Blue's niece, wicked zutopang. Yuh, understan', mon?"

"Yeah, Blue, I understand, but I see another side of Missy. A softer side. This is my last chance, Mr. Blue; I have to talk with her. For me, for my family, and for my dad, Luke. I have to escape this ghetto."

Man, I love that boy for sayin' he needed that scholarship for him, but also for his fam. Did y'all hear that, people, he said for us and his dad!

For Luke!

"Bwoy seh 'ave ta, 'stead of want ta. Blue big up on dat. Blue not know, doe, if Reverend bwoy know Luke was Blue's key, mon. Luke was don. All di while. 'At's why bwoy still 'ere and nuh salt. Blue know 'dat bumboclot, No Neck. 'Es quash. 'Is screw face jester, mascot. Yuh, mon, Blue nuh. Come from da door, siduag and Blue make wicked niece talk wit jerusalem bwoy. Like Luke, you bredren. Come in from da door, mi seh, 'ave a siduag."

"Thank you, Blue, thank you so much."

"Nuh tenk, Blue. Neba tenk fuckery 'til yuh can beat it, mon. Truss, Blue, Reverend bwoy."

"Yeah, Blue, I hear ya. But thanks anyways for the chance."

Blue laughed loud again and said, "Yuh yutes search always for jester and nuh know w'en ta laugh."

"Who da fuck dis nigga in mi yard? Damn, Blue, mi busy. Mi hear all dis ruckus outside mi window when I'm wit' mi man, da fuck goin' on? Yuh 'ave any idea what time it t'is, nigga?"

REVEREND WENT WALKING

"Don't give Blue screw face, mascot. Back to yuh room. Blue got t'is."

"Well good ten, nigga. Your ass be t'inkin' you run shit."

"Quiet, quash. Blue cutlass yuh even if yuh Blue's sis."

"Oh, nigga, whatever."

Reverend entered Missy's mom's place for the first time ever through the front door. He sat down gently on a leather sofa. A real leather sofa. Beneath some real expensive chandeliers. He saw amazin', hand-blown, glass bongs, beautiful stained glass, art work he knew was money from the books he'd done read at the library, and had no idea why they was hangin' so fabulous in this ghetto apartment off Nazarene.

But they were.

I'm talkin' some goddamn Picasso's maybe.

Maybe, not.

But Rev was diggin'—or intimidated by—the immaculate apartment with the fine art and money fixtures. Thought about how he wished he'd seen them before. Was crazy confused by the house tucked away on South Nazarene End, that shouldn't have been so tucked away.

Rev saw Blue smile.

"Blue wake wicked niece. Jerusalem bwoy, wait."

"Blue, hang on. I heard from the street that Missy might be going back to Philly. Is that true?"

"Yuh, mon, truss, but wicked niece nuh leave 'til two more morn'."

"Word? I've got a chance?"

"Word, at steppa, 'cause Luke is key, yute got a chance."

Rev sat back again on the fine leather couch. Took in the custom love of the comfort. Wondered why Missy never shared this beauty with him before. His eyes glazed over. Shit, people, he was mad tired. He saw fire hangin' on the wall in some picture he recognized but couldn't place. Another one he knew was worth mad money from a book he'd read. Reverend felt like he was soaring. His waxed wings could never melt now. He was nearly home.

But, Rev was so tired.

He tried to stay awake.

Blue.

Missy.

Luke.

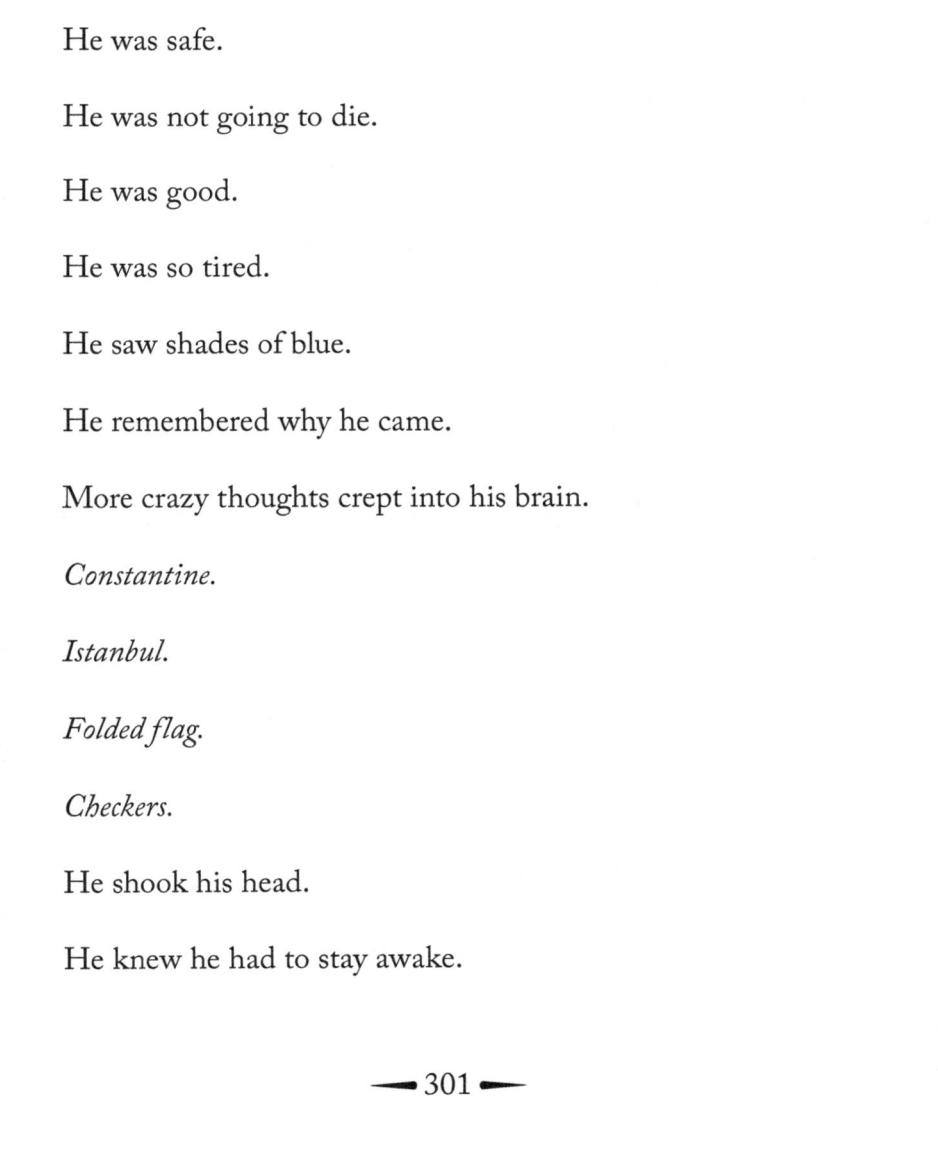

The full leather couch was invitin' Rev to sleep.

He was safe.

He was not going to die.

He was good.

He was so tired.

He saw shades of blue.

He remembered why he came.

More crazy thoughts crept into his brain.

Constantine.

Istanbul.

Folded flag.

Checkers.

He shook his head.

He knew he had to stay awake.

WILLIAM TEETS

He was so close.

Mighty Missy walked out of her bedroom.

Blue made her do so.

Blue was gone.

Missy stood in the archway to the room with the first hint of dawn gloaming behind her.

The soft light made Missy seem an angel.

An angel from above.

Her curves pulled against her white tee and her hair whispered gently.

An angel for sure.

Rev tried to stand up from the leather couch.

He fell.

Reverend couldn't speak.

Fall, Icarus, fall, I told you not to fly so high.

Chapter 32
Promises

Yeah, my dudes, yeah.

Groovy, right?

An angel in Rev's midst.

Or was that just a thought in his mind?

Was Missy another Devil hidden behind another disguise?

A trickster?

Man, I love that word—trickster. Sums up Satan all at once.

Who was the he/she Satan?

Chill, y'all, I know I'm playin' with y'all, but relax, people, relax. Let me tell y'all what happened next. Let me speak the truth.

Rev felt a spark run through his body. A yearning. Know what I'm sayin'? His eyes became moist and shined such light and beauty. His heart skipped the lover's proverbial beat. He felt like Heaven.

Missy looked so good.

Beautiful—she always was beautiful—none ever doubted that, but don't forget a serpent is still a serpent.

And our superhero Rev wasn't alone.

No siree.

Many a hero been slain or laid to ruin due to a women's beauty. Driven to madness, booze, death by lost love or a siren's song. Or jealously. Hell, how did things turn out for John the Baptist, Samson, Othello, because of a man or woman's love?

Just askin', of course, just me askin'.

And Missy, let's just say she was all woman, my people. The ultimate vixen. Fem Fatale—or somethin' like that—is how the French say it. Yeah, man, Missy was an avenger for Eve eatin' that apple.

But Rev was convinced he could convince Missy to help him out. Told me later that no one ever saw the side of Missy that he saw when the two of them were alone and sharin' dreams. Said she was so damaged and ravaged by the streets, her family, sexually abused by men and women, she had wounds that could never heal, but that she also had a goodness within her that was beautiful and few ever saw. A piece of her soul she hid from most and protected to the fullest. That's what Rev told me. Said he knew her goodness.

Anyways, Reverend was smacked back into reality when Missy pulled up a chair—red panties and all showing beneath her too-small-tee—and said, "Damn, Rev, what you doin' here?"

"Missy, I ca-came t-to- ta-talk with y-you about something," Rev stuttered.

"Well talk then. You ain't never stuttered before."

"It's j-just you look so beautiful. So beautiful in the first light."

Missy turned her head around and looked over her shoulder; she knew she was bangin' in the glory, folks, and she appreciated Rev's compliment more than he could know. She knew his words were honest and heart-felt and sincere. She played the praise off, even though Reverend always made her feel special. She felt bad for doin' what she'd done to him. She said coolly, "What's up, Reverend? I thought you were locked? Don't try no dumb shit, neither. No get back. I got a blade. You know I'll use it, too. It was business, Rev, it was never personal. I always liked you, I loved our time together, thought about you a lot. By the way, you look like hell. I mean you still fine and all, playa, but you look played yourself."

"I went AWOL, Missy. Went AWOL from juvy to talk with you. Fuck our letters. I'm out of time. We need to talk face-to-face. I've been on the run since midnight. Made a promise to someone who helped me out and I need to keep that promise, but I'm running out of time."

Damn, my people, sound familiar?

We all still runnin' out of time down here in the hood.

Everywhere.

All where.

Runnin' out of time.

Always!

"I've been through hell, that's why I look like hell," Rev continued. "Chased by five-o and a K-9—let's just say a lot of shit has happened since I've been in juvy, Missy, a lot of shit."

"Yeah, son, I remember you writing you got busted in the head and things were fucked for a while."

"Yeah, but that's not important, now. I met this teacher—real cool—gave me this college entrance test to take and I aced it. I scored real high. Got offered a scholarship to a great college. I wrote that to you. Remember? Did you read that letter? I never got a reply. Well, it's not worth anything if I can't get my charge, the charge you and No Neck pinned on me, dropped."

"Yeah, my uncle been hasslin' me 'bout that, but I don't pay him much mind. That motherfucker be buggin'. Hey, wait a minute. You wired, nigga? You *wired*?"

And Missy jumped up from her chair. Took two steps back from Rev, wide-eyed.

"No, Missy, look, chill," Rev said, as he pulled off his hoody.

Missy sat back down.

"Sorry, Rev. Sorry again, it's just the street in me. You know, baby, it's just me. But what then, Rev? What can I do? Fuck, I ain't got no time machine like in that story you told me. I can't go back in time and change shit, baby. Wish I could though. To help you and get that dirty-ass No Neck. He tried to turn me out. Pressed up on me. If it wasn't for me remindin' him Blue's my uncle—couldn't get my blade out to stick his fat ass—he was gonna rape me. Anyways, Rev, what the fuck am I supposed to do for you now?"

And as Rev told me this story later, folks, it hurt me inside. Made me feel like I was stuck in my gut by Missy's blade. This is what growin' up too fast does to young people. Growin' up in the hood. Them two kids should've been sittin' at home at some Sunday dinner table with fam, sayin' excuse me and pass the peas, please, and does anyone want desert, but instead they was talkin' 'bout set-ups and wires and rape and dreams being destroyed, 'cause that's just the way it is.

Wrong my, people, so fuckin' wrong.

I don't want to rant on, y'all, but do you see how America is divided, people. A great divide between those who have and those who have not? How some of our children are playin' Scrabble and Monopoly and watchin' family sit-coms, while other folk's children is runnin' and gunnin' and tryin' to keep their noses above the waterline so they don't drown completely.

Just sayin' and all, folks, as always, just sayin'.

But, damn, sad shit like that boils my blood.

Nature or nurture shouldn't be a choice hand dealt by fate, but a winnin' hand dealt to all. Don't that constitution of ours say liberty and justice for all? I may be misquoting, I might not be the most educated government academic among us, but I know damn sure the Declaration of Independence says *all men are created equal.*

Just ain't happening, folks.

Just ain't true.

Kids talkin' about death, while they playin' Hopscotch.

REVEREND WENT WALKING

And that's the biggest disgrace this great nation—and I fought in 'Nam, damnit, I'm a soldier, damnit, a Vet, got a purple heart and all so don't you dare tell me to love America or leave it—but nowadays, America is a lie, and will always be a lie, until we *all* are equal. That's not some old crazy man's rhetoric rant you be hearin', but the truth.

Hell, have you all been hearin' the story?

Ray Charles could see shit be broken.

Not fair, my dudes.

Not fair.

Yeah, and don't say nothin' to me. I know I went on a tangent again. Did so 'cause y'all needed to see or be reinforced by the truth. By justice. By the *real* American way.

Right?

Righteous.

Let me tell on.

How many Reverends and Missys exist in this great nation of ours who ever have a chance? How many? You, sir, you, wearin' that fly suit and tie, you obviously successful, how many?

Right, sir, right, hardly none!

WILLIAM TEETS

I hope, sir—and Old Man ain't puttin' ya down, you seem like a solid brother and you were here from the start of the story and done stayed—just hopin' that fine suit and that fine white starched shirt ain't a undercover uniform for the KKK. For more hidden racism.

Just sayin', sir, just sayin'. You appear righteous, though.

I hear ya.

I respect you, sir.

I believe you're not.

Just sayin', that's all, just pointin' towards the truth, usin' examples is all.

Y'all know the racist is underground.

Hidden.

No, sir, not you.

I dig you.

Just sayin', your brethren, they wear starched collars instead of hoods nowadays.

Yeah, man, I'll take a swig with ya.

Shit, we was better off when we could identify them.

Word.

No, sir, you're cool and the gang. Respect to you, too. Thanks, for the swig, brother. You're good in my book.

Let's me get back to Rev and Missy, though.

Rev explained everything to Missy. The whole shit and kaboodle. How she needed to go see the DA and sign a deposition that No Neck coerced and bribed her into settin' Rev up with the gun. Told her Billy Jackson would get her immunity from any prosecution. Told her if she did all this, Rev's charge would be dropped and he'd get into that good-ass school, and she'd even get payback at No Neck for pushin' up on her.

And before Missy could ask Rev the question he thought was comin', Rev said, "I'm not going to lie. I got nothing for you, babe. No cheddar, no wears, no ice. All I got is my dreams. Are my dreams enough?"

Missy held Reverend's wrist in her hand. Felt the warm honest blood flowing; sincere and strong. Saw the glint in his eyes, the passion, the love, and gently brushed his lips with her fingertips.

"I wasn't gonna ask you for nothin', Rev. Just a promise. A promise you'll go to that school and never come back to these streets or me or this life. That you'll finally soar above it all. Like that dude, Icarus, you done told me about so many times. But promise me your wings won't melt, that you'll soar so high can't nothin' bring you down ever again."

"I will, Missy, I will, but you can come, too. We both can get outta these streets. You can get your GED, get into college just like me. We'll both make it, baby. Both of us."

"You're sweet, Rev, but we know that's your future, not mines. Besides, if you make a promise you know you can't break it."

"I haven't promised anything, yet."

"No, playa, no you haven't."

Rev and Missy sat in silence starin' into each other's eyes. Like kids, like the kids they were. Missy's eyes welled up and she quickly stood and fake-laughed and turned her back to Rev. She said, "Oh, hell, I'll do it. Philly can wait a little longer for me to burn it down. Who knows, doin' somethin' good for someone might make an honest girl out of me yet."

She fake-laughed again.

"What's that sayin', Rev, about a good deed never going . . . ?"

Missy turned back around and Rev was standing face-to-face with her. They kissed. Rev was hard, about to lower Missy's red panties, both of them heavy breathin', when they heard, "Oh, hell nuh, nigga, hell nuh, whore, nuh one 'bout to get glamity on mi leather couch before morn'. Hell nuh, not 'ere," Missy's mother shouted.

Rev and Missy laughed.

REVEREND WENT WALKING

Rev grabbed and threw on his hoody.

Him and Missy ran out to the alley.

Day was breakin'.

Rev got Missy's digits for her phone, as Missy stood shivering in the cold November air.

Rev said he or Solly or Billy Jackson would be in contact with her, shortly.

Rev kissed Missy, again, and said he had to leave.

Had another promise he had to keep.

Rev jetted towards the six, swore he'd be back, told Missy he loved her.

Missy smiled and waved and jumped in the air as she watched him jog down the block towards the underground.

Her eyes welled up again.

With happiness.

Happiness for Rev.

Even a little for herself.

Somewhere near, a Jamaican could be heard laughing loud like thunder.

Chapter 33
Row That Boat Ashore

Rev caught his train upstate—his return ticket still stuck in his sock—and rode the northbound to Silver Bridge station. He called the Hall up on an old pay phone, yeah, folks, you can still find pay phones, and the SOD picked him up and brought him back to campus.

All by ten a.m.

He was seen by a social worker, diagnosed as OK to return to the daily program, checked out by the infirmary, deemed healthy clean and sober, and his AWOL warrant was vacated.

Rev was back in the school building by eleven-thirty a.m.

He didn't go to his scheduled class, though, he went to Josh's classroom.

The big man was sittin' at his desk, vacant-eyed, his face in a hurry. He wasn't accomplishin' much durin' the first of his two prep periods.

"Got any lunch to share, Mr. M? Brotherman is starved."

"Rev! Oh my God, Rev!"

Josh jumped up and hugged Reverend.

Hugged him tight.

Real tight.

"I was so worried, Rev, so worried. I called in sick this morning, but came in late hopin' you would show up. And here you are. Alive. In one piece. Safe. Reverend, you don't know."

"We made a promise, I couldn't break that, but chill, Mr. M. It's all good. It worked. I'm good. And I wouldn't have been able to do any of what I did without you. Without your faith in me. You took a chance on me, Mr. Moriel, man, you saved me. Thank you, thank you so much. But, seriously, dude, you got any food?"

Josh and Reverend laughed.

Josh gave Rev a Snickers bar he had in his desk draw.

Josh called the main office on the intercom and said he had Rev with him if anyone was lookin' for him. Rev heard Josh say, "No, he's not AWOL again. He's with me."

Josh and Reverend laughed again.

"So what happened? Where we at? Oh, thank God you're safe. I was shook, Rev, real shook. I had this crazy dream, anyway, tell me all about it. Tell me what went down," Josh asked.

And before Reverend could start his tale, Josh said, "No one sliced your throat then?"

"What?"

"Never mind, Rev. Tell me what's up."

Reverend told Josh all the details. Told him how Missy was OK with everything. That she was goin' to speak with the lady DA. Told Josh 'bout running the streets, about Blue and Missy and Missy's mom and how goddamned tired he was.

And hungry.

And happy.

So fuckin' happy for the first time in a long time.

"That's awesome, Rev. We have to call Old Man, Solly, and my guy at the school. We have to get the ball rolling now. By the way, Rev, you look like hell."

"Yeah, so I've been told. You ain't looking so good, yourself, Mr. M. Rough night?"

"You can't imagine, son, no idea."

REVEREND WENT WALKING

Josh and Reverend laughed a third time that morning.

Now remember, people, remember, me and Solly still had no idea what was up with Rev and his AWOL. Had no idea how Josh conspired with Reverend. Had no idea 'bout Rev meetin' Missy on the low. Still thought his ass was AWOL, were still scared to death—sweatin' bullets—when the phone in Solly's shop rang.

"Yes, this is Mr. Burke. What? What's that you say? Ah, man, cool. Yes! So fuckin' cool. Pardon my French, ma'am. When can I speak with him? Tonight? After six? OK, thanks, thank you, thank you so much. He's safe, right, he's good, right? Thank you again, ma'am, thank you."

Me and Solly let go of a big exhale.

One of the good kinds.

We started high-fivin' and dancin' 'round the shop like schoolgirls on leave. Poured us selves a couple of long whiskeys and smiled, my dudes, smiled. As you all know, wasn't often we heard good news in the hood, but that was some *real* good news from the Hall. Lettin' us know Rev was safe and sound. In juvy—granted—but safe and sound for the moment.

WILLIAM TEETS

My celly rang.

It was Josh.

"Old Timer, my brother, you're on speaker with guess who?"

Solly put my phone on speaker.

Reverend told his story again.

Left out the part of Josh bein' an accomplice. Both Rev and Josh agreed no one needed to know about that. A secret. Their secret. Another secretus, set-apart, well, y'all know 'bout that, now, right? But anyways, me and Solly got busy, instantly.

It was happenin', folks, *it* was *real*.

One for the righteous.

Fuckin' one for the good guys!

Solly called Billy Jackson in VA and lawyer-man said he would make some calls and be in town in forty-eight hours, depending on the lady DA keepin' her word. I told One Shoe to find Blue and see if Blue could meet me and Solly at the shop.

With the quickness!

Shit, my people, lives were on the line here.

Dreams.

Ultimate dreams.

Savior dreams.

Calls were made.

The last call that needed to be made was to Mighty Missy Brown.

She was the cog in the wheel, the fuel to run the engine, the only person on Earth who could make or break all of our wishes.

Word.

Solly called Missy with the number Rev gave us.

No answer.

Solomon called again.

No answer.

He called again.

Yeah, you got it folks, no answer.

"That fuckin' hood rat. We got to depend on her? Naw, Old Man, I trust her like I trust a crackhead with my money. I've known her kind all my life. Bitches that are down wit' you, then screw you over in the end. Naw, Old Man, I don't trust her."

"Be easy, Solly, be easy. We're close, son, *real* close. You heard what Rev said. Patience, my brother, patience, faith."

But I ain't gonna front, folks, I was nervous too. *All* our dreams, *all* of Rev's success, *all* of *all*, was ridin' on wildcard, Mighty Missy Brown.

Hell, my dudes, I'm sure y'all know so many people who say they gonna do things for you and then don't do shit. Tell you they gonna save you from the fire, but your ass still burns. Tell you they gonna take you home, all honorable and shit, and you end up somewhere you ain't never been.

Right?

Word.

Me and Solly were still excited, but oh so tense.

We waited to hear back from Missy. Hell, Solly done closed shop early again, said he couldn't concentrate on no cuts—and y'all know how brothers are serious 'bout their cuts in the hood—when we heard a knock at the front door.

REVEREND WENT WALKING

It was Blue.

And Missy.

And as much as I love Rev and want everythin' to pan out, a part of me was wishin' I was on Mars.

Jamaican Blue and Mighty Missy at the door, together?

Jamaican Blue and Mighty Missy in the same space?

Shit, let Satan take me now.

Solly unlocked the door to the shop.

"Solly, Old Timer, yuh 'ave sum acid for Blue?"

Solly poured Jamaican Blue a deep Bacardi.

"Blue tenks yuh, Solly. Blue wit' wicked niece yuh, mon? Yuh been callin' 'er all di while, nuh? Blue come ta yuh yard, 'cause Blue see at steppa jerusalem bwoy early in the morn'. Taught 'e was a tief, mon. Lucky for 'im and Blue, Blue recognize 'e Luke's bwoy. Yuh, mon. Blue 'as big up ta Luke yuh know. Luke was Blue's key, mon. Ain't ways, mi wicked niece wanna big up, neba meant 'arm ta Luke's bwoy. Speak dis true, zutapong girl."

Damn, people, like I said before, that patois is a motherfucker, but when spoken by someone like Jamaican Blue, you find yourself understandin' exactly what he be sayin'.

Missy spoke.

"Solly."

And Blue thwacked the back of Missy's head.

"Wicked niece, show da respect ta Mr. Solly, nuh?"

"Damn, alright, ya crazy fool. Mr. Solly, I just want to say what I did, settin' up Rev, was trife. I wanta help Rev now. I'm willing to go the DA and tell it all—with that guaranteed immunity of course—and get Rev into that college. I know you don't like me and ya think I'm shit, but really, I wanta help Rev and help you and fuck No Neck while doin' it all."

Blue glared at Missy.

"Sir, Mr. Solly, sir."

Well, y'all, me and Solly were dumbfounded. Here we are with two of the biggest gangstas in the hood, I mean two of the baddest motherfuckers you never wanta know, and they both agreein' to come correct, and *save* Rev from these streets.

Who saw that comin'?

I ask you again, folks, who saw this comin'?

Hell, we always know sunny days can be followed by rainy

ones, but damn, my people, the sun was shinin' bright now. I didn't even have that sick feelin' of the proverbial other shoe droppin' no more. Of some ragin' storm blowin' in all over us again. This shit was *real.*

Rejoice, my people, rejoice.

Forget Michael.

Reverend row that boat ashore, hallelujah.

Reverend row that boat ashore, hallelujah!

Yeah, my people, life was lookin' up.

Sunny side up.

Row that boat, Rev.

Row that boat ashore.

Chapter 34
Whirlwind

The following few days, people, were a whirlwind.

Billy Jackson arrived in town to make sure everythin' was on the up-and-up, and him and Missy met with the DA.

But let me back track for a sec, folks, let me tell y'all a *real* interestin' sidebar to our story.

No, y'all, I ain't gonna rant.

Ain't gonna go off the rails.

Just relax and listen up, folks.

Enjoy what I'm tellin'.

Listen up, now.

Seems that after Blue and Missy left Solly's shop, Blue paid a little visit to that scoundrel, No Neck—'nother great word,

REVEREND WENT WALKING

my people, scoundrel, right?—but anyways, as I was sayin', Blue walked up to No Neck on the corner and *invited*, word on the street was *told*, No Neck to join him at Arthur's Bar for a drink and a talk and a siduag.

Blue sat with No Neck at one of the back tables in the bar. In that beautiful bar darkness of an early afternoon—you drinkers all know what I mean—anyone who digs barrooms and drinkin' durin' the day knows what I'm sayin', but anyways, Blue had a little talk with No Neck.

No one chillin' at the bar heard what was said between the two of them—all were watchin' though. Arthur told me Blue spoke *real* low to No Neck with diamond eyes.

Eyes like diamonds.

One Shoe, who was at the bar knockin' a few back, told me later, Blue's eyes were more like the eyes of a rattlesnake.

Just sayin', folks, just sayin'.

That's what Shoe said.

Rattlesnake eyes.

Remember, people, remember?

Usman?

Rattlesnake eyes?

WILLIAM TEETS

Sure, ya do.

Shoe and Arthur said Blue was talkin' all serious and low to No Neck. Looked real menacing. Horror-like. Sends shivers down my spine just thinkin' 'bout it. They also said that No Neck's eyes looked like sparrow's eyes, face-to-face with a waiting-to-strike Cobra. All bugged out and hypnotized and scared-like.

Like a person facin' a heart of blackness.

A heart of darkness.

Scared eyes that held no hope.

Eyes that knew they were seein' their jury judge and executioner.

Yeah, man, Blue's eyes.

I'm tellin' y'all this, brothers and sisters, because the DA woman said to Missy and Billy Jackson, upon their arrival at the court house for their meetin' with her, that two hours before, No Neck had already copped to the set-up of Rev.

Done turned himself in.

Gave that lady DA a full blown verbal and written confession.

On his own, folks, on his own.

DA lady said she was shocked as all get out.

She asked Missy and Billy Jackson if they had talked with No Neck, or knew anything about his confession. Was No Neck's confession coerced? Lady DA didn't want the confession voided in court later on if No Neck was forced to tell it. Lady DA didn't want to be blindsided. She wanted the truth. They both said, no. Hell, my dudes, they were just as shocked as the DA.

But we know better, right, folks?-

Yeah, dawgs, we know better.

Blue never shared the conversation he had with No Neck that day in Arthur's Bar with anyone. Never talked about their convo. Wasn't Blue's style. But after No Neck's confession and subsequent charges and conviction—he ended up bein' sentenced to a two year bid—he was never seen on the block again.

Ever.

No Neck was told to leave Dodge, by Blue, and No Neck did.

'Nother one of them urban legends, people?

Hell, I don't know.

What do y'all, think?

WILLIAM TEETS

Just askin'.

Just sayin'.

After that meetin' between Blue and No Neck in Arthur's Bar, though, Blue would laugh low, like a rumble—not thunder—whenever someone mentioned No Neck's name.

Justice?

I think so.

Serves that two-bit hustler, No Neck, right, if you askin' me. Fuckin' with children. Spreadin' pain and poison. Thinkin' he's bigger than the horse he be ridin'. Hell, there's always a bigger horse.

Believe that.

But, y'all decide for yourselves.

Anyways, between No Neck's confession and Missy's statement—which wasn't even needed according to the DA and Billy Jackson—she wanted to still give her testimony, though, said to *make shit right, to finally do somethin' good, to show Rev her love*—Reverend's charge was vacated and the court wrote an order to release him immediately from the Hall.

But hang on, brothers and sisters, hold tight.

What's that you ask?

Naw, no surprises, people. No crazy twists and turns.

I see you all high-fivin' and celebratin' for Rev, but the story ain't done bein' told yet.

Hang on, y'all.

Don't share the Henny, yet.

I knows y'all happy.

Happy for Rev.

But, let me finish.

Yeah, give me a swig. Yeah, young-un. Should've cracked that Olde E, earlier. Good lookin' out for the old man, though.

Good looks.

OK, settle down, everyone. Let me tell y'all what else went down.

Luke's main man, Billy Jackson, wasn't done yet. He sued the Hall for a cool one-point-five mil for Reverend bein' assaulted. Rutherford B. Hayes Haven Hall, anxious to forget about how Too Bad hit Rev in the head with that iron—an improperly stored weapon with a complete lack of adult supervision as well as with total staff neglect and implicitness—was how lawyer-man Jackson said it, settled out of court for five hundred and fifty thousand.

WILLIAM TEETS

U.S. dollars, that is.

Billy—hell, me and lawyer-man are on a first name basis now—still wasn't done yet. Servin' as Rev's executor, he set up an even heftier trust fund than the one Luke left for our main man, Reverend. Solly and Rev, with the assistance of Billy again, bought a big house upstate.

And we still ain't through, folks.

Mr. Billy Jackson—without chargin' a dime—oversaw the entire transaction of Solly sellin' his shop in the hood. He then helped Solly in buyin' a new barbershop upstate. In the same town the house was in. All with a healthy profit for Solly.

Lawyer-man Jackson was a *real* blessin'.

Said he did everything he did because he dug us as *real* people.

And did what he did for justice.

And for righteousness.

But mostly because Luke was one of the greatest brothers he'd done ever known. Said Luke saved his ass once. Literally. Wouldn't get into details, just that he owed Luke big time, and Billy said he had to pay his debt to Luke. Billy Jackson said he always pays his debts.

He paid lovely, brothers and sisters, lovely.

And Luke, in another crazy supernatural way, saved the day again.

God bless, Luke.

Between the money Luke left Rev, the settlement from the Hall, and Solly's profit on his shop, we was all able to finally *buy* a slice of that American Dream. We had to buy that Dream, folks, but we finally got a piece. Phony as the Dream is, we were allowed to partake. Only because of money, not because of who we are. We got it, people, but please don't get the bigger idea twisted. Took Rev gettin' locked up on a bullshit charge and damn near dyin'. Took meetin' Billy Jackson 'cause of Luke's . . . well, y'all know why we met Jackson, but yeah, folks, we were out of the hood and livin' large for real.

We was movin' on up.

I say we, 'cause the house Rev and Solly bought got one of them mother-in-law apartments attached. Me and One Shoe moved in rent free, 'cept for helpin' out as needed.

I'm talkin' nickels and dimes, my people, nickels and dimes.

Damn, life is good.

Solly married his girl, Donna, she's expectin' in a few more months, gonna be a boy. They gonna name him Luke Blue

Reverend Burke. And Josh, hell, Josh came through with his word and crazy plan from jump street and Rev got into Rodgers.

Solly opened his sweet shop upstate cuttin' crazy suburban boys' heads. Crazy designs and all. They all love him. And, he's makin' a pretty penny. No more sippin' rye in the shop, eatin' ox-tails, or blowin' smoke rings, but like I said, the shop be boomin'.

Go figure.

Missy went to Philly as she'd planned, probably burnin' down the City of Brotherly Love, but we never heard nothin' from or about her.

She never reached out to Rev again.

'Cept for one time.

She got our address from Blue, who got it from One Shoe on the low, and Missy sent Reverend a letter.

No return address.

She wrote in the letter for Reverend to soar. To soar so high above the clouds, greater than Icarus, can't nothin' bring him down. Wrote that if her heart, her soul, her spirit, could've loved, was capable of love, she would've loved Rev more than herself. She wrote in that letter she did love Rev more than herself. Loved Rev for bein' him. For believin' in her. For sharin' a world she could never imagine. A special world of dreams and ideas and books and hope. Told Reverend to soar so high, for both of them, that maybe she could be free one day, too.

She wrote that, folks.

I seened the letter.

Rev wept.

One more thing, my peeps, one more gravity fact.

Missy signed her letter to Rev, *Love, Icarus' girl.*

Reverend wept again.

And Mighty Missy Brown was gone.

Straight up ghost.

Another urban legend.

Maybe Missy did soar, but fell into the sea. Maybe not. Maybe her waxed wings melted from her fire world and she fell into despair and nothingness. Maybe not. Maybe a Baku grabbed her in the night and feasted on her soul. Maybe not.

Maybe she soared real high and owns Philly. Maybe not.

Maybe we'll hear from Mighty Missy Brown again.

Broke Rev's heart, nonetheless.

Hell, though, my peeps, he's young, he's strong, oh, so strong. He'll get over her and life's set-backs and he'll rebound.

Shit, Reverend always does.

Don't he?

That boy been to hell and back. Triumphant like some cursed Greek god. He'll get over Missy.

I thought of Tasha.

Thought of burnin' rubber on the road and tall blue spruces sheddin' snow.

I felt for Rev.

You always remember your first.

Anyways, I still talks to some of the old heads in the hood and visits. Kick it with the youngbloods. On a southbound, now. I spread the wealth. I try to bring brothers and sisters up. That's why I'm lampin' on this stoop now sharin' my story of Reverend with y'all.

For youse who don't know, folks tell me shit is changin'. Hipsters movin' in, sippin' green tea and eatin' curry goat wraps, and brewin' their own beer. Like that shit ain't been happenin'—minus the wraps and green tea and brewin' sumptin' other than Olde E—forever down here.

The almighty dollar rises again.

Another shell game.

Another hustle.

Someone always loses.

Someone has to lose.

And it ain't ever the Man.

The hood still got segregation and them *Savage Inequalities*. Pardon me, Mr. Kozol, but no one has ever said it better than you. I had to use your line, again. Respect, sir, respect.

Yakabus is still open for business, so is Arthur's Bar, barely. Ol' Arthur refuses to change with the times and serve any beer that you got to stick a lemon or orange slice in. Any beer called Strawberry Bacon Delight. Who the hell can blame him for that? Charlie Chings' is a Tai restaurant now and Pacheco's Pool Hall is a thrift shop where thrown out clothes and old furniture and silly lookin' hats is fetchin' major league dollars.

Abdula is dealin' in fine wines. Really?

Let the gentrification of a hood, continue.

Let the gentrification of our souls . . .

WILLIAM TEETS

Two tears in a bucket, fuck it.

Bring in the hipsters.

Hell, maybe they'll do better.

Pastor Goodman-Brown is still sellin' unanswered dreams and a hymn at St. Pete's. Still sweepin' up vials and collecting his tithe. Still preachin' to the masses that don't need to hear the Word.

Makes me think about Crazy Constantine sometimes.

She ain't been heard from since she left for down south.

What if she was right?

Naw, I doubt it.

A few eggs are always gonna break.

We can all still make a cake, though.

Anyways, y'all, bad news to share. Jamaican Blue was gunned down in a shoot-out over who knows what.

With Haitians.

Haitians and Jamaicans.

People so close and similar, yet two peoples who despise one another so violently.

Catholic and Protestant.

Jew and Gentile.

Democrat and Republican.

Black, Brown and White.

Uptown, Downtown.

My Gang, Your Gang

The Haves and the Have Nots.

When will it stop?

Oh hell, y'all know what I'm sayin', folks.

Anyways, Blue took out three bad ass ghoulies, before he died with six slugs in him, on cold and lonely blood-stained concrete. On 148t Street and Society Could Care Less Boulevard. Another death on another lost sidewalk in another lost city. I have nightmares 'bout it, because I know he had to have rattlesnake eyes when he died and his thunder was stolen.

Doesn't mean much now.

I mean his glory.

Just another urban legend, who laughed louder than thunder, and who will soon be forgotten. His laugh and his legacy will lilt like unheard whispers on the wind.

WILLIAM TEETS

Like the rumors of so many lost saints from so many lost religions.

Rumors.

I hope not.

I pay homage to Blue in my prayers.

Yeah, folks, he was as gangsta as they come, lotta blood on his hands, but he was a main force in helpin' Rev. And helpin' his community and doin' the best, the best way he knew how.

Seein' us all through.

Just like Luke.

Ain't none of this story, none of this dream come true, would've happened without them and the goodness in their souls.

That little bit of light.

That little bit of darkness.

Word.

Believe dat.

I hope Blue is chillin' somewhere good with his key, mon.

His key, Luke, mon.

Bredda man Blue was a hard soldier of the streets, but I thank the Universe and *all that is*, he was on our side and showed us love. Me, Solly, and One Shoe always pour out some acid for bredda Blue, whenever we toast.

We never hear nothin' back, though. No Island patois on the wind.

R.I.P. Blue.

You're missed and appreciated.

Most of all, you all best believe, not a day goes by that we don't think about and thank and pray for Luke. Regardless of everything that went down, with and without Luke, alive and in spirit, we all would've been dragged back into the bucket and left to whisper hollowed hymns without his guidance and force. Instead, we shared some truth. Some facts. Some hope. Much Love! At least I think we did. Not a better man, a greater influence, ever lived than Luke.

Was he a saint? Hell, no.

He was *our* savior!

Well, that's the story, my dudes. My story 'bout an amazin' kid named Reverend. A superhero from the hood. Thank you all for listenin'.

WILLIAM TEETS

Wait, though, hang-on, before y'all get ready to jet, hang-on, hang-on, for one last talk. I just thought 'bout somethin'. This story ain't quite over.

Yeah, I know I'm a little tipsy, but let me finish up.

Gather round', now, stop huggin' and celebratin' 'bout Rev. Right, sister, right, what about, Josh?

Thank ya, sister. That's what I'm talkin' 'bout.

Yeah, youngblood, I hear you, what about Josh?

Even though Rev earned this celebration, some of y'all screamin' too loud, gather 'round, let me wrap up. Hear an old timer. Thank you, my people, thank you. I knows I told an awesome story. But it ain't over yet. Yeah, brother, we gonna talk about Mr. Joshua Moriel.

Yes, sister, Josh.

Y'all hear up?

Let me wrap everything up correct-like and go on one more rant.

Dig it, my people!

Dig.

So many of you are shoutin' 'bout Josh, now. Chill.

REVEREND WENT WALKING

Give me a taste of your cup, brother.

Let me wrap this up.

Hang on, my dudes, yeah, calm down, y'all, I ain't done tellin' yet.

Old Man ain't done sharin' yet!

Chapter 35
Salvation Teacher

While y'all got crazy celebrating a happy endin', I forgot, and heard a lot of shout outs from the crowd askin' me about Josh. Let's come correct and righteous, y'all. Need to tell you how Josh ended up in all this. Y'all reminded me. Like I said I'm a bit tipsy. But let me finish this up with Joshua Moriel.

Let's start by sayin' Josh is fam.

Always will be.

But I gots to be honest with, ya. Needs to give you a reminder. Remember—even though shit worked out—by the grace of the Universe, Rev's AWOL worked out, I still knew nothin' 'bout Josh helpin' Rev AWOL. The two of them done kept that a secret from all of us, but I never told y'all, how I found out 'bout their collusion. How I found out about Josh's stupid-shit involvement until much later.

I'll tell you how and when.

We all was havin' a party at the new house upstate. Me, Solly, One Shoe, Donna, Rev, Josh, Billy Jackson, Arthur, and a few more homies from the hood, toastin' our good fortune. Drinks were slidin' deep, questions were asked, answers were given, and Rev slipped up. He said-she said followed, and that's when the alley cat of deceit was let out of the bag. Not until then did the truth come out regardin' Rev's AWOL.

And like I said, I was heated.

I was vexed.

I thought Rev pulled that whole AWOL stint off by himself. Never knew, like I told y'all a million gazillion times, 'bout Josh's crazy involvement. Well, like I said, the cat done burped up the canary yellow feather. On a slip up.

I went beserker.

Straight up fruit.

Flashback City!

Charged Josh.

Solly and One Shoe grabbed me up and told me to chill, but I was so angry I was gonna hit Josh. Over his stupidity. His unprofessionalism. Him puttin' that boy in danger even though everything went for the good. And everyone started arguing and tellin' each other to chill, grabbin' up and pullin' on each other's shirt collars and sellin' woof-woof tickets, and then Rev stood up on the coffee table and shouted, "Listen, everyone!"

Commandin' like.

Loud.

Not Rev's style.

We listened to brotherman.

"You all want to judge, Mr. M? Hell, if not for Mr. M none of us would be here. You want to ask if the ends justify the means? Well, I guess sometimes they do. Look at us all now—chillin'—as opposed to being in the ghetto, not even that long ago. Was Mr. M right? Wrong? It's not for any of you to say. Only he can answer for his act and if he's found or needs absolution. Or me, and what I chose. But are we going to let this tear us apart? Tear us down? Like in the hood? Like crabs in a bucket?"

We all sat back down.

Josh was uncomfortable and downed his Canadian Club. He walked to the kitchen for a refill. When he returned to his seat, Rev continued, "Believe what you have to. Garner your opinions based on your beliefs, but don't ever judge this man for believing in—or for doing—what he believed to be right. Isn't that what you all were running from in the first place? Now that everything is fire, let's find something wrong? Is that how we want to live? Could it have been catastrophic?

Sure. But Mr. Moriel didn't make his decision lightly. Neither did I. But I made a choice. He made a choice. Decisions. We have free will to do so."

Oh, no, not that free will shit again.

I coughed, sarcastically.

"Old Man, no, be *real*. You've been watching out for me, forever. And I thank you. I love you. But haven't you been reading books I shared with you, and still do, and that Mr. M still shares with you? Isn't there so much truth in those books? Haven't you loved the truth those books shared? Haven't you learned? You also looked out for Luke and Solly back in the day, right? You were their mentor, right? Well, let's be honest, you were a great mentor but not always the wisest, right? The booking, the weed, remember? Does that erase all your good? Of course not. Same as you made the decision to reach out to Mr. M because of your love for him and for all of us. Because of your courage and Mr. M's courage we came out on top, finally. You are still one of the best mentors, ever, even with a few bad transgressions. Isn't that so?"

I squiggled in my seat.

"One Shoe, you too. I saw how you stuck up for me when No Neck was messing with me. Solly, my God, Solly, need I say more? You're my dad, now. My center. But Luke, Luke would have told me to keep everything a hundred. To never give up. To prove justice. He would've told me justice must prevail.

Has to prevail. At any cost. And he did tell me. And he told me never to lose my self-respect, never lose me. Right? To be honest, have courage, fight against inequality, fight for my life, my future, me. Everything about my father's love was at risk, and Mr. M helped me attain all those virtues. Every last one. Helped to save me. Us."

We all was mad quiet.

I sipped at my rye.

Rev continued.

"I don't want this party to be ruined, this celebration, by what I say. But listen up, just know, Joshua Moriel for the months of hell that I was at juvy, held me down, taught me so much knowledge from books and philosophy I never would've known. And then got me into Rodgers. But, all before that, when the chips were *really* down, he believed in me. Like you all do. But he gave me a chance and believed and I promised I would keep a promise. A promise made through love and education and trust and . . . oh, hell, you all know what I'm saying. Joshua Moriel gave his all and I gave my all. He only asked that I come correct and fulfil our promise. Faith. So before you crucify him, thank him. Thank him for not succumbing to your simple man-made thoughts and rules, and societal ideas about right and wrong, but thank him for being *real*. I thank you, Mr. Joshua Moriel. Thank you for being my salvation teacher."

Well, hell, folks, everyone got *real* hushed.

REVEREND WENT WALKING

Donna started cryin' and hugged Solly, they hugged Rev, who hugged me, and I hugged Josh and told him I was sorry for my judgment of him.

We all started weeping.

We all wept.

A child had truly led us.

Then One Shoe broke the party open by sayin', "Who's gonna hug Shoe? One Shoe can't get no love?"

We all shared a shot of rye.

Even Rev.

Even though the whiskey made Rev's face twist up and he didn't like the taste.

We were all thankful.

Thankful we were saved by love.

Reminded of that love because of Rev.

Because of a love seed planted by Luke so long ago.

WILLIAM TEETS

Speakin' of Josh, though, the last update y'all didn't get is he's still at the Hall teachin' English to those juvy convicts. Still got them wanna-be-gangstas reading Shakespeare and eatin' out of the palm of his hand.

Still hittin' the sauce too hard.

Still tryin' to save too many souls.

But, ah, hell, that's just Josh.

I love him so much.

The great thing, people, is he's only 'bout a thirty minute drive from where we all be livin'.

We see each other all the time.

He spends his mini-visit-vacations and summers visiting us now.

Allows me to gets to keep a proper eye on him.

Just sayin'.

Someone's got to.

Don't we all have them dreamers and lost ones in our lives, the ones we need to watch over and love and handle with extra special care?

Sure we do.

Chapter 36
Reverend Went Walking

Now I'm gonna keep you all a few more minutes more 'cause I need to apologize.

And my apology will be short, brothers and sisters, but my summary strong. And Lord, this story needs a summary. Not just about the players, but about the future, as deep as that may sound.

Now, just because everything is groovy, don't you dare think for a moment that I'm righteous with Lady Liberty or that bitch Justice or the American Dream.

Hell, no.

That bitch still needs to be flogged.

And I say that loud and proud.

I say that, because this great nation of ours is still unfair, unequal, and still has to pay back past dues to so many. Repay so many bounced checks like Dr. King said, that are stamped *insufficient funds.*

So much is owed to so many.

All of us.

Black and white.

Native and immigrant.

Urban and rural.

A nation, my people, a nation.

United we stand, divided we fall!

Thank you, Ben Franklin.

Through the grace of God, Karma, and a*ll that Is,* our boy, Reverend, came out on a winnin' end.

Me, Solly, and One Shoe, too.

And even Josh, kinda.

Shouldn't we *all*, though?

Luck?

Shouldn't be that way.

Luck—even though I'm thankful—we *all* should be entitled to the Dream.

They're still too many lost superhero children in America.

That's wrong, my brothers and sisters.

But this is the part I apologize for, my dudes.

Remember I told y'all superheroes don't exist, fairy tales don't come true, Baku's will snatch your soul in the night, alcoholism, addiction, bein' born a shitty hand is gonna happen?

Remember, folks, remember?

The whole false American Dream?

How man-made organized religions strangle spiritualism?

Remember, brothers and sisters, remember?

Well, I'm here to say that's all true, still!

Unfortunately, shit ain't changed.

But, I'm also here to say I'm sorry because there are superheroes in our midst.

Just like I told y'all, not too long ago.

Let me review.

WILLIAM TEETS

Not Marvel's heroes.

Not some politician with his hands buried in some lobbyist's pockets.

Surely not the government or the Man.

Surely not religions that OK hate and poverty and false . . .

And definitely not big business and corporate government.

Not some Baku.

Not some stick-up boy.

But *common* superheroes.

Every day *common* ones like mom and dad.

Like grandma and pop-pop.

Superheroes like Luke.

Superheroes like Solly.

Like Billy Jackson.

Like a great teacher.

Like an awesome coach.

'Specially, like Joshua Moriel.

For breakin' *the rules*.

For giving enough of a shit to break *them rules* in the first place.

For strivin' and takin' a chance to make a life better.

For someone besides themselves.

Even though Josh may be crazy, he's a superhero because he took a chance on a youngblood, showed him the way, was a teacher, a mentor, became involved, invested.

Shared love.

What else is there?

A savior in his own right, yes, indeed, a savior.

And even a superhero like Missy.

Yes, people, Missy.

She was someone who exceeded her own perceived self-worth, her perceived wellbeing, and rose above her own imagined faults in order to assist someone else and help them to rise above their own. She loved, even when she was incapable of love, or thought she was, people, she delivered.

I'm talkin' 'bout superheroes that can't fly or stop a speedin' bullet, superheroes that can't swing from skyscrapers or solve everything with a six gun, ridin' a white steed, but people that exist every day amongst us. Who struggle every day and fight the injustice that life throws at us.

That we *all* overcome.

That *we* must overcome.

Foster parents like Luke, and yes, even Crazy Constantine, who set and built and maintained a foundation for their child against the wild winds and horrors of this time.

To give more than wantin' to receive.

To pull up and support each other 'cause it's the *right thing* to do.

Oh, hell, people, to love.

That's all I've got to say.

Need I say more?

That's all I've got to tell.

Hell, I could probably ramble on all night.

I'm a little boxed and tired myself, y'all.

So is you, I bet.

I will tell y'all this in closin', though.

REVEREND WENT WALKING

Reverend is doin' great at Rodgers.

Is finishin' his second semester already.

He just left the other day after visitin' us all.

I saw him walk to the car on a blusey spring day, me and One Shoe on the front porch of the big house sippin' spicy Bloody Mary's, ballgame on the radio, Josh gettin' ready to drive Rev to Rodgers, and I shouted out, "You made it, Rev. You the *realest* superhero I know."

He waved his hand over his head, backpack strung up across his shoulder and strong chest.

Man, he grew up strong.

And Reverend smiled.

Yeah, man, he smiled.

His million dollar smile.

He bounced his walk.

That Reverend walk.

That precious walk.

Hard and fast and strong.

He waved goodbye.

WILLIAM TEETS

Told us all he loves us.

He was back off to Rodgers.

Off to his future.

The sun shone brightly.

His wings expanded.

Reverend soared.

Above all the crabs in the bucket, above any Baku.

High above the streets in the hood.

High above the world.

Reverend soared.

Yeah, man, he soared.

I was there.

I watched.

I seened.

Reverend went walking on a clear spring day.

Acknowledgements

The author would like to thank Gabriel and all the folks at Word Werks, Inc. for their outstanding effort, professionalism and expertise in editing, *Reverend Went Walking*. This novel would not have been possible without their support and guidance. A special thanks to Barbara and Dawn for their *early eyes* and as always to Kathy and JD for their unwavering commitment and conviction.

CPSIA information can be obtained
at www.ICGtesting.com
Printed in the USA
LVHW090713050819
626450LV00062B/72/P

9 781478 773931